Liar's Fire

Quantity discounts are available on bulk orders. Contact sales@TAGPublishers.com for more information.

TAG Publishing, LLC
2618 S. Lipscomb
Amarillo, TX 79109
www.TAGPublishers.com
Office (806) 373-0114
Fax (806) 373-4004
info@TAGPublishers.com

ISBN: 978-1-934606-05-6

First Edition

Liar's Fire

Dee Burks

About
The Author

Dee Burks has been in the publishing industry for more than a decade. She has written numerous Amazon.com #1 bestsellers as a ghostwriter and is the author of *Picks & Shovels: Cashing in on the New Gold Rush in Ghostwriting*, *The Trouble With Money: 8 Strategies to Eliminate Financial Chaos From Your Life*, and *FREE Your Inner Millionaire*.

Dee also writes historical romance under the name Kerri Marshall and has started a historical series beginning with *Yours Again* (January 2011). She has taught novel writing, ghostwriting and freelancing on the collegiate level and has an MBA with a special emphasis in international marketing. Having worked in the jungles of corporate America for more than a decade, her experience lends a level of believability and compassion to her characters' voices.

Dee is Editor and Publisher at TAG Publishing, LLC and is committed to helping authors build long term audiences for their work. www.deeburks.com

Chapter 1

"He actually said you need a man with a leopard skin loincloth?" Nolea Brown stood in Serena Finley's office peering over her bright red frames. "Is that some kind of psycho babble reference to the fact that he's boring as hell?"

"I guess." Serena tapped a pen on her desk. "He said I needed a Tarzan type that took direction well and preferably didn't speak English."

Nolea flipped her long dark curls and grinned. "You know, that doesn't sound half bad."

Serena ignored her. "He said I wear him out."

"As in—great in bed?" Nolea's eyebrows popped up.

"As in high maintenance and hot tempered."

"So let me get this straight," she made finger quotes in the air, "*Doctor* Jeffery Scott is looking for a butt ugly woman with zero personality, no skills, and no goals, right?" She leaned forward. "Do those even exist anymore?"

"Not that I know of. I think he hates the competition. He may have to start cruising the feed stores and bait shops to find some babe with overalls and a crew cut. That might suit him." Serena gazed out the glass that separated her office from the newsroom.

She had always been on guard with Jeffery, never able to relax, be herself. He'd spent every minute they were together trying to analyze her, assign reasons for her actions and attitudes, as if she were his pet project.

Serena had never wanted to reveal that much of herself to anyone, but some of his comments still rattled around in her head, eating away at her confidence. "I mean, I will admit that I try to look decent, but I am not hot tempered. Am I?"

Nolea cleared her throat and glanced away. "I wouldn't say that—exactly."

"What would you say, *exactly*?"

"You just like things your own way, which is fine. At least you know what you want, and what you don't." She paused, then shrugged at Serena's frown. "It's a redhead thing; he should know that, and you were sick of him anyway. I'm glad you finally got it over with."

"Me too. I'm more relieved than anything I guess."

"Which cemetery did you pick him up at anyway?"

"He came highly recommended by the infamous Aunt Macy."

Nolea snorted. "Well, no wonder. What is her deal anyway? Every time she comes around here she's got some dreaded disease."

"It's just the way she is, part hypochondriac, part cupid. She means well, though. She just doesn't want me to be alone when Justin leaves for college."

"I can't believe how fast he's grown up."

"He graduates in two months." Serena couldn't bear to think of him as a grownup. Justin had always been with her. Through the good and the bad. At the end of the summer, she'd be completely alone for the first time in her life. She'd refused to think how things would be after he left, instead concentrating on getting him into a good school, planning the finances, and being sure he was ready. But was she?

"Makes me feel old," Nolea said.

"Thirty-five is not old. You're the same age as me."

"Yeah, and the only thing I've been able to raise is my boobs, courtesy of contestant number three." Nolea stood and stretched her shirt across her chest. "One of the better parting gifts I ever received from a man."

And she had received a lot. The woman attracted men in droves, and they all showered her with gifts and marriage proposals. It dumbfounded Serena and annoyed her at the same time. She considered herself above average in looks, but compared to Nolea she felt like a twinkle light in the shadow of a neon sign. "Why can't I ever get that?" She mumbled.

"You want better boobs? I can get you my plastic surgeon's number."

"No." Serena glared. "Why can't I get fabulous parting gifts? Or even a guy worth talking to for five minutes?"

Nolea plopped her hands on her hips. "You want the truth, or you want me to tell you the same old crap?"

"The truth." Serena blew out a breath.

"It's your attitude."

"What attitude?"

"That, 'if you come within a foot of me I'll cut your dick off' attitude. You have to let the past go, Serena."

"I do not have an attitude, and I certainly don't have *that* attitude."

"Do."

"Do *not*."

"Do."

"And the past is not the issue here."

"It's always the issue. So you made a mistake. You were a teenager for God's sake. You've spent the last eighteen years raising a fabulous kid. It's time to move on already. Men are not the enemy."

Easy for her to say. Nolea divorced every mistake she'd made; Serena's life was never that simple. "I *am* moving on. I got rid of Jeffery didn't I?"

"Yes, you did and I'm proud of you." Nolea flashed a grin, showing perfect white teeth framed by hot red lipstick. "So what's next? Are you off to the happy hour jungle in search of Leonard Loincloth?"

"Very funny. Although it might make another good fluffy piece of reading for our Lifestyles section." She held up the morning edition of the *Cranfield Reporter-Star* that the copy editor had placed on her desk. "I can see it now: 'How to Find Tarzan, and Still Remain Sane.'"

"You may have an idea there. Every woman wants to be Jane."

"I said, *sane* not Jane, and the two don't necessarily go together." She shook a finger at Nolea. "And don't you go giving Uncle Frank any ideas about having me write more fluffy crap."

"Are we going to go through that again?" Nolea sank into the chair in front of Serena's desk and propped her four-inch heels on the edge. "You do a great job on the *Lifestyle* section and you know our female reader base has really expanded. I can't figure out why you fight it. Your uncle is very proud of what you've accomplished."

"Not proud enough to let me cover any real stories or, heaven forbid, political issues."

Nolea grabbed the paper and scanned the front page. "Oh yes, here's a story worth covering. A man in San Antonio is being sought for bilking women out of more than $200,000 in an investment scheme. Said one woman, 'He promised we'd marry after I turned over my money.'" Nolea tossed the paper down in disgust. "Now do you really want to have to do that kind of reporting on the scum of the earth?"

"No, but I would like to write about important issues, things that can help people move forward with their lives." Serena had fantasized for years about working for a national publication, one that made a real impact.

She'd intended for her job here to be a stepping stone to bigger publications and eventually New York. But life had gotten in the way of that dream. Raising her son had become her number one priority during the last 18 years, and she'd done her best, but now it was her turn to chase that long set aside goal, and no one in New York would be impressed with her latest article on geraniums. "I wouldn't even mind being editor of this section if he realized women do more than putter around their gardens and worry about what style is 'in' this year."

"There's that attitude again. I hate to break it to you, sweetie, but many women love to garden, and I, for one, always wonder what is 'in.' Women spend money, and our advertisers know that." She tapped two perfectly manicured nails together. "Hmm. That reminds me. We need to start coordinating the advertising for the bridal season."

Serena moaned. "I *hate* bridal season. It's like sending a vampire to a garlic festival."

Nolea hopped up. "Oh, it's not so bad. I should know. I've been a bride four times in ten years." She strolled to the door and leaned against the jamb, striking a provocative pose. "And I've become very adept at sucking every drop of cash from my victims, not to mention receiving a variety of great perks." She patted her chest.

"How is it that you get all the perks, and I get all the jerks?"

Nolea arched a brow. "Faulty selection process I'd say. Men are to be conquered, not put up with."

Harsh, but probably true. Serena had never been able to climb the first bunny hill of love, let alone plant her flag on top of the mountain.

"You have to look at the whole thing as a challenge. You should do what I did after my first divorce. Get a few sexy negligees and try them out on some unsuspecting guy just for fun. You might be surprised at the reaction."

A voice outside the door chimed in. "Where does someone as old as you get anything sexy to wear? Victoria's Catacomb?"

Nolea glanced behind her. "Back off, Skippy, or I'll drive the heel of my shoe through your heart." She waved to Serena and disappeared down the hall.

Will Mason grinned and glanced at Serena, "Hey there, Captain Old Maid. I hear the latest contender bit the dust."

"Already?"

"Small office. So, who's the next victim to be drawn into your lair?"

"There is no 'next victim.' And at least I have a lair and don't live with my mother."

Will feigned offense. "My mother happens to love me. Besides, she does laundry and cooks for free."

"It doesn't bother her that her son is a thirty-year-old broke troll?"

"Twenty-nine and nope. She knows I'm saving up for the right girl."

"Saving up? Like you're going to order the *right girl* off the Internet or something?"

"Maybe." He rubbed the top of his cleanly shaved head. "I'll have you know that there are women on this earth who would suck face with a toad for cash, and we both know one." He jutted a finger toward Nolea's office. "I figure if I live with Mom for the next six years or so I'll be set. Then Nolea will regret not giving me a chance and fall at my feet begging for a date."

"Bet not."

"You'll see. I'll wear her down, eventually." Will's dogged determination in his pursuit of Nolea was admirable, but hopeless. Both women viewed him as the lovable little bother type, not any kind of serious love interest.

"Well if you're that determined, then take my advice and ignore her for a while."

"Ignore the love of my life?" He feigned disbelief.

"Absolutely. Play hard to get."

He snorted. "Like she'd even notice."

Frank Walker breezed into Serena's office. He wore the official uniform of all old school newspaper men: white shirt, dark suit, red tie with the knot pulled down a few inches and sporting the required coffee stain. "Morning, sweetheart."

Serena stood, allowing him his routine peck on her forehead. "Hey, Uncle Frank. How are you?"

"Great, and you will be too in a few minutes."

Nolea slid into the room behind Frank and gave Serena a helpless shrug.

It immediately put Serena on guard. Uncle Frank regularly had ideas to increase circulation, advertising, and market share for his newspaper. Trouble was, Serena usually ended up doing the work to pull it all together.

"I've come up with the perfect plan to kick off this year's bridal season," Frank announced.

Serena held her breath.

"You will write a series of articles about how to find the right person to spend the rest of your life with." He paced around the small office intent on his mission. "With all the mush and romance you can pack in. The advertisers will love it!"

"*What?*" Serena's chest tightened. She wouldn't even know where to start. She'd had very few relationships and certainly had never experienced anything that approached "the right one."

"Her?" Will cackled. "She can't even get a Mr. Right Now!"

Serena glared at Will, annoyed that he'd voiced her thoughts.

"I've taken that into consideration, and I have a plan. Oh, and I'm sorry about Jeffery, dear. I never liked him anyway. Too stuffy for you."

Great. The gossip wagon had even stopped at the editor-in-chief's office this morning. Serena cringed with the knowledge that every person she passed in the hall this morning was probably hanging out by the water cooler right now talking about her love life or lack thereof.

She mentally braced herself, dreading the revelation of "the plan." The last plan Uncle Frank devised resulted in her wearing a chicken suit at a parking lot of a car dealership for four hours in 100-degree heat. Somehow she had a feeling this would be much worse.

"You know how we have the personal ad section on our website we've been trying to promote as *the* place to find your mate?"

Serena nodded.

"Well, you are going to try it out. Each date could be the beginning of a lifetime of love."

"Oh, noooo." Serena dropped her head in her hands.

"Oh, yes," Frank grinned. "It was your idea to put our resources into going virtual. Print is dead for news, you said, if I remember correctly."

Yes, she had said that in a fit of frustration, and Frank had listened. She understood that more and more people didn't want to wait for a print edition to get the news, and she'd been right. As print subscribers dropped off, their online subscriptions had boomed. But dating complete strangers was another thing. She could tell by Frank's tone he was serious.

"You want me to go out with these losers? What if I get an ax murderer?" she argued.

"They're lonely not losers, and customers not ax murderers. We'll send a staff member along for protection. Say young Will here." Frank popped Will in the arm. "He'll observe at a distance, take a few photos, maybe. It could be quite a boost to our revenue."

"Photos? You're increasing revenue by pimping out your editors?"

"Nothing so dramatic, Serena," Nolea piped up. "It might be a lot of fun. Think about it, the first article could be about meeting in a coffee shop. There are three that are on the verge of signing advertising contracts. Then the next segment could be a romantic dinner at an Italian restaurant."

"One that's planning to advertise with us as well?"

"Well," Nolea hesitated, "More like one that's thinking about cutting his annual advertising in half, and this might make all the difference."

"Not to mention the fact that it would really beef up the personals section, which you know has a great margin for us," Frank added. "C'mon kid, what'd you say?"

"This isn't reporting, it's fantasy." And not one she wanted any part of.

Nolea frowned. "We're doing it as a special advertising section, not a news feature, and it will only run for a few weeks."

"Absolutely." Frank always carried a newspaper and now he rolled and unrolled it in his hands. "We'll call it "Lone Star Love Affair." What do you think?"

It's absolute crap. Drivel. A complete and total waste of my time, energy, and talent. New York seemed farther away than ever right now. They all three leaned toward her, waiting on a response. "And if I say no?"

Nolea tugged at one of her long curls. "Well, we thought you might be a little hesitant, so I already called a few for you that looked promising and left your number."

"You *what?*" She narrowed her eyes at Nolea. "You knew about this, and sat here chatting this morning and didn't say a word? Were you trying to soften me up?"

"That's one way to look at it, but it really could be fun if you would just go with it." Nolea scooted out of the room, not giving her the chance to argue.

"Your Aunt Macy thought these sounded pretty safe."

Serena stared at her Uncle. "Aunt Macy? Is she the real reason I was chosen for this little adventure?" Aunt Macy had made it her personal crusade the past two years to find Serena a man. The only good thing about having Jeffery around was the fact that Macy had backed off her quest. Now it seemed she was at it hard and fast once again.

"Oh, no. Well, not really." He stammered. "It's a great idea for the paper, but you know how things are these days. You can't ask an ordinary staff member to go on company-sponsored dates, but you're family, and I know you always put the good of the company first like I do. The fact that it will get you back out there again makes it a win-win for everyone." He smiled and patted her arm. "Let me know how things go!"

The minute Frank was out of earshot, Will let out a huge peal of laughter. "Dust off your cape, Captain Old Maid. Love is in the air."

"Hey, you have to tag along too and protect me."

"Of course. You know I'd never miss a meal on the company dime. Besides, I can't wait to see the love-starved loser parade." He winked at her and left.

So this is what her love life had come to. Play-by-play of her inability to relate to the lowest level of man on the planet, all while being chaperoned by the company leprechaun. It would almost be funny—if it were someone else.

The phone on her desk rang. Serena yanked it off the hook. "What?"

"Bad morning?"

Her son's voice soothed her a bit. At least Justin had no desire to get his mother hitched. Last night when she'd shared the fact that Jeffery was history, he'd done his touchdown victory dance, followed by a loud "Whoopee, we's free" yell.

"Yeah, kind of. What's up?"

"I was going over to Terry's after school to watch the game if that's okay."

"Sure that's fine."

"And there're some messages on the machine. Did you put in that ad to rent out Jacie's room?"

"Not exactly, but I'll do that today."

"Okay. See ya mom."

"See ya kid." Serena chewed on her bottom lip and stared out her window. She'd meant to place that ad for the last few months but hadn't. Jacie, the copy editor's niece, had rented their extra room for four years while she attended college. The money helped fluff up Justin's education fund. Serena wanted to have him to herself the last few months before he left for school, but now it was time to start looking for additional income. Not that her salary at the paper was bad, but Cranfield, Texas, was not a large market, and college tuition presented a daunting financial concern for a single parent. She had to be sure the money would be there if they needed it.

Serena glanced at the printouts Nolea left on her desk. There were large black circles around several ads and big numbers denoting the ranking of each one. She hated to think what kind of suggestive message Nolea left while pretending to be her. Now these men were calling her house. They could be stalkers for all she knew, and she had to write some mushy crap to sell more advertising?

The line between good reporting and pleasing the advertisers blurred a little more every day, and this was the kind of situation that turned professional journalists into outright liars. And that's what this would be: a complete and total lie.

Serena knew the odds of an actual relationship were pretty much nil, which suited her fine. She had no intention of getting involved with anyone or putting off her plans to flee this place for the lights of Manhattan. She wasn't about to share her nonexistent love life with the whole world, either. Too bad she couldn't find some guy, take a few pictures, and fabricate a racy affair. Her heart picked up pace as she turned the idea over in her mind.

Why couldn't she? Uncle Frank didn't say it had to be real. Newspapers used to run serial novels all the time, and as long as it was presented as a special advertising section, that gave her a great deal of freedom. It would serve them right if she wrote copy so hot it melted off the page. If they wanted Tarzan, she'd give it to them.

Now all she had to do was find the right guy—one that could be convinced to play along, but keep it strictly business. Maybe an out-of-work actor or someone who might be interested in some free advertising. She glanced down at the circled ads and smiled. *Wonder if any of these guys have a leopard skin loincloth?*

Chapter 2

A wet, rough tongue slathered Tyler Cooper's face. He tried to push it away, but only succeeded in getting two paws firmly planted on his chest.

"Off, Shadow." The tongue continued. "*Off!*" The dog backed away, sat, and waited. Tyler opened one eye, then the other, wiping dog slobber off his cheeks at the same time. Morning came so early these days and so brightly. He raised his head and looked down. He'd fallen asleep on the couch with his clothes on. Again.

The chef smock he wore still smelled of the grill, and he hadn't even taken his shoes off. He sat up and ran his fingers through his hair, trying to wake up. Unbuttoning the top two buttons, he pulled the shirt over his head and tossed it in the corner on top of a few other articles of clothing in similar condition. The smell of barbecue, steaks, and grease clung to his skin and hair.

He hoisted his tired body off the couch and walked to the window. The boxer followed, prancing and wagging her stunted tail in anticipation. When he failed to notice, she yapped a half-bark. The noise echoed around the empty apartment. Tyler scanned the room. He should do something about this place. A TV, the couch that sometimes served as a bed, and his recliner.

Krista took everything else. *Everything*. The furniture, the money, and John Suther, his best friend and business partner. They'd left him nothing but a struggling restaurant and piles of bills. Every time he got a few dollars ahead, some other financial disaster crashed in on him. Most, courtesy of Krista. She was like the damn Ghost of Christmas Past, revisiting his mind and raping his bank account with some leftover or undone business every time he turned around.

He didn't really blame John. Tyler had fallen for Krista's crap for two years until she'd wiped out every resource he'd had. John was her next meal ticket, and that thought provided Tyler with some small comfort. Tyler went to the kitchen and filled Shadow's bowls with food and water. He watched the dog munch.

John would get what was coming to him in time, and what a hard lesson it would be, too, as Tyler had already found out. That woman went through more cash than Donald Trump. Being raised on cash and weaned on a trust fund had given Krista the attitude that money was to spend, not pay bills, and that's exactly what she did. Everything from old student loans to IRS debt arrived on his doorstep in little white envelopes from this lawyer or that one. The threats ranged from arrest to liens on the business.

At least he still had this condo, such as it was. Krista had subleased it from her uncle, and as long as he paid the rent, no one said anything. Somewhere in the past year he'd ceased to view Krista as human, deciding it was safer and more accurate to define not only her, but the entire sex as a mutant species—the financial black holes of the universe.

The dog nudged him in the back of the knee. Tyler had worked like a slave for a year and a half trying to run the restaurant by himself, and hadn't cared about or even noticed anything else. Except Shadow. He bent down and scratched the dog's ears. Now this was a loyal companion, incapable of lying, cheating, or scheming. She also couldn't talk. Another big plus in his mind.

Tyler located the leash, and they started outside for her morning walk. As Shadow trotted down the hall, the door to Mrs. Lathem's condo swung open. She frowned over her half-glasses at his bare chest. Grasped snug in her arms was Rat Dog. Some kind of exotic hairless Chihuahua, the thing couldn't weigh three pounds and was completely naked, except for white tufts of hair at the tips of his ears. It growled at Shadow, who wagged her tail at the bite-sized mutt.

"In this complex, Mr. Cooper, residents are expected to present themselves fully clothed."

"Yes Ma'am, just taking Shadow out for a walk." As if on cue, Shadow sniffed at the woman's knee, then tilted her nose higher. Tyler ignored the dog and smiled at Mrs. Lathem, watching panic light in the woman's eyes. He tugged the leash back as Shadow's nose grazed Mrs.Lathem's crotch. She gripped Rat Dog tighter and glared at Tyler.

"You would do well to control that dog of yours, too. It has been leaving gifts in the geraniums again."

Gifts? She wouldn't even lower herself to call it dog pooh, let alone anything else. "What makes you think it's my dog?"

"I watch, and it doesn't happen during the day. You are the only one coming in at all hours of the night when I'm trying to sleep. You can't fool me, you know. I'll have it tested if I have to, to prove it's *that* dog." She gave Shadow a disgusted look. "And if it continues to happen I will take it up with the homeowners association." The door slammed in his face. He clenched his teeth.

Ah, swell. Another woman determined to make his life miserable. What was wrong with people? She *would* take it up with the association, too. Probably even have the offending droppings DNA tested if it meant getting rid of Shadow, and him in the process. Tyler had no idea what he'd ever done to piss the lady off, but she clearly hated him for some reason. He'd been made well aware that several of the older couples disapproved of a single man in residence. They didn't think it produced a family-friendly environment.

All he did these days was work, and if the Rat Dog patrol had been watching, they would also know that no female had passed his threshold since Krista left. He could be voted monk-of-the-year at this point, and if that wasn't family friendly, he didn't know what was.

Tyler took Shadow out to the garden and sitting area the association had spent years cultivating, and unhooked the leash. As expected, the dog ran on the lawn sniffing and playing. Not giving one hoot about the flowers and certainly not squatting on any of the precious geraniums.

Tyler caught a movement in his peripheral vision. Mrs. Lathem peered out of one of the first floor condos, alongside another woman with matching blue hair. Their gazes latched on him like two prison guards.

Tyler's temper surged. As if he didn't have enough crap going on in his life, he had to deal with a snooty, petty, nosey old biddy. Tyler walked over to the flowers. Several of the blooms were bent and broken. He leaned down and examined them while Shadow roamed the grass. He sighed. It was another no-win situation. Tyler smiled and waved to the ladies who just glared, then whistled at Shadow to head back in.

Just as Tyler opened the door to his condo, he heard his cell phone beep with an unanswered message. He frowned at the number, and put the message on speaker to listen, not in the mood to talk to anyone. His sister, Chelsie's, perky voice squealed, "Hey big brother! Just called to wish you a happy birthday. Jim and I are having a little get together this afternoon about three and would love for you to come."

Tyler grimaced at the phone. He'd have to make up some excuse. There were a million things to do today to get ready for the weekend run on the restaurant. He had no time for a tea party and hadn't even thought about it being his birthday. Thirty-eight and broke hardly seemed like something to celebrate.

Her voice continued, "And you can't say no or I will ambush you at work." She would, too. His sister was one of the most determined people he knew.

"I have a big birthday surprise for you!"

Tyler groaned and flopped onto the couch. He'd bet the "surprise" came in the form of some friend she wanted to hook him up with. Chelsie thought being single ranked right up there with having the plague. Like being alone was some hideous disease she had to save him from by parading eligible prospects in his path. Why couldn't she accept that he preferred being alone?

He didn't have the patience for a relationship, having to tiptoe around and worry about making someone else happy. Without a woman in his life he could be himself all day, every day, and that's the way he intended to keep it.

Chelsie could be very determined, but so could he, and maybe it was time to lay down the law. Get her to back off and let him breathe. He'd stop by for a second, have a firm chat with little sis, then be on his way.

Just as Chelsie's message finished, his phone rang again. The name on the caller ID flashed *JT's*. Tyler had a sinking feeling. The restaurant only called this early if it was bad news. He picked up.

A thick Spanish accent boomed through the phone. "We have problem right now." Lydia was the head server and his all round right hand at the restaurant.

"Yeah, so what else is new?"

Lydia ignored the comment and went on full steam ahead. All business, as usual. "The truck this morning is short chicken and no New York steaks. Arty called in sick, and the ice machine is no working again. You want I should call somebody to look at it?"

Tyler glanced at the clock. Lunch rush loomed two hours away and no repair guy ever moved fast. "No, I'll do what I can. See if you can get Jamie to come in and send him over to buy fifty bags of ice. Maybe I can get it up and running by then."

"*Si.*"

The dial tone hummed in his ear, and he scrambled to the bathroom for a five-minute shower. Twenty minutes later, Tyler weaved his Jeep through the alley to the back door of the restaurant. Tony greeted him on the back step, his 6-foot-4, 260 pound frame blocking Tyler's way. A large, imposing man, Tony looked more like a bouncer than a chef.

"You don't wanna go in there." He shook his head and stepped into the alley, pulling a cigarette out of his pocket.

"Why's that?"

"It's too long a list for one smoke." Tony lit up his smoke and took a deep drag.

"Great." A small pickup loaded with bags of ice screeched into the alley.

"You mind unloading while I try to get the ice machine running?" Tyler asked.

Tony nodded. "No problem."

Tyler walked through the busy kitchen. Within seconds, Lydia trailed behind him, talking non-stop. A tiny woman, she had the tenacity of a pit bull and the temper of one. Tyler chalked it up to her Latin heritage. Lydia could get things done, and in his mind that outweighed her occasional lack of people skills.

"We got more chicken from Ken's Wholesale, but we still short. The New York steaks are a no, everyone's out. Jamie went to get ice, should be back by now."

"He is."

"A guy called from Brown, Lankley and something and said they send some kind of papers over."

Tyler checked the hoses on the ancient ice machine as she talked. Frozen over again. He'd have to get it melted before he could unhook it. The phone up front rang, and Lydia scrambled around the equipment, leaving him in peace for a few minutes. He retrieved a heat gun from the office that he kept for this particular recurring emergency and plugged it in. It roared to life and the lights flickered.

The building was historic for the area, and so was the wiring. Hopefully the ice would melt before they overloaded the circuits. His cell phone buzzed. He didn't recognize the number and clicked it off, shoving it into his front jeans pocket. *Probably just bill collectors anyway.*

Lydia waved her hand in front of him to get his attention. He turned off the heat gun.

"Your sister is here."

"Shit." Handing the heat gun to Lydia, he wiped his wet hands on his jeans. "See if you can get the rest of that ice off the hoses."

He turned and almost ran over Chelsie.

"Nice to see you too, Ty." She crossed her arms over her expanding stomach and frowned at him.

"Just have lots to deal with today, Sis."

Tyler directed her to the front of the restaurant and grabbed them two glasses of water. She slid into a booth across from him.

"I figured you wouldn't come to the cookout, so I decided to chase you down. Happy Birthday, by the way."

"Thanks. How've you been feeling? How's Jim?"

"Fine. I'm fine, the baby's fine, Jim's fine. Don't change the subject. I came to give you your birthday present."

"I don't need a present, I'm fine."

"That's what I thought you'd say, and no you're not. It's like you're this shell of your former self. All you do is work. You never do anything else."

"I *have* to work. I don't have time for anything else."

"You don't make time. But you will now."

"Why's that?"

"You need to get back out and meet people. Since you seem determined to avoid any of *my* friends, I placed a personal ad for you online."

"You did *what*?"

"You heard me. It started today. By the time you get home, there should be an avalanche of phone calls from women who would love to meet a, she cleared her throat and quoted, 'Single white professional male, seeking professional female for companionship, maybe more. I'm six foot two, wavy blonde hair and blue eyes. Like to dance and enjoy cooking for that special someone."

"This is a joke right?"

"Nope."

"I swear to God, Chelsie, what gives you the right to mess with my life?" She'd gone too far this time, stepped over the line. His temper boiled.

"It's your own fault. You refused to work with me on plan A, so I switched to plan B." She leaned toward him. "And if this doesn't work, then there's a plan C."

"No." He got up. "I'm not doing this. I will decide who is in my life, and you will keep your nose out of it from now on, or I'll…"

"You'll what?" Chelsie stood in front of him, the top of her head barely coming halfway up his chest. "Beat a pregnant woman? Ooh, I'm so scared." She waved her hands at him exactly like she used to when she was little and he threatened her.

"Don't tempt me." His bluff hadn't worked much better back then, either.

"*You're* not even in your life anymore, Ty." She bounced her finger off his chest. "You'll thank me for this someday." Turning on her heel, she didn't give him time to argue.

"Don't bet on it," he yelled after her. He shook his head—at a complete loss. What could she have been thinking? You don't intrude on someone's life, set that person up with the whole world by running a personal ad and then spring it on him like it's a good thing. This could possibly go down as the worst birthday he'd ever had, and it wasn't even noon yet.

Lydia and Tony looked very busy when he got back to the kitchen, pretending they hadn't heard every word. He took the heat gun and bent down to start on the hoses again.

"So, boss," Tony's voice held a hint of humor, "when do we get to meet your first virtual Miss Maybe?"

Tony and Lydia dissolved into laughter. Tyler clenched his teeth. These two would never let go of this one. He'd likely hear about this everyday for a month. He flicked on the heat gun to drown them out.

The rest of the day sped by, as the restaurant filled and emptied through the lunch rush and refilled with patrons for the evening. Tyler cooked side by side with Tony until the last order was filled and the last ticket paid. When he finally glanced at his watch, it was well past midnight.

Driving home in a blur, Tyler collapsed on the couch. Shadow rubbed her head under his hand until he scratched behind her ears. He pulled his wallet out of his back pocket and tossed it on the end table. He pulled the phone from his pocket to toss it on the table as well, but stopped. Remembering his little chat with Chelsie, he powered it up.

The display flashed 18 messages. *Eighteen?* What had Chelsie done to him? He blew out a slow breath. What that girl needed was a good swift kick in the butt. He stared at the flashing number. How many desperate women were there anyway? Eighteen, at least. He closed his eyes, physically and mentally exhausted. Too bad he couldn't hire a buck-toothed biker chick to take to Chelsie's next cookout. That'd shut her up.

His eyes popped open, and he focused on the number again. Why hire someone when there were 18 possible biker-chicks calling for free? He could pick the worst, most desperate woman of the lot. How hard could it be? Tyler chuckled to himself. Chelsie was going to learn the lesson of a lifetime, and all he had to do was push "play."

Chapter 3

Serena sat at her kitchen table and looked over the names on her notepad. It had been easier than she thought to set up her plan. She'd taken half a day off to make the calls in privacy while her son was at school. At least Nolea gave out her landline number and not her cell. She could always cancel her home phone if one of them turned out to be a stalker. She scanned the list. She'd planned for one each hour from 5:30 p.m. to 7:30 p.m. If she had to do this, no reason not to be efficient about it. She had two set up already, and only needed one more. She could teach a course on speed dating: three dates, three hours, no commitment, no kidding.

She'd picked Friday as designated date night. Nolea and Will agreed to accompany her as chaperones and keep watch at a distance. Distance was the key word. They had to believe she was really serious about this, not that they wouldn't be on her side if she told them what she was up to. All single people hated blind dates. Neither one of them had any ability to keep a secret, and if her uncle caught wind of the charade, it would be off. Then Aunt Macy would be back on again, hounding her to find a good man.

The rolled up T-shirt on the coffee table kept attracting her attention. Justin entered the house every day dropping clothes, papers, shoes, whatever in a trail as he went. She walked over and picked up the shirt, an odd sock stuffed in the side of the couch, and a Rangers cap hooked on the lamp, intending to deposit them on his bed. She swung open his door and paused.

The place was a pigsty, and she'd had enough of nagging him to clean it. Besides, the ad to rent out the extra room started running today, and she would be horrified for someone to get a glimpse, or a whiff, of her son's living habits.

Serena used her feet to scoot laundry into the center of the room, having no idea if it was dirty or clean. She held one shirt to her nose and quickly jerked it away again. *Definitely dirty.* In fact, it could almost walk to the washer on its own. Trying to hold her breath, she hefted a huge pile of clothing off the floor.

Boxer shorts tumbled from the pile. She shifted the load and bent down to grab them. The phone rang just as she stood. Serena grimaced and dropped the laundry, picking up the handset off her son's desk.

"Hello?"

"Hello," a deep voice said. "Is this Serena?"

"Yes."

The man cleared his throat. "This is Tyler." He waited a moment for her to respond. "You know. The ad."

"Oh, well, the room is 12 by 14 and has plenty of windows." She shuffled the stack of school papers and books on Justin's desk, looking for a pencil and something to write on. "You'd have your own private bath, and the house has a security system." She yanked open the side drawer and found a pen. "Where do you work, if you don't mind my asking?"

"Um. I really didn't expect to move quite this fast. What kind of thing did you have in mind?"

The laughter in his voice immediately pricked her temper. "Well obviously not the kind of *thing* you have in mind, *mister*. You know I really don't appreciate prank calls."

"Hey now, you called me first, and *you're* the one offering a sleepover," he chuckled. "By the way, is a continental breakfast included?"

"I did *not* call you first. I don't have any clue who you are, and I am not about to stand here and…" She threw the pen back in the drawer. It bounced off a small blue box. She frowned and picked it up. Two words riveted her attention.

Lubricated Condoms.

"You answered my ad."

Serena ignored him and stared at the box in horror. How long had Justin been using these? And with whom? She flipped open the top and counted. Six left out of? She squinted at the box. *Twelve?* A vision passed through her mind of herself a year from now, wearing an ugly burp-stained shirt bearing the word grandma while pushing a stroller down the sidewalk.

"Hello? Are you still there?"

"Uh. Yeah."

"You answered my ad. Said you were interested in coffee or something. Is this the something?" He was still laughing.

"Oh, *that* ad." Heat flamed her checks. "Um, I'm sorry. I have an ad running to rent out an extra room."

"So are we on for drinks or whatever?"

"Drinks, yes. Whatever, no. How about Friday at 7:30?" Serena stared at the blue box again. She'd have to confront Justin and figure out what exactly he'd been up to or *who* he'd been up to. The thought made her stomach churn. Did he not realize how easily his life could be turned upside down by one careless moment? Or one broken condom? She would certainly fill him in on that one. Not to mention the fact that he could catch something that could endanger his health.

"Tomorrow? Fine by me. Where would you like to go?"

"How about Chuck's over on Condom Street?"

"Condom Street?" He laughed. "I hate to admit it, but I'm not really familiar."

"*Camden* Street." Serena gritted her teeth, grateful he couldn't see how red her checks had turned.

"Oh, of course. So it's Friday at 7:30 at Chuck's?"

"Yeah."

"How will I know you?"

"Red hair, medium length, green eyes, black business suit."

"Sounds like you've done this before."

"Actually, it's a first for me." *And hopefully a last.*

"Uh huh." He didn't sound convinced. "See you there."

She set the handset back on the base, put the box back down and slowly shut the desk drawer. *What to do?*

Her first instinct was to demand to know what was going on, but she knew that was futile. Justin inherited her stubbornness and independent attitude, which was good most of the time. But it produced a lengthy silent treatment when she demanded information or cooperation. A gentle persuasive technique worked best, but unfortunately she lacked the skill or patience to use it effectively.

She'd have to figure out how to go about getting him to talk. Something like this could change his whole life. And not for the better. The front door opened, and Serena spun around grabbing the pile of laundry. Justin met her at his door.

He dropped his backpack on the floor with a thud, and nodded at the clothes. "So what's that?"

"I'm doing your laundry."

"*You're* doing *my* laundry? What's the occasion?"

"I ran the ad to rent out the spare room."

"I hope this doesn't mean you're going to start cooking too." He made a face.

"Very funny. Why don't you clean the rest of that mess?" She started down the hall.

"I'll consider that." He yelled. "I'm a busy man, you know."

Busy? The word took on a whole new meaning today. Serena stuffed Justin's clothes in the washer and dumped laundry detergent on top. He appeared in the doorway of the laundry room. "Are you sure you're doing that right?"

She glared at him and dumped in more detergent. "I'm not totally without homemaking skills. Who do you think kept you in clean diapers when you were little?"

"Weren't they disposable?"

She arched a brow at him and motioned to the papers in his hand. "What's that?"

Justin followed her to the kitchen. "I went by and picked up that financial aid stuff." He shuffled through the stack. "Lots of paperwork."

"I remember. We'll get started on it this evening."

"Kind of early don't you think?"

"It's *April*. You can never be too early with college forms, especially the ones for the grants. They are slower than Christmas."

"There's a whole section that has to be filled out by the non-custodial parent." He flipped through papers. "Tax returns, contact info, lots of stuff." He paused, but she said nothing. "How are we going to handle that?"

"Same as always. You only have one parent. They'll have to be satisfied with that."

"I told the lady at the Financial Aid office that. She said no way. They have to have it filled out to prove he isn't hiding money that can be used for school."

"They can't do that."

"They can. She also said that if it's because he's in prison or something, they still need official documentation. She said if they don't get it, they can refuse to accept the financial aid application."

Serena took the papers from him and glanced though them as pinpricks of panic stung her neck. "Hmm. I'll think of something." Financial Aid had been part of her plan for his college education from the start. It had been there to help her, and she didn't have enough to plop down cash for one of the better schools.

"What's the big deal? It's not like I even care at this point. Why can't we just tell them who he is?"

"It's nobody's business but ours, Justin."

"Well if it's *our* business, then why won't you at least tell me?"

Serena hesitated. He had every right to know, and she had every reason to keep it from him. Although given the evidence in his room, it might put a halt to his extracurricular activities.

"I know. I'll guess." He wiggled his brows with a half grin. "You were one of the original artificial insemination guinea pigs?"

"No."

"You adopted me from a band of roving gypsies?"

She laughed. "No."

Justin half smiled and lowered his voice. "So, am I Mick Jagger's love child?"

"Absolutely not."

"You can't fool me, you know. I've seen you wander home in the middle of the night with your pantyhose stuffed in your purse."

"Justin!"

"Well, I have. I bet you were one of those groupie chicks that chased the roadies, right?"

"I wish. At least Mick could help pay for college."

Justin picked up his keys. "I gotta get to work." He started for the door then turned around. "You're gonna have to deal with this sooner or later, Mom. It makes me no difference, whoever he is. It's not like I'm gonna run off and try to find him or anything, you know."

She nodded. "I know." And she did. Justin had never even hinted that he wanted to be anywhere else. Most parents weren't so lucky. He was a great kid.

"I mean unless he can do laundry *and* cook, now that would be something worth looking in to."

"Go already!" Serena smiled.

She went to the window and watched his truck pull out of the drive. She'd done all she could for him, but he deserved better. Better than her. And better than the truth. Serena walked over to the large rolltop desk and ran her fingers along the top edge. It had been her grandmother's and had occupied a prominent location in every home they had lived in since Justin was born.

The desk reminded Serena of family, of home, of secrets best left hidden. She took the key chain from her pocket and unlocked the top drawer. It only had the one key, and she kept it with her at all times. She pulled open one of the tiny drawers reveling a small silver cross encrusted with green and red stones.

It pulled her mind back to a sweet childhood, before her dad died, before she got pregnant, before she was sent away. Anger and resentment rose in her chest as she flipped the piece over and rubbed a finger across the inscription. She'd been told it was an old Gaelic saying, but she couldn't remember what her father told her it said. Something about the heart. It didn't matter. She'd worked hard to change her life, correct mistakes, provide a better life for her son, and she'd succeeded. But it didn't take away the hurt or make up for all she'd suffered. She tossed the necklace back in its drawer and pulled out a file labeled Baby Boy Finley.

Adoption? Artificial insemination? Those would be easy to explain compared to this. She stared at the birth certificate. Two little footprints on either side of the name, Justin Lee Finley, 7 pounds, 8 ounces. The fancy scrolled writing listed mother on the left and directly below that, her name, Serena Lee Finley. More scrolled writing occupied the right side announcing father and directly below that the space appeared exactly as it had that morning more than 18 years ago.

Completely and totally blank.

Chapter 4

Serena leaned toward her bathroom mirror and applied more lipstick. Only 20 minutes until her first "date" of the evening, and while she had no intention of trying too hard for this farce, she still wanted to look good. Brushing the front of her business suit with her palms, she glanced at her reflection in the full-length mirror on the back of the bathroom door. Not bad. The black skirt grazed her knees and the heels weren't too high. Nothing remotely suggestive about this outfit, which made it perfect. This was business after all, just business. She heard a key in the front door. "Justin?"

"Yeah?"

The faint sound of cereal hitting a bowl drew her to the kitchen. She stared as he filled one of her large mixing bowls with fruit rings and topped it off with a half gallon of milk.

Justin carefully picked up the bowl and met her gaze. "What?"

"Don't you work at a restaurant?"

"Yeah."

"You should eat there."

"I did. This is a snack."

Serena groaned. The boy was a bottomless pit. She grabbed her purse off the table.

"I was thinking about applying for a second job when school gets out," Justin mumbled. "A day job." He shoveled cereal in his mouth and let the milk drip off his chin back into the bowl.

Serena raised an eyebrow. Hard to believe he was about to be unleashed on the world as an adult. She handed him a paper towel. "That will be a lot of hours. Do you think you can handle it?"

"'Course."

"I mean it won't leave much time for friends or whatever." Whatever being uppermost on her mind. Not that she wanted to push him into working himself to death, but it sure would keep him busy.

He shrugged. "Not much going on anyway."

Serena hesitated a moment. This might be her chance. "You mean there are no hot women after you these days?"

"Oh sure, but I can fit them into my schedule."

Not the answer she had hoped for. "So who are you fitting in? Someone I know? You didn't say anything about going to the prom."

"Prom? Why would I spend money on that kind of crap?"

"So who is she?"

"Who is who?"

"The girl?"

"What girl?"

Serena glared. She had no patience for this. "The girl you're so hot and heavy with?"

"Gee. Hot and heavy? I don't know, but if you figure it out get her number for me."

His teasing smart-aleck expression irritated her beyond belief. She picked up the roll of paper towels and took aim at him. It was tempting, but it wouldn't get him to talk. Especially about anything important. He always tried to be funny when she needed to be serious. And the subject of sex at his age was very serious. She set the roll back on the counter and opted to pop him on the arm as she headed for the door. She'd have to try again later.

He laughed. "I'm cute when you're angry."

She slammed the front door and got into her car, catching sight of her red cheeks in the rearview mirror. Not exactly a great frame of mind to start the evening. Of course, she would be faking her love life tonight while her son was off somewhere *not* faking his.

Serena arrived at Chuck's five minutes late. Nolea and Will were already in position at the bar. Scanning the few occupants, she walked over to her chaperones carefully avoiding the peanut shells scattered on the floor. While Chuck's exuded the typical western theme, at least no dead animal heads were perched on the walls, and drinks were cheap.

"Thought you'd wimp out." Will slugged down a beer.

"You thought wrong." Serena climbed onto a bar stool.

Nolea craned her neck to see everyone else seated at the bar. "So who is the first guy? What should we look for?"

"His name's Bill something or another, and he's in his fifties." Serena searched for the notepad in her purse.

Will snorted. "Look for the motorized wheelchair and oxygen tank."

"Very funny." Her notes were difficult to read in the dim light. "Don't forget you two are supposed to rescue me if things get scary."

"Define scary."

Nolea nudged Serena's arm. "Ooh. White hair at twelve o'clock."

A man strode in Serena's direction. Six feet tall, stocky, dressed in a sport coat. Not bad for his age. His hair was totally white, but at least he still had it.

The man walked up to her and smiled. "You wouldn't be Serena, would you?"

"Yes, and you're Bill?"

He nodded and extended a hand. "Nice to meet you." His gaze passed over Will and settled on Nolea.

Appreciation lit his eyes as he took in her long curly hair, and scanned the full length of Nolea's shapely legs and dangerously high heels. Good. A roving eye is a great excuse to get rid of this one. Nolea gave him a wave and he grinned.

Serena suppressed a smile. The woman couldn't help herself. Nolea loved men and attention, which worked perfectly for Serena.

No danger of anyone falling for her with this kind of distraction around. Will thumped Nolea's fingers, and Serena cleared her throat, once again capturing Bill's attention. "Why don't we find a table?"

Bill nodded and followed her across the bar. Serena chose a table for two and took the seat with her back to the bar, giving Bill a full view of Nolea. The waitress placed menus in front of them.

"I'm not really hungry." Serena handed the menu back to the girl and looked at Bill. "I thought we might have a drink and see how things go. Is that all right with you?"

He grinned. "Suits me just fine."

"Great. I'll have a margarita on the rocks."

"And I'll have tequila. Straight up. A double."

A double? Either this guy was incredibly nervous or an alcoholic. "So, Bill. What made you place an ad?"

"Oh, you know, seeing what's out there." He shrugged. "What made you answer it?"

"You sounded like a nice guy. What do you do for a living?"

"I'm in sales."

"What kind of sales?"

"A little bit of everything."

Uh oh. A car salesman. They were always evasive.

The waitress set their drinks down, and Bill took a huge gulp. "What line of work are you in?"

"I'm a writer."

"What do you write?"

"Little bit of everything." This was going nowhere.

He grabbed a handful of peanuts from the bucket on the table and chewed with his mouth open, throwing the shells on the floor. "These babies sure make you thirsty." He motioned to the waitress for more drinks.

Serena shook her head. "I'm fine thanks, but you go ahead." And he did. While they chatted about the weather, he drained another and ordered more. She narrowed her eyes at him. "You really like tequila."

He gave her a lopsided smile. "Yeah, you see I'm hypoglycemic, so tequila has almost no effect on me at all. And yes, ma'am, I *do* like it." He raised his glass to her and drained the whole thing.

"Did your doctor tell you that?"

"No, my mom did. She ought to know, she's the same way. Drinks a fifth a day and never had any problem with it." He leaned toward her. "Say, how close are you and that pretty friend of yours?"

Tequila-laden breath floated across the table, assaulting her senses. "We get along all right." Her eyes watered.

"I bet you two make a great team." He tried to wink, but failed. "I've been known to be a team player myself on occasion."

Team player? *Oh my god!* Time for a little rescue. While Bill ordered another drink, Serena moved her purse to the other side of the chair in the predetermined signal for Will to show up. She waited.

Nothing. She glanced behind her. Nolea shrugged and pointed to the restroom.

"So, Honey." Bill reached over and grabbed her hand. "What's say we find somewhere a little quieter?"

Serena's heart pounded. She willed herself not to panic as she tried to tug her fingers from his large sweaty hand.

"Serena?" Nolea appeared next to her chair. "We really need to get going."

"Hey there, sweet thang." Bill's drawl became more pronounced and much louder. "We's talking about a little get-together over at my place. How about it?"

"How about what?"

Serena finally snatched her hand away from Bill's drunken grasp. "Why yes, Nolea. You see Bill is a *team* player."

Nolea raised a brow. "Oh *really*? How convenient." She trailed a finger down Bill's arm. "Just what we were looking for."

"I am?" Bill seemed shocked.

He wasn't the only one. "He is?" What in the hell was Nolea up too?

"Definitely." Nolea grinned. "We brought along most of the equipment. The chains and dog collar are in the trunk. You don't mind a little blood do you, Bill?"

"Blood?" he squeaked.

Serena tried not to laugh. The man turned ashen, and his drinking hand shook. She played along.

"The last time was an accident, Nolea. I'm sure Bill is man enough to take it." She scrunched her nose at him and smiled.

Bill jumped up. "Uh, ladies, I don't really think I'm what you're looking for."

Nolea wiggled up against him, and he backed away as if burned. "Oh you're exactly what we need. No attachments, no commitments, no relatives to ask questions."

Bill staggered backward and reached into his pocket. "Uh. I gotta be going." He tossed cash on the table and hurried past the bar, almost knocking Will over in his attempt to escape.

"That guy looks like he saw a ghost," Will said as Nolea and Serena joined him.

"More like a Dominatrix," Serena said.

Nolea glared at Will. "And why did you pick now to inspect the porcelain?"

"When you gotta go, you gotta go. What did I miss?"

"A used car salesman aka porno king wanna be." Serena motioned to the bartender for a glass of water and climbed onto a barstool next to a cowboy. He turned and gave her a polite nod then proceeded to mind his own business, thank God. Nolea and Will scooted their stools closer to her.

"How much time 'til the next show?" Will ordered another beer as Serena glanced at her watch.

"Twenty minutes." The evening already dragged.

"What's the scoop on date number two?" Nolea asked.

Serena consulted her notebook. "Tall, has an IT degree, is almost thirty. His name's Michael."

"*Almost* thirty? So since you couldn't rob the grave with the last one, you're going for the cradle with number two?" Will snickered.

Nolea glared. "Listen Diaper Dan. You're thirty too, and if that is what works for her, then that's fine."

"Twenty-nine. So are you saying an old chick, like yourself, would be willing to have a go at a younger man?" Will wiggled his eyebrows at Nolea. "Like me?"

"Not on the darkest night, on the loneliest island at the end of the earth." Nolea sipped her drink.

"I love it when you play hard to get." He grinned.

Serena ignored them, and leaned back to get a better look at the door.

The cowboy glanced over his shoulder at her. "Am I in your way?"

"No, you're fine." She looked up into deep blue eyes. He smiled. *In fact you're very fine.* Too bad this kind of guy didn't run an ad. She dragged her eyes away from his and tried to focus on the business at hand. He turned around and sipped his beer, ignoring her again. Though he wore a casual shirt and jeans, the old crinkled straw hat gave him away as the real thing, not some kind of drugstore cowboy.

A tall lanky man with spiked blond hair walked up to Nolea. "You're Serena, I hope?"

Will laughed. "Strike one, lover boy."

Serena thought she saw the cowboy smile as she scrambled off her stool and around to the man. "I'm Serena. Why don't we get a table and talk for a while?" She pulled his sleeve, leading him away from the bar.

The waitress followed and Serena ordered another margarita.

"I'll have milk," Michael said.

Milk? Did he actually say milk? Who orders milk on a date? She cleared her throat. "So, Michael, what do you do?" His baby face sported what looked like the first whiskers he'd ever grown, and they barely covered his chin. He could be her son's age. Obviously he'd exaggerated a bit in the ad. He'd be 29 all right, in about 10 years.

"I test software."

"Oh really?" He might look young, but at least he had a real job. That was something. "What kind of software?"

"Video games."

So much for a real job.

"Do you play?" he asked.

"No. Not really."

"Why not?"

Because I'm a grownup. "I guess I never really got into it."

"Man, that's too bad. I mean," he leaned forward. "You have no idea how good it feels to beat a program that people spent months or even years designing." He motioned with his hands as he talked, his excitement building. "I mean, take the one I'm working on now. I've been trying to get out of underworld for almost two months now. Tried everything. Firing the granite, worshiping the maker, you name it. Finally last week I got out of the afterlife tunnel and figured out the sequence to steal the Roman life skill."

Was this guy even speaking English? Serena sat and listened as he babbled, trying to keep her mind from wondering. Wondering how to look interested. Wondering if the next guy would be this bad. Wondering how long it would take to get another margarita.

He paused to take a breath. "You know, I hear video games really help older people keep their minds active." He looked at her expectantly.

She narrowed her eyes at him. "Meaning?"

"That you should go ahead and give it a try. Why wait 'til the last minute?"

The last minute? That's it. Serena pointed to the back of the bar toward the restrooms. "Would you excuse me for a little bit?" She moved her purse to the opposite side of the chair hopefully signaling the cavalry.

"Okay. I'll wait here."

"Yes, Michael." She tried not to sound sarcastic but the margaritas were getting to her. "You wait here and drink your *milk*." *Granny's got to pee.*

Chapter 5

Tyler paced around his condo trying to figure out why he had the jitters. He'd seen four women this week. All ranked somewhere around average. Which was nowhere near bad enough. Not a chipped tooth among the lot. Oh, they had their issues all right. From chronic unemployment to five kids in tow. He'd sure seen some fearful baggage this week.

But nothing that would scare off Chelsie, and when he'd presented his plan to one of the women, she'd smacked him right in the mouth while ranting on and on about how he dragged her out on a date under false pretenses. Fat chance. Of course, telling her he wouldn't touch her with a 10-foot pole probably didn't convey the warm fuzzies his date had envisioned.

So why the nerves for this one? He still hadn't figured out why her voice sounded so different. The message Serena left on his phone had a deep sultry quality, but when he'd called back, she'd sounded completely different and completely distracted. He grinned to himself. *Condom Street*. There had to be a story behind that one. If nothing else he could use a good laugh.

Tyler glanced at the clock. Only 6:00 pm. No sense in hanging around here. Might as well show up early, have a beer or two, and relax a little. He jammed his favorite straw cowboy hat on his head and tried to open the door. Shadow jumped on it, then on him, wanting to go. Tyler scratched her ears. He hadn't been home but a few minutes at a time all week with his biker chick shopping.

Poor dog needed some attention. As Shadow settled down, he moved around her, then quickly slipped out. He heard her yelps from the hall.

"At least my poor Reggie won't be listening to that noise much longer." Mrs. Lathem stood in the doorway to her condo. Rat Dog quivered at her ankle. The thing shook like a naked cat on crack. He couldn't tell if the dog was nervous or scared, but he could understand it. Mrs. Lathem had that effect on a lot of people, too.

"Are you and," Tyler pointed to the dog, "*it* moving somewhere?"

She yanked the dog off the floor as if he'd attacked the thing. "It's okay, baby, the mean man will be gone soon."

"Gone?"

She glared. "I've discovered that condo was subleased to Dick Rawlin's niece, not to you."

"So? I pay the bills."

"You're a squatter, Mr. Cooper." She pointed a finger at him. "And you'll be gone within the month if I have anything to say about it." She stepped back and slammed the door.

Tyler wasn't scared. Last he heard, Dick Rawlins was in Mexico somewhere, and the reason he'd subleased it in the first place was to have some income and get someone to take care of it. Krista never paid anything on time or in full, but Tyler had. Mrs. Lathem would have a heck of a time convincing Dick to kick him out. He shrugged off the threat as he steered his Jeep to Camden Street.

Arriving at Chuck's a few minutes later, it looked like the happy hour crowd was breaking up. He had no trouble finding an empty seat at the bar and ordered a beer.

"So how do you want me to get rid of the next one?" A man a couple of seats over asked.

"Does it matter? It's not like you didn't get caught with your pants down a minute ago." The sultry voice tapped Tyler's memory. The same one on his phone. He tried to look around the guy between them, but couldn't see her face. All he could see was legs on one side of the bar stool, long curly hair on the other. Odds were good that she was pretty, and in his book that spelled disaster. He concentrated on his beer, knowing he would leave as soon as it was gone. No use wasting his time. She obviously had some kind of sick mind game going on with her junior bodyguard anyway.

A woman sat next to Tyler, looked at him, and he nodded an acknowledgement but didn't speak, anxious to leave. He only caught bits and pieces of the conversation during the next few minutes. Not that he cared anymore. The woman laid her notepad on the bar next to his elbow and turned back to her friends. He glanced down at the notes. There were several names on the page. The name Bill had a line drawn through it. The next on the list was Michael, then Tyler. *Tyler?*

He glanced at the woman out of the corner of his eye. Red hair, black business suit, green eyes. That's the description Serena had given him. He frowned. Well if this was Serena then who was Miss Legs at the end of the bar? What in the hell kind of game were these people playing?

Serena jumped off her barstool and tugged on the sleeve of the biggest geek Tyler'd ever seen. He knew he should leave while he had the chance, but curiosity kept him glued to his seat.

"So what do you think about this one, Will?" Miss Legs asked as soon as Serena was out of earshot. Tyler could see her clearly now in the mirror at the back of the bar, and his first instinct proved right. Pretty, but not as pretty as she obviously thought she was. Just the type to expect men to worship her and her little turned up nose.

"Not a snowball's chance." Will grinned.

Serena led her date to a table and they sat. She wasn't bad. Petite and curvy, more on the cute side than anything, though she'd hidden it well in that business suit. Or tried to.

The waitress returned to the table with drinks a few minutes later, and Miss Legs laughed. "Did she just bring him milk?"

Tyler squinted at the glasses on the table. Sure enough it looked like milk to him. The geek started talking, and Tyler would swear his mouth moved a mile a minute.

He'd had one of those dates himself this week. At the time he'd wondered if the girl would ever stop talking long enough to take a breath.

Miss Legs leaned back resting her elbows on the bar. "You buying any of this, Will?"

"Nope. Can't quite figure out what she's up to though."

"Me neither. She gave in *way* too easy on this idea."

They all watched for another few minutes, then Serena got up and started toward the back of the bar.

Will put his beer down. "There's the signal. This loser's history."

He strutted over to the geek and poked him in the chest. The guy shook his head no and stood up. He towered over Will by a good foot, but acted scared. Will poked his chest again and the guy backed up a step then turned and hurried past them out the door. Tyler looked at Will amazed. Bald and no more than five and a half feet tall, he had all the attitude of a bouncer. And the geek just got bounced.

Will strutted back to the bar as Serena reappeared. She climbed back on the stool next to Tyler. He stared at the liquor bottles behind the bar, pretending not to listen.

"That was horrific. The guy is underage and into video games." Serena squirmed and tried to straighten her skirt. "How did you get him to leave?"

Will puffed out his chest. "I told him you were my wife."

Serena elbowed him hard in the ribs.

"What did you want me to say?"

"Not that! I don't want people to think we're fuck buddies or something. Eew!"

Tyler choked on his beer and tried not to laugh. She sure had a mouth on her. This was turning out to be the best entertainment he'd had all week.

"Whoa there, Red," Will laughed. "I think them margaritas are going to your head."

"No, they aren't," Serena said. "Not yet anyway."

"When's Act Three supposed to show?" Miss Legs motioned to the bartender for some more pretzels, but the man ignored her. She banged the bowl on the bar, forcing his attention to her.

"Nolea!" Serena snatched the bowl out of her hand, then consulted her notepad. She crossed off the second name. "Not until 7:30. His name's Tyler. Tyler Cooper. No clue what he does."

"Gee, don't sound so excited." Nolea leaned back and looked at her. "Somebody might think you weren't really into this."

"Oh, it's not that. I just hate having to wait."

Too quick on the denial, hon. Tyler saw a knowing look pass between Nolea and Will.

"I'm hungry." Will rubbed his stomach. "Is the company buying dinner?"

"No." Serena stuffed her notepad back in her purse.

"I think I'm gonna walk down to the bar on the corner. They give away free hot dogs on weeknights. Y'all want anything?"

Nolea shook her head, "You are such a cheap bastard."

Serena nodded. "You'd think free was his favorite four letter 'F' word."

"Second favorite." Will departed, leaving the ladies to themselves.

"What are you up to?" Nolea glanced at Serena.

"Up to?"

"You know we're not buying this little charade, don't you?"

"What charade?" Serena stuffed a pretzel in her mouth.

"You know exactly what I mean. And don't give me that innocent look. I can tell your heart's not in this." Nolea waited for a response, but Serena remained silent. Finally Miss Legs spun around and hopped off the barstool. "I'm going to the sandbox; save my spot."

Serena nodded and watched until her friend disappeared. She propped her elbow on the bar and leaned her forehead on her open palm. "Oh shit," she groaned, "This is such a nightmare."

Tyler cleared his throat, "You never know, the next one might be better."

Her head snapped up. "Excuse me?"

He turned to her and smiled. "I said, the next one might be better."

She smiled back. "He couldn't be much worse."

"So is this some kind of new speed dating?"

"Not exactly. It's ummm, well," she groaned again, "complicated."

"Maybe you'll get lucky, and the next guy will cancel."

"I wish. Nolea and Will would never buy it though."

"Sure they would, if you made it look good." He wiggled his cell phone between his fingers. "Be easy to arrange a phone call at the right moment."

Serena looked at him as if he'd tossed her a life preserver. "Would you really do that?"

He grinned. "What's your number?"

Nolea sat down as Tyler stuffed the napkin with Serena's cell number in his shirt pocket. "I wish I'd had Will get me a hot dog," she said.

Serena frowned. "You're just as cheap as he is."

"Only about some things."

"I swear you two are opposite sides of the same coin."

"What coin?" Will sat an extra hot dog in front of Nolea.

Serena pointed to the food. "See?"

"Whatever." Nolea shrugged and took a big bite.

Tyler slid off the barstool and walked to the back corner of the bar. He dialed and waited as Serena searched her purse and finally picked up.

"Make it look good," he whispered.

"Oh *hi*, Tyler."

Nolea and Will leaned closer.

"No problem at all. We'll reschedule for another day."

Reschedule? Like he was a dentist appointment? This was the first time he'd ever helped a girl break a date with himself. Looked like they were buying it though. Serena could act, and given the right motivation she might be nervy enough to scare the hell out of Chelsie —if they could ugly her up enough. Tyler waited a few minutes, then returned to his seat. Will and Nolea stood, ready to go.

"You two go on, I think I'm going to get a burger here and then head home." Serena waved and turned back to the bar, watching in the mirror until they left. The second they were out the door, she gave him a huge grin. "That worked great! I owe you a big favor, and I mean *big*! Can I at least buy you a burger or something?"

"Sure, I'd love one."

"Great, I'm starved. Oh, I didn't even get your name." She stuck out her hand. "I'm Serena."

He took her hand gently, but firmly and waited until her gaze met his. "I'm Tyler. Tyler Cooper."

Surprise lit her eyes as the smile melted off her face. Serena tried to pull her hand from his, but Tyler held on refusing to let her get away. He leaned closer. "And I intend to collect on that favor."

Chapter 6

Serena followed Tyler to a table, goose bumps still rippling across her flesh. What did he want? He'd succeeded in helping her get rid of another bad date, or had he? After all, he *was* that date. Maybe all he'd really been trying to do was get rid of Nolea and Will. And now he had her cell phone number too! Her eyes traveled down his back as he walked, and settled on his jeans. The undulation of taunt muscles under the faded fabric seemed almost hypnotic.

What a rock-hard butt! The thought forced her gaze upward again. She had to keep her wits about her and could not afford to get distracted by his anatomy or by another foray into Margaritaville. Trying to calm her nerves, she glanced around. More people had filled the bar in the last half hour. He seemed smart enough not to try anything in public. She hoped.

The waitress came to their table immediately and flashed Tyler a big smile. He ignored it and ordered first.

"We'll have two burgers, medium, I'll have a beer and she'll have a margarita." He handed the menu back to the waitress.

Serena squashed her annoyance. Not that he didn't get points for ignoring the flirty waitress, but she could order her own food. "I'll have water, thanks." He looked great but came across a little high-handed for her taste, and she wasn't about to drink anything else until she found out exactly what he wanted.

"Oh, and a large order of onion rings," he said. The waitress nodded and left.

"Onion rings?"

"You don't like them?"

"Well, it's not exactly date food."

He smiled. "Well, this isn't exactly a date, now, is it?"

"What is it?"

He moved the ketchup, salt, and pepper out of the middle of the table. "Stuff should be over here." He looked up at her and hesitated. "I get the idea that you aren't interested in a real date anymore than I am, and . . . "

"I'm not," Serena cut in.

He nodded. "Good. Me neither."

"Then why did you place an ad?"

"I didn't. My sister did. She seems to think I might wither away without some woman in my life."

Serena frowned. "So why did you call me and come here tonight?"

"Why did you set up the date and then want to break it?"

She paused. "It's, umm . . ."

"I know. It's complicated, right?" He smiled. "Why is that?"

Serena didn't even know where to begin. "You first."

"Fair enough." They both paused as the waitress set two large steaming burgers in front of them. Tyler poured ketchup on his fries as he talked. "See, I have this plan."

A plan? Great. All she needed was another man with a plan. Maybe he and Uncle Frank should get together.

He held up a hand at her expression. "Now, hear me out."

He seemed to sense her irritation and impatience. Interesting, most men she knew couldn't sense an alligator in their underwear. She arched a brow and waited.

"I figure the only way to get my sister to stop butting into my life is to scare her off."

Serena frowned as she cut the large burger in half. She hadn't realized how hungry she was. "How?"

"I decided I'd find the worst woman I could from the ad she ran, then take that girl to one of Chelsie's cookouts. Hopefully it would scare little sis good enough to get her to mind her own business."

"So, I'm the worst example you could find?"

He paused mid-bite and looked at her. "No. But you're a decent actress when you want to be, and I figured we could work on the looks thing."

"The *looks thing?*" Serena, while relieved that he wasn't after a real date, had a difficult time not being offended.

"You know." He popped another french fry into his mouth. "Need to ugly you up a bit."

No wonder the man didn't have anyone in his life. Tact was not his forte. "Have you mentioned this plan to anyone else?"

"Yeah. One girl last week."

"What happened?"

"She hit me."

Serena laughed so hard it drew looks from nearby tables. "Imagine that." She found herself liking Tyler for his absolute honestly, in spite of his horrific way with words.

"It wasn't funny," he said, then smiled as she continued to laugh. "Maybe it was a little funny. So what's your story?"

Serena sat back and thought a moment. If he can be blatantly honest, so could she. It's not like she had anything to lose at this point. This guy might actually be the business arrangement she was looking for. "My uncle owns the paper, and I'm one of the editors. I was supposed to answer a few ads and then write some mushy copy to sell advertising."

"Why? Are they hurting for cash?"

"Not really, but more is better. And I know it's really another one of my aunt's ideas to get me a man so I won't be alone when Justin leaves for college."

"Justin?"

"My son." She saw him frown, and it piqued her curiosity. "You have any kids?" *Or ex-wives?*

"Nope. Have a dog, Shadow. Man's best friend, you know."

"Man's only friend?"

"That too." He shrugged. "You don't look old enough to have a kid in college. That the reason you're renting out a room?"

"Yes. College isn't cheap these days."

He nodded. "So what was the deal with Condom Street?"

Heat flashed across her face. "Oh that."

"Couldn't be that bad." He laughed.

"It could." She lowered her voice. "I found a half empty box of condoms in my son's room while I was talking to you on the phone. I guess it distracted me a little."

Tyler nodded. "If my mom had found a box of rubbers in my room, she'd been more than a little distracted."

"Not a box. *Half* a box. Which is frightening at his age." Serena poured out information to this man she'd known less than 30 minutes with no clue as to why. Normally she was exceptionally guarded where her personal life was concerned, but then Tyler wasn't interested in getting involved, so he posed zero threat.

"So you'd rather he not be using them?"

"No. I rather he be celibate until he graduates from college."

"It certainly has its advantages."

He glanced up as if realizing what he said, then quickly resumed eating. Serena swore she saw a slight pink color in his checks. How revealing. No girlfriend, no dating, no sex. Normally she would assume a guy like that was gay. But Tyler Cooper exuded sensuality from his scuffed cowboy boots to his crinkled straw hat. She nodded at the hat. "You a real cowboy?"

"I suppose. Used to rodeo in high school."

That seemed to fit him. She could imagine Tyler atop a horse in a rodeo arena. "So all you do now is work? You must love what you do."

"Not really. I own a restaurant. JT's."

She knew of it but had never been there. Some kind of barbecue joint from what she'd heard. "Why don't you like it?"

"I do like it, most of the time. But lately all I do is work, and there's never enough money."

"Is that why you don't date?"

"That's part of it."

"What's the other part?"

He shrugged but didn't answer. That was fine. She really didn't care. He would be perfect for the fake romance. Little low on social skills, but she didn't need those anyway. Just a guy that looked good and didn't want to get in her pants. Or pantyhose as the case may be. Tyler got an A+ in both areas. He wasn't the kind of guy she usually dated in that he wasn't a professional, had no cash flow, and worked all the time, so there was no chance of her getting attached. She had plans for her life, and they didn't involve a hunky cowboy.

Excitement flittered through her chest. Could she really get lucky and find the perfect guy on the first try? She peered at him again.

No baggage, no romantic interest, no complications. Yes. Tyler Cooper seemed perfect in every way, for her purposes at least. Serena finished off her burger and snagged one of his onion rings. "These are good."

"Not as good as mine." He smiled. "Always have to check out the competition."

Serena pushed away her plate. "So, let me see if I understand this plan. If I help you with your sister, will you agree to help fake a hot love affair for the paper?"

He piled his empty plate on top of hers. "What would I have to do?"

"Work with me on a few ideas for articles, maybe pose for a photo or two. I mean, I'd use different names or initials or something so you wouldn't be bothered."

"Doesn't matter. I don't mind being bothered."

"Well, I do. I have no intention of becoming a Dr. Ruth for the *Cranfield-Star*. No one will know it's us, except for family."

"Good. They're the ones causing the problems anyway."

"Exactly."

"So what names will we use?"

Serena thought a minute then smiled. "They call me Captain Old Maid, so I could use the initials COM."

He laughed. A deep, vibrating laugh that tingled down Serena's spine. "Okay. Then you can call me Lieutenant Rolling Stone."

"As in Mick Jagger?"

"As in gathers no moss. Or anything else for that matter."

"So, Lieutenant. Do we have a deal?" Serena grinned and stuck out a hand.

Tyler shook it. "That we do, Captain."

Chapter 7

"Wow. I almost need a cigarette after that." Will handed the paper to Nolea.

Serena watched Nolea's expression as she read silently. The first installment of "Lone Star Love Affair" had already hit the newsstands, and Serena braced herself for the fallout. She hid a small, satisfied grin as Nolea's jaw dropped.

"Oh my god." Nolea glanced at Serena, then read aloud. "The tingle of his lips on mine as his fingers slid gently up my spine?" She read on in silence, emitting only short gasps, gulps, and one sharp inhale before she tossed the paper on the desk.

Serena waited for her to say something. Anything. "So? What did you think?"

Nolea shifted her gaze to Serena. "I think we all may get fired."

"I'm not going to get fired, and neither are the two of you." Though the notion sent a small tremor of fear through Serena. The article wasn't *that* bad. Nothing worse than anything on TV these days and certainly nothing that a child couldn't read. She glanced at the last paragraph that detailed the final kiss of the fantasy evening. Well, maybe an older child.

Silence descended on the trio. Nolea pierced Serena with her gaze. "This comes across as very passive-aggressive, Serena. If you didn't want to write this column, you should have said so. What is it going to prove to get yourself fired by making this stuff up?"

"You sound just like Jeffery. I didn't make it up."

"Then who's Mr. Happy Hands?" Will asked.

"A cowboy I met after the two of you left the bar."

"*A cowboy?*" Will grinned. "Does this mean the next column will include some interesting activities involving spurs?"

Serena smiled. "It might."

Nolea punched Will's arm. "Don't encourage her. What cowboy?"

"You know. The one sitting next to us at the bar during the dating game."

"I remember." Nolea nodded slowly. "Beat up hat, great butt. Not bad."

A jolt of excitement went through Serena. This might work yet. Nolea remembering Tyler was her first break. Now they would believe her. "He thought the whole date thing was funny, and we got to talking, and that led to dinner, which led to— well . . ." She shrugged.

Will leaned forward. "So did it really end with just a kiss?"

"I'll never tell." Serena wiggled her eyebrows.

"Did you have to make it so, well, sensual?" Nolea asked. "A lot of our advertisers are older people with established businesses. There may be a backlash from this."

"I don't think it will be as bad as you think." *I hope.*

Mary Jo Clark hurried across the newsroom and stopped at Serena's office, puffing for air. Uncle Frank's secretary had been at the paper for 15 years and knew every tidbit of gossip there was to know about the place and the people in it. She held a hand to her ample chest as the cord from her headset dangled. "Oh Lordy." She heaved another breath. "Dalton Reid is on the phone, yelling something about us printing pornography and wanting to pull all his advertising."

"He's my biggest account." Nolea jumped to her feet and hurried out the door.

Mary Jo continued, "Frank's talking to him now, but the phone has been ringing off the hook both in our office and in circulation. One of the subscribers even threatened to have you arrested."

"Holy shit." Will picked up his camera and started toward the newsroom. "You're on your own on this one, Red."

"Thanks a lot." A sinking feeling pressed on Serena's chest. Had she really gone too far? She watched the newsroom as activity intensified. The phones picked up pace, and the noise level of the whole building seemed to climb a few decibels.

This could be bad. Really bad. Advertisers pulling out, subscribers canceling, angry letters to the editor. It hadn't occurred to her that this could endanger her job. What would she do if Uncle Frank had to let her go to pacify their readers? It could happen. Easily. Then what? How would she survive? How would Justin get through college?

The *Cranfield-Reporter Star* was the only newspaper in town, and New York was still a dream, which didn't leave her many options. Not to mention the fact that everyone would know why she got fired. That would put a big damper on any job interview. She needed to smooth this thing over before things got out of hand. They could print a retraction and say she had a hormone surge or a breakdown of some sort. This thing could be salvaged. Maybe.

Serena had to talk to Uncle Frank. She went to her doorway and glanced down the hall. His office door was closed. She called Mary Jo's desk and left a message for him to call her as soon as possible. Nothing to do now but wait and allow one horrific scenario after another to run through her mind like a string of old horror flicks. Frank screaming. Justin starving. A big scarlet letter painted on her chest.

She tried to stay busy, answering e-mail, editing stories, and reshuffling every piece of paper on her desk. Twice. Anything but answer the phone.

The voice mail light flashed relentlessly until curiosity got the best of her, and she dialed in. The monotone electronic voice came on the line.

"You have seventy-three messages."

Seventy-three? It would take the rest of the day just to listen to them all.

"You have a minute?" Frank Walker stood in the doorway.

Serena quickly hung up. "Sure." She tried to sound calm and confident but had no idea if she succeeded.

He closed the door and sat down, his expression somber.

Serena waited, the tingle of panic at the base of her skull growing. Co-workers hovered and hesitated outside her window, no doubt tossing more rumors into the feeding frenzy. Serena feared her whole life could change in the next few minutes, and she would have to sit here and take it while the world observed her like a fish in a glass bowl. Her mind grasped for the arguments and calming statements she had formulated during the course of the morning, but they all seemed to disappear.

Frank cleared his throat and gave her a small smile. "I have to say we're certainly getting some feedback this morning."

"We are?" Serena mentally kicked herself. She hadn't intended to start this conversation by playing stupid. "I mean, of course we are. I only intended to start things off with a bang." A bang? Poor choice of words. The image of her standing before a firing squad flashed through her mind.

"You certainly did that. Did you have any idea the kind of hornet's nest this would stir up?"

"To be honest, Uncle Frank, I hadn't expected quite this level of interest." Which was true. Nor had she expected this to be over so quickly. She'd had grand expectations that these articles would be the answer to so many nagging problems in her life. From Aunt Macy's interference to her lackluster career, she'd hoped "Lone Star Love Affair" might provide a welcome distraction to her otherwise boring life. Now it threatened to decimate that boring life she'd clung to for so long. "So I guess you'll be pulling 'Lone Star Love Affair?'"

Frank leaned back and crossed his ankles. "I've thought about it all morning, and I think we'll let it run for a little while longer."

"You what?" The shock must have registered on her face as several passers-by stopped and stared. "What about the advertisers, the subscribers?" She leaned forward. "The porn police?"

Frank laughed. "You heard about that one? Gave me a chuckle for sure."

A chuckle?

Frank sat up and smiled. "Oh, sweetheart, don't take it so seriously. A wise old editor once told me that you're not a real newspaper man until you get sued."

"Meaning what?"

"Meaning we're not doing our job unless we get a reaction out of people. Doesn't matter if it's positive or negative, it's all good for business. The fastest way to kill a newspaper is with reader apathy, and everyone seems to have an opinion on this column."

"How can it be good to lose all our advertisers?"

"We haven't actually lost any, yet. But even if we do lose a few, we'll pick up others. That's the nature of the beast. No, I think we'll let things go along as is for the time being. That sit good with you?"

Serena nodded as waves of relief flooded over her. Frank left her to her thoughts, and Serena shut the blinds over her glass partition closing out her curious co-workers. Let them wonder. This thing wasn't over yet. Far from it.

Uncle Frank would have to rethink things if their revenue slipped too far. But for now, Serena had a temporary reprieve and a little more time to give her ideas a chance to actually become a plan. One that included keeping her job, helping Tyler, faking a romance, getting to New York as soon as possible, and a partridge in a pear tree. It was going to be about as easy as juggling Jell-O. She'd have to work fast, but with a little luck and some dogged perseverance, she could make this happen. All of it, she hoped.

Liar's Fire

Chapter 8

Tyler loaded Shadow into his Jeep and followed the directions to Serena's house. He'd called this morning to make sure she really understood how bad he needed her to be. Hopefully, this would actually work, and he could have some peace in his life with no female interference for once. Serena came across as a really good sport and seemed to have a great sense of humor. She wasn't bad in the looks department either. Not that he was interested. After all, this charade was supposed to get women out of his life, so he could focus on turning his business around, not open the door to any possibilities.

He drove down Serena's street looking for the address he'd written on a small scrap of paper. Parking in front of a tan brick house, he noticed water running from the driveway where someone washed an old truck. Tyler looked the vehicle over as he walked up the sidewalk. A 1972 Ford, dirty white to rust in color, depending on where you looked, except for the right front quarter panel which was primer gray. Tyler shook his head. That kind of truck hardly seemed worth wasting water on.

"It may not look like much, but it rolls." A teenage boy walked around the back of the truck toward Tyler. He stuck out a hand. "I'm Justin."

"Tyler." They shook. "That yours?"

"Yep. Got it off a farmer real cheap, but the engine's good." He gave Tyler's Jeep a skeptical glance. "Nice wheels."

Tyler followed his gaze. The bright yellow paint was chipped off both bumpers, and the roll bar had a good size ding in it. "May not look like much, but it rolls." He grinned, and Justin grinned back. "Got it off my brother. He has a Jeep tour company in New Mexico."

"Cool."

Serena's son didn't look anything like her. Almost equal to Tyler in height, Justin sported a full head of dark hair, cut close, and a deep tan with no apparent tattoos or body armor in his nose or lips. That right there said a lot about Serena as a mom. The boy seemed a sharp contrast to her white complexion and bright red hair. The only feature they shared, as far as Tyler could see, was deep green eyes.

"You a friend of my mom's?"

"Yeah, she's helping me with a little project this afternoon."

The front door opened, and they both watched Serena walk carefully down the front steps in the tallest stiletto heels Tyler had ever seen.

The black dress she wore was short and very tight, especially across her chest. She'd curled her hair and put it up on top of her head. She looked years younger.

Wow. Tyler hadn't really noticed what a great figure she had, and this getup showed it off. Every bit of it.

She strutted up to him and smiled. "So what do you think? Do I look like a bar fly or what?"

Tyler had a hard time keeping his eyes on her face rather than staring at her deep cleavage.

"Y'all going to a Halloween party or something?" Justin laughed. "You look like a hooker."

"I feel like one too. A hooker on stilts." Serena looked down at her shoes, giving Tyler an even more distracting view down the front of her dress.

He cleared his throat and frowned. "I thought you were going for disgusting."

"Oh, don't you worry about that one." She gave him a mischievous grin. "I've got it covered."

"Was that why you had guacamole for breakfast?" Justin asked, then smiled at Tyler. "Oh man, are you in for it."

Serena climbed into Tyler's Jeep, and he joined her. "In for what?"

She smiled. "You'll see."

As Tyler navigated the Jeep toward the highway, Shadow stuck her nose into the back of Serena's poofed-up hair. She jumped and turned, frowning until she saw the dog.

"Hey, you have a boxer?" Serena petted the dog's ears. "You must be Shadow." The dog rubbed her head under Serena's hand, loving the attention.

Tyler nodded. "Have to warn you, she has a jealous streak. Doesn't like any women coming around. Wants me all to herself."

"She can have you." Serena continued to scratch the dog's ears.

The smile faded from Tyler's lips. Not that he cared, but it would be nice if she were a *little* interested in him. Nothing hot and heavy or anything, but it would be easier if she at least found him attractive.

He frowned at Shadow. That dog never liked any girl. Figures she'd like this one since Serena wouldn't be hanging around for any length of time. Tyler's eyes gravitated to Serena's enticing breasts again, and the Jeep swerved.

"Hey!" She shot him a glare. "I'd like to get there in one piece."

"Sorry." He stared at the road and tried to concentrate. This girl could be dangerous if he let his mind wander. Another incident like that, and some cop would pull him over for driving under the influence of great cleavage.

An awkward silence settled between them until Serena cleared her throat. "So, tell me about your sister. What do I need to know and what should I focus on?"

"What do you want to know?"

Serena thought a minute. "The standard stuff. How old is she? What does she do? What's her relationship to you like? What do I need to do to really shake her up? That kind of thing."

"She's about thirty-three now. Five years younger than me, two younger than Sam."

"Sam?"

"A brother. There are four of us. Jeff is the oldest, then me, Sam, and Chelsie. She's been married for eight years to Jim Lohan."

"What does Jim do? Do they have any kids?"

"Jim is a veterinarian. She's a kindergarten teacher. Their first kid is due in a few months."

"We're antagonizing a pregnant person?" Serena made a face. "I don't know about that."

"She'll be fine. Hasn't had one problem and loves being pregnant."

"What is her relationship with you like?"

He shrugged. "I'm kind of the bad seed. She did everything right, went to college, started her career, got married."

She raised a brow at him. "And you?"

"Dropped out of college, went to work in a restaurant and liked it. So here I am."

"And your brothers?"

Tyler inhaled. This was more information than he ever gave anyone, let alone a near stranger. But it was worth it to teach his meddling sister a lesson.

"Jeff's an attorney. Sam runs a Jeep tour company. He might even be there tonight. I heard he's in town."

"They have families?"

"No. Jeff's a workaholic, no time for anyone. Sam likes keeping his options open, if you know what I mean."

"Oh." Serena smiled. "A playboy."

Tyler chuckled. "More like a boy who wants to play. He's a good time though."

"What about you? You ever been married?"

"Once. For four weeks."

"*Four weeks?* What happened?"

"Long story."

She frowned at him. "It couldn't be that long if it only lasted four weeks. Didn't you ever want a family and all that?"

"Not really." She looked at him like she didn't believe him. But it was the truth. No kid would want a father like him. And time had proven no woman wanted a steady relationship with him, let alone marriage. It's not like he felt deprived in any way or like he'd missed anything. Besides he'd made a complete disaster of his own life; why be responsible for messing up anyone else's? He glanced at her and tried to change the subject. "Justin seems like a good kid."

"He is. Very." She smiled.

Tyler rolled the Jeep to a stop in front of Chelsie's house. Just the place one would expect a schoolteacher to live. Red brick cottage, white rail fence, the clay pots on the porch full of bright flowers. Serena leaned forward to get a better look.

"Cute place."

Tyler got out and Shadow followed.

Serena walked up by his side.

He looked her over again and raised his eyebrows. "You ready for this?"

She grinned and leaned close. "I was born ready." Serena slipped her hand into his, jolting a small charge up his arm.

Tyler squeezed her hand and they walked up the sidewalk. "We're a couple now, remember? We have to act like we're hot for each other." Not that *he* would have any problem with that. His gaze scanned the back of her dress that showed skin almost down to her rear end.

"No problem." She gave him a saucy grin. "I can fake anything." Serena stumbled across a loose brick in the sidewalk and Tyler's hands encircled her waist. He pulled her up against him. His fingers on the bare skin of her back sent tremors of pleasure through his body. They held onto one another for the space of three heartbeats. He pulled away first, forcing himself to concentrate on guiding Serena the rest of the way up the walk.

Tyler collected his scattered thoughts as best he could. One thing, however, had become crystal clear. The only one *faking* a hot attraction tonight would be Serena.

Chapter 9

The door swung wide, and a tiny woman with short blond hair leapt into Tyler's arms. "Hey! I can't believe you actually made it."

"Hey yourself." Tyler hugged her carefully. "This is Serena."

Chelsie's big brown eyes grew as she took in Serena from the top of her teased and puffy red hair to the bottom of her very short skirt.

Serena stuck out a hand. "Hey there, you must be Chelsie, or a paternity suit waiting to happen." Serena leaned over to Tyler and pointed at Chelsie's stomach. "You didn't have anything to do with this, did you?"

Chelsie gasped, and Tyler tried to stifle his smile. "No, she's my sister."

"Heard that one before." Serena elbowed him playfully, and then cocked an eyebrow at Chelsie. "So are we gonna stand here or what?"

"Uh, no. Please come in."

Serena brushed past a stunned Chelsie and walked into the kitchen. Jim and Sam sat at the table, with a deck of cards between them.

Sam jumped up and rushed to Tyler. "Hey, bro." He smacked Tyler's back and they shook hands. "Long time no see." His gaze shifted to Serena. "What have you been up to?"

"Serena, this is my brother Sam." She smiled and strutted over to Sam, looped her arms around his neck, and planted a big kiss on his lips. "Hey, brother Sam." She looked up at Sam's battered cowboy hat, almost a duplicate of the one Tyler wore. "I just love cowboys."

"Yes ma'am." Sam backed away and frowned at Tyler.

Serena glanced at Jim, who had stood now too and was eyeing her with a deer in the headlights expression. "Well now, who is this?" she purred.

Tyler went on as if her behavior were completely normal and made the introduction. "This is Jim, Chelsie's husband." Serena walked around the table toward Jim, who moved too, keeping the furniture between them. Serena stopped and put her hands on her hips. "What's the matter, Honey? Don't you want a hug?"

Jim held up his hands and waved her off. "Uh, no. I've got a little bit of a cold, and I might be contagious." He coughed to convince them. No one was fooled.

Tyler watched his three family members. They all looked like they expected Serena to leap across the table and pounce on Jim any second. And she just might.

He hadn't ever seen them this scared. Or speechless. It was all he could do not to burst out laughing, but he wasn't about to ruin this show.

Serena winked at Jim. "Too bad, I'll have to be *extra* friendly when you get well." She slinked over to Tyler's side and gave him a little pout. "I thought you said we were going to eat. I'm hungry."

"It'll be ready in a few minutes, as soon as Jim gets the meat on the grill." Chelsie smiled tightly.

Serena jerked back like she'd been stung and turned on Tyler. "Meat? We're eating meat?" She glared at him. "Didn't you *tell* them I'm a vegetarian?"

"Uh, no." Vegetarian? He'd seen her scarf down a huge burger in five minutes flat.

Tyler wished he'd asked her to give him a playbook so he could keep up. He thought a minute and opted for the stupid guy act. "I guess I forgot."

"You forgot?" Serena shouted. "You know how important it is to me. How could you forget? Don't I mean anything to you?"

Her voice became a high squeal. Definitely one of the most annoying noises he'd ever heard. He saw Sam grit his teeth and cringe.

"It's okay," Chelsie rushed in. "We're having grilled vegetables too and a salad. Will that work for you?"

A long moment passed as Serena continued to glare at Tyler. "I guess it will *have* to do, won't it?" The whole room breathed a sigh of relief.

"Why don't we sit down and play some poker for a little bit while the grill heats?" Sam motioned to the table. Tyler and Jim sat.

Chelsie pointed to the other counter where several large squash rested. "You can help me chop these up if you want, Serena."

Serena gave her a disgusted expression. "Me? Touch raw food? Gross." She plopped down next to Tyler on the bench and smiled at Jim. "So, can you teach me anything?"

Jim stared at her, and Chelsie banged a plastic bowl a little harder than necessary on the counter.

Serena's voice was smooth and sexy as she continued to smile at Jim. "About cards I mean?"

Jim said nothing. Tyler squeezed Serena's hand. "I can teach you, babe." He caught a disgusted roll of the eyes from Sam and a look of relief from Jim who dealt the next hand.

Serena peeked at her cards and tossed two. "So, Sam, what do you do?"

"I run a Jeep tour company in New Mexico."

"Ooooh. That sounds exciting. I always wanted to see what the desert was like."

"It's up in the mountains, so it's not really desert."

"Have you ever been to the desert, Sam? I hear it's really hot."

"Most deserts are." Sam tried not to let his annoyance show but failed miserably.

Tyler could tell Sam thought she was dumb as a stump.

"I went to Phoenix once, and it was pretty hot," Sam offered.

Tyler motioned for Serena to bet and she tossed in a chip and looked thoughtful. "So how far is Phoenix from the coast of Arizona?"

Sam paused mid-motion, the poker chip still in his hand. Chelsie's angry whacks with the knife on the cutting board ceased. Everyone stared at Serena.

Serena gave Tyler an innocent expression. "What?"

Sam smirked. "What makes you think Arizona has a coast?"

"Well, hello!" She gave him an exasperated huff. "You know the song about oceanfront property in Arizona."

Tyler struggled not to crack a smile. The other two men looked at him like he was crazy.

Serena pointed to Sam. "You should read more, Sam. You know what they say; a mind is a terrible thing to waste."

"No kidding." Sam's forehead gleamed a bright red. He tossed in a chip and called. They all showed their hands.

Serena clapped like a little kid. "Oh look, mine are all red!"

"That's a flush, babe. Way to go." Tyler hugged her shoulders and gave his brother a wink. "Beginner's luck."

Sam frowned and tossed his cards in. "Yeah, whatever."

"Uh oh." Serena leaned toward Tyler.

"What?" As soon as the word left his mouth a noise ripped through the kitchen, followed quickly by the worst odor Tyler had ever smelled in his whole life.

Serena grinned. "Excuse me." She shrugged at their stunned expressions. "It's part of being a vegetarian, you get a little gassy sometimes." She casually went on playing cards like nothing had happened. Jim's eyes watered, and Sam pulled his T-shirt up hooking it over his nose.

Tyler's neck muscles and face ached from trying not to laugh. And here he thought she didn't understand disgusting. Boy, did she.

The smell finally dissipated, and everyone relaxed again. Except that now there was little to no conversation.

Sam went to the refrigerator and pulled out a bottle of beer. "The iced tea isn't cutting it." He took a big swig and set it down.

Tyler raised a brow at his brother. Serena would have them all crying in their beer before the night was over. After a few minutes, she leaned over the table and reached for the beer. Tyler saw Sam's eyes widen at the view down her dress.

"I know a really great trick with a beer bottle." Silence greeted her along with frightened stares. Several beer bottle *tricks* he'd seen in the past flew through his mind—all of them shocking.

"I learned it when I worked at Hooters. See, you take the bottle and hold it between your boobs like this." Serena slid the bottle down her cleavage, adjusting her dress to make room.

The men stared. Chelsie slammed her knife down and gave Tyler a murderous look. If Chelsie got any madder, she was going to blow a gasket. Perfect.

He took Serena's hand. "Why don't we get some fresh air, babe?"

"Okay. I can show them this later." She smiled as if completely oblivious to the discomfort of the rest of the people in the room. "We'll be right back." She set the bottle back on the table.

"Great," Jim said with zero enthusiasm.

Tyler barely made it to the front porch before he doubled over in laughter. Serena joined him, laughing so hard tears welled in her eyes. "So, was I disgusting enough?"

"Oh, yeah. Definitely."

"It's the guacamole. Works every time."

Tyler regained control of himself. "We probably won't stay too much longer. I think Chelsie is about ready to stab me in the back with that knife."

Serena feigned offense. "What? You mean I won't get an invite to Thanksgiving?"

He chuckled. "I don't think so. And don't expect a Christmas card either." He looped an arm around her and squeezed.

She glanced at the window behind him. "We have an audience."

He didn't look back. He knew it was Chelsie. "How about a grand finale?"

"What kind of finale?"

"I was thinking about a grope fest."

She gave him a grin. "You or me?"

"How about both?"

"Right here?" Serena glanced around at the houses. A few of Chelsie's neighbors were out and about.

"Yes. Right here in front of God and everybody."

She laughed. "That would do it, I think."

He gathered Serena into his embrace and turned slightly so little sis could get a good view. Tyler lowered his mouth to hers and kissed her long and hard. Serena ran long fingernails up his back and then down. Lower and lower until she grabbed his butt and squeezed.

It sent an unexpected jolt of need through him, and Tyler pressed their bodies closer. The heat and electricity flowed between them unhindered. His lips traveled down her throat and she rewarded him with a moan. Serena flattened her body up against his until he could feel every curve. She had to be the best actress on the planet.

It excited and almost scared him to think how hot she might be when she meant it. He slid his fingers up her thigh and just as his hand grazed her bare butt, the screen door slammed into the side of the house. They jumped apart.

Chelsie glared. "Dinner is served," she gritted out.

Serena rubbed a hand down Tyler's chest as she held Chelsie's gaze. "Great, I'm starved." She bounced across the porch and into the kitchen. Chelsie banged the door shut in Tyler's face.

He placed a hand on the door jamb and leaned on it for a moment, trying to cool off. He still felt the heat of Serena's body on his. Her sexy voice rang out from inside the house.

"Tyler, hun? Aren't you hungry?"

Hungry? Man was he! Starving in fact, but not for food. He clinched his fist trying to erase the feel of her naked flesh. He'd set out to teach Chelsie a lesson, not torture himself with a woman he couldn't have.

Serena popped her head out, winked at him, and smiled. She motioned for him to join her.

Good thing this wasn't for real, or he'd be a goner.

Chapter 10

Serena put her hand on Tyler's arm as they stepped inside the door. She leaned into him and whispered, "I'm going to disappear to the ladies room and give them a chance to chat with you."

"Gee, thanks."

Slipping into the bathroom, she gazed at her face in the mirror. Her skin still burned a bright pink and her lips looked a little swollen. Tyler's kiss shook her to her knees. It's a wonder she'd been able to walk on the high heels after that one. She glanced down at her feet. They ached terribly, and she could see they were starting to swell. Hopefully this acting gig was almost done.

A little twinge of guilt gnawed at her. She'd behaved horribly, which was the whole point, but Tyler's family seemed like nice people—the kind she could really like. Of course, there was no hope they'd ever like her now. She took a deep breath. Not that it mattered. This was all part of the plan, and it had to work fast, even if this did seem a little extreme. Her eyes focused on her lips again and she brushed a finger across them, remembering the feel of his mouth on hers, and his hand on thigh, moving up to…

Oh! Serena shook her head, trying to erase the image from her mind. She fanned the heat from her face. That was it. No more kissing. This was a business deal, and she needed to treat it that way. Loud voices drew her attention. She quietly opened the door and crept down the hallway, crouching outside the kitchen where she could hear.

"Have you lost your mind?" Chelsie ranted.

"I think she's cute."

Serena could hear the smile in Tyler's voice.

"Cute?" Chelsie screeched. "Oh my God! How far is Phoenix from the coast of Arizona? That's cute?"

Sam laughed. "Where did you scrape her up, anyway?"

Silence fell on the group, and Serena inched closer. Photographs lined the hallway. Serena could barely make out Sam and Jim's reflections in the glass. Chelsie paced around the room. Tyler's back was to her.

He finally spoke. "Chelsie put a personal ad online for me as a surprise for my birthday."

"You what?" the men said in tandem.

"I thought we discussed that?" A note of censure crept into Jim's voice.

"We did, and I did it anyway." Chelsie crossed her arms daring Jim to say something. "It's not right for him to be alone."

Sam snorted. "Oh, and this is better?"

"Hey," Tyler said, "I'm getting the feeling that you don't like my girl."

"Your girl?" Chelsie seethed. "You mean your dime store hooker-vegetarian-doesn't touch raw food-gassy wonder woman?"

"Where'd she go?" Jim lowered his voice.

"Probably to check her drawers," Sam said. "Talk about damaging the ozone layer." Jim and Sam both laughed.

Serena almost giggled out loud and had to put her hand over her mouth. They were totally falling for it. The photograph underneath their reflection drew her attention. Two boys, maybe 12 or 13, all decked out in their cowboy hats and boots with ropes hanging on their shoulder. She smiled, a warm feeling flowing through her. They were adorable in a cowboy kind of way. She knew Tyler was the one on the left, but the other kid she couldn't place. It looked a lot like Jim. The conversation in the kitchen picked up again.

"If that's the way you feel about her, I think we need to leave." Tyler even managed to sound angry. "This was your idea, Chelsie, and now that it's working out for me, you want to go back to the way things were. You can't have it both ways."

That was her cue. Serena walked gingerly back into the room, her feet throbbing.

Tyler took her arm. "We're going."

"Oh, good. Now we can go get something decent to eat." Serena headed for the door.

Chelsie rushed after her. "Serena, I really enjoyed meeting you." She tugged on Serena's arm. "I hope you come back sometime."

Serena glanced at Chelsie. She really felt sorry for her. Even if this charade was provoked by her meddling tendencies, it still seemed a little cruel. Serena wanted to let Chelsie, and all of them, off the hook. They could have a good laugh, sit down, and enjoy the rest of the evening. Serena looked at Tyler, who gave her a warning glance that said, *Don't do it.* But she so wanted to.

"We'll see," Serena said, and almost ran out the door. Tyler quickly followed.

"Hey, what about your date? I mean dog?" Sam stood on the porch wearing a big grin and holding onto Shadow by her collar. He certainly wasn't sorry to see them go. Tyler whistled to Shadow and she jumped into the back of the Jeep. They sped off, leaving his family staring after them.

Tyler pulled around the corner from Chelsie's and parked. He grinned at Serena. "Looks like I underestimated your talents, Miss Finley. You ought to get an Oscar for that one," he laughed.

"You think so, Mr. Cooper?" She laughed with him.

"Oh, I know so."

"You know I feel bad. Chelsie took it really hard."

"She took it all right; she was just mad that I outfoxed her on this one. She's probably planning her next move right this minute." Tyler smiled. "I could tell you were wavering at the end, but you played it out like a trooper." He grinned, his excitement contagious. "The topper was the grope fest. That *really* ticked her off. She'll be hearing about that one from her neighbors for weeks."

Tyler looked at her, an odd expression on his face. "You know I really appreciate you getting into it. We never talked about, you know, anything physical being part of the deal. I hope I didn't go too far."

"No, not at all." She shook her head. *In fact you didn't go far enough.* She tried to push the thought from her mind, but it was difficult with him staring at her lips like that.

He leaned toward her and she felt herself drawn to him, closer and closer until their breaths mingled and the lightest touch of his lips brushed hers.

A digital version of an old rock tune blared from his hip and he jerked back, grabbing his cell phone. "Sorry," he said as he flipped open the phone.

Serena thunked her head back against the headrest. *Damn, damn, and double damn.* He'd almost kissed her and not five minutes after she'd promised herself no more kissing. She wasn't irritated that he'd tried to kiss her, but that she'd wanted him to. Was she that sex starved? She looked at him out of the corner of her eye. Or was he that sexy? Either way this was a dangerous game. Very dangerous.

Distance could be a good thing if there was enough of it. She leaned toward the door not listening to his conversation. She'd stay over here and mind her own business. No talking. No looking. No thinking. She watched his mouth move as he spoke. What great lips. She jerked her gaze to the road. No looking. And definitely no thinking.

He snapped the phone shut. "I have to get back to the restaurant." He started the Jeep and steered into traffic.

Her shoulders drooped with disappointment. She'd had a fabulous time with Tyler and wasn't ready for it to end so soon. "What's wrong?"

"Half our wait staff didn't show, and only one busboy came in. We're getting slammed."

"Is there anything I can do to help?"

"Only if you know how to wait tables."

"I used to, but it's been about fifteen years." She sat up straight. "And Justin is off tonight. He works at a restaurant in the Winslow district. I'm sure he wouldn't mind pitching in too."

"That would be great, but…" He looked at her dress and cocked a brow at her.

"He can bring me some regular clothes. Can I borrow your phone?"

"Yes, ma'am." He smiled. "You know, I'm beginning to think we make a great team."

Chapter 11

Tyler parked the Jeep in back of the restaurant and escorted Serena through the kitchen. Though she tried to hide behind him, several staff members stared openly. He dragged her into a small office and flipped on the light. The tiny space barely had enough room for two people.

A rickety desk occupied one corner and had papers, mail, and invoices in piles, one of which had spilled onto the floor. Napkin and paper towel boxes stacked to the ceiling took up most of the remaining space. Shelves lined one wall and displayed a haphazard arrangement of tools, parts, extension cords, and gadgets.

"You can change in here," Tyler said.

"Oh my." Serena hesitated even to move for fear one of the boxes, or worse, one of the shelves might tumble down on her.

Tyler scanned the room. "I didn't have a chance to tidy up."

She pointed to the desk. "Is there actually a computer under there?"

"I prefer to think of it as a very large paperweight."

"Then how do you keep up with your book work?"

He shrugged. "If someone calls and yells, I send them a check."

"Oh my."

"You said that already."

Tony stuck his head in the doorway. "Did you come to work, or . . .?" His smile spread as he took in Serena's outfit. "So is this the first Dial-A-Date?"

"No." Tyler frowned.

"Yes." Serena smiled. "In a manner of speaking. I helped him give his sister a scare." She stuck out a hand. "I'm Serena."

"If I know Chelsie, you gave her a good one." Tony laughed.

"You woulda loved it," Tyler said. "Serena is going to change clothes and give us a hand. Her son is coming in to bus tables, too."

"Great, we need some help bad." Shadow pushed her nose through the crack in the door. Tony widened it to let her into the office. "You know customers get kind of weird about seeing a dog in the kitchen."

Tyler frowned as Justin rounded the corner with his arms full of laundry. The boy squished his shoulders between Tony and the office door giving the cook a nervous glance as he passed. He dumped the clothes into Serena's waiting arms.

"Thanks," she said. "Are you sure you want to stay and help out?"

He shrugged. "Yeah, I know a girl that works here."

Knows? Knows how well? Serena kept the questions to herself, not wanting to embarrass Justin in front of the two men. She pointed with her elbow. "This is Tony." He nodded at Justin who returned his acknowledgment.

Tyler dug in his pocket. "Justin would you mind running Shadow over to my place first?"

"Sure." Justin took the keys he offered, and Tyler scribbled the address on the back of an envelope and handed it to the boy.

"Is that something important?" Serena pointed to the envelope.

Tyler gave her a frustrated glance. "I told you if it's important, they call." He waved Justin on his way. "Get back as quick as you can." The boy disappeared and reappeared a second later. He jerked a hair brush out of his back pocket and handed it to Serena, then was gone again.

"Thanks!" she shouted.

"Good, I was worried about . . ." Tyler motioned to her hair. "That."

"Well, if you'll make yourself scarce, I'll take care of *that*."

He hurried out the door and shut it behind him. Serena looked for an empty place to put her clothes. There wasn't one. She dumped the pile on top of the cluttered desk, causing several papers to float to the floor.

How could he let this office get into such a mess? Her urge to straighten and tidy nearly took hold, but her aching feet won out. She was ready to lose these heels and put on her comfortable tennis shoes. The entire evening had been an adventure, and she hadn't wanted her time with Tyler to end so soon. Helping him out gave her the perfect excuse to hang around. Shimmying out of the dress, Serena slipped into her T-shirt and jeans in two minutes. She struggled to sit in the only chair and put her tennis shoes on, but it kept rolling backward time and again.

Finally accomplishing the task, she stood and grabbed the hair brush off the edge of the desk. *God bless that boy for remembering it.* She tried to find something that she could see her reflection in and finally settled on the clock on the wall. It was almost face height, and she could see enough in the glass to brush out her highly teased hair. Each stroke brought a wave of pain as she tugged and yanked. "Now I know why big hair will never come back," she mumbled.

Grabbing a rubber band out of the desk drawer, she pulled her hair into a small ponytail. She gazed at her reflection. Thank God she hadn't done a wild job on her make-up for tonight. She now looked and felt like herself again.

This evening seemed to be working out perfectly, too. She'd have the chance to observe what Tyler was really like, see him in action so to speak. He came across as a guy completely at ease and in control of his life. Her gaze focused on the pile of bills covering the desk. All evidence to the contrary not withstanding.

She opened the door and came face to face with a small dark-haired woman who had one hand raised as if to knock. The woman nodded at her. "I'm Lydia. Tyler said you came to help?" Her Latina accent was thick and distinct.

Serena nodded. "I'm Serena."

Lydia studied her, not seeming pleased. If she'd wanted to see the hooker costume, it was a little late. Lydia glanced behind Serena into the office.

"Tyler's out there somewhere," Serena said.

Lydia narrowed her eyes. "I know that. Follow me."

Serena tagged along behind the woman trying to place her heritage. The accent was not exactly Spanish. Puerto Rican maybe.

Her straight, jet black hair hung to her waist and her dark skin gave her an exotic appeal. Lydia wasn't exactly pretty, but interesting just the same. She didn't act the least bit happy that she had to babysit Serena, though. And what self-respecting waitress would when they were this busy?

Serena quickened her pace and closed the gap between them to be sure Lydia could hear her. "I've waited tables before, and I can tend bar a little."

They had almost reached the dining area. The woman snatched an apron off a shelf and flung it back at Serena. Lydia pushed through the swinging doors to the drink station that was a buzz of activity.

She faced Serena and lowered her voice. "Keep the glasses full of ice. Bring water, tea, and coffee. Stay out of trouble. Tell me when a table needs cleaned."

Serena nodded, though Lydia's tone begged for a tacky response. She took a deep breath and bit her lower lip to keep her mouth shut, trying to remember that this wasn't about Lydia. This was about helping Tyler, and she was determined to lend a hand any way she could. Even if that meant schlepping tubs of dirty dishes to the kitchen and putting up with Senorita Nasty.

Lydia turned to leave, then stopped and glared at Serena. "Don't touch the tip money."

As if! Serena squelched the smart remark that almost leaped out of her mouth. Grabbing a pitcher, she scooped up ice. Another waitress came by and stopped. "Hi, I'm Debbie. You must be Justin's mom."

Jerking upright, Serena looked at the girl. Short and cute, she had a bandana tied as a headband. Her brown wavy hair fell about shoulder length. "You know Justin?"

"Yeah. I met him a minute ago in the kitchen."

Serena smiled in relief. She really didn't want to meet her son's lover over a pitcher of ice.

"Hey, I can show you an easier way to do that."

Serena nodded, grateful for the help. For the next half hour, she followed Debbie around learning where things were and the layout of the restaurant dining area. Lydia watched her. Serena sensed the woman's gaze, but every time she looked up, Lydia glanced away. She was probably making sure Serena didn't lift any of her precious tips.

In college, Serena enjoyed waiting tables, chatting with the customers and keeping them happy. She'd always had great tips with her outgoing personality and sense of humor. Which was a good thing. It kept her in college books and Justin in diapers those first few years.

Serena watched Lydia out of the corner of her eye. The woman hardly ever smiled and seemed irritated when someone asked for something extra. No wonder she was so worried about her tips; she probably didn't get very many.

The first hour flew by, then the next. Serena filled glasses and fetched bread, passing Justin as he hefted tubs of dishes onto the cart and rolled them to the kitchen. She finally took a break and went back to see what occupied Tyler.

Scraping a spatula across the grill with one hand, Tyler tossed ingredients in a saucepan with the other, then set it back on the fire.

An impressive display of multi-tasking at its finest. Serena watched him for a few minutes as he plated up a slab of delicious looking ribs. Serena's stomach growled. Tyler caught sight of her and smiled big enough for dimples to show. Strange, she hadn't noticed he had dimples before. "So how's it going out there?"

"Great, but busy. How are things back here?"

"Hot. But it's slowing up a bit."

"She can leave now. Nothing more for her to do." Lydia had followed Serena and stood behind her, arms folded.

Tyler took Serena's hand and led her toward the back door. "I'm taking a break, Tony." They stepped into the cool night air. The alley behind the restaurant seemed eerily silent after the chaos of the kitchen.

Tyler put his hands on his hips and breathed deep. "I get sick of inhaling mesquite smoke sometimes."

"I kinda like it." She stepped closer to him, the chill rippling gooseflesh up her arms.

He looked down at her. "I can't tell you how much I appreciate you and Justin helping us out of a bad spot tonight."

"No problem. Though I don't think Lydia likes me at all."

"Why is that?"

"She made a point to tell me not to steal the tips and has watched me like a hawk all night."

Tyler laughed. "She probably heard you came in here dressed like a hooker. She's a little sharp with people sometimes. I wouldn't worry about it."

"I'm not."

A shadow moved from behind the dumpster, and Serena scooted back toward the door. Tyler took her hand and led her to the man that was now limping up the alley.

"Hey, Bobby Jack, how ya' been?" Tyler waved at the man.

He looked somewhere between 50 and 150 to Serena and was whisper thin. A long white beard hung part way down the red plaid shirt he wore over dusty blue jeans. She supposed him to be one of the homeless wanderers that she saw around the city on occasion—from a distance. What connection did Tyler have to him? Bobby Jack smiled a greeting, then stopped short when he saw Serena.

Tyler pulled her over to the man. "Got someone here I want you to meet." He tugged her closer. "This is Serena."

"Nice to meet you, ma'am." The voice sounded like he'd gargled sandpaper. He grinned at them, "You go and git yourself a girl, Ty?"

"I sure did."

His response surprised Serena. Tyler didn't have to keep pretending now; they were away from his family. Why would he introduce her as his girl? Even to a homeless man?

Bobby Jack looked her up and down. "She's a winner, all right."

Tyler looked at Serena, "She sure is."

Debbie ran out with a bag and handed it to Bobby Jack. "Got your dinner ready." She hurried back inside.

"Much obliged, Ty," Bobby Jack said. "Nice to meet you, ma'am." He nodded at Serena and hobbled off into the darkness.

"How do you know him?" Serena asked.

"He started coming around right after we opened. We'd give him a sandwich, and he'd tell us stories about roughnecking in the early oilfield days."

"What happened to him?"

"The way I understand it, he lost his wife and baby boy in a gas explosion of some kind in the late sixties. Never got over it."

Serena shook her head. How would someone ever get over that? And how many people would care enough to even give the man a sandwich? "It's great that you take care of him."

"It's no big deal."

A humble hero. Quite different from the self-important jerk she'd spent the last two years with. Dr. Jeffery only did good deeds if he got public credit for it or a bronze plaque he could put up for all to see. He'd never see the value in letting a man buy his dinner with a good story.

Tyler stood behind her and rubbed her arms, warming them up. "We're about through for the night. Would you like me to take you home?"

"Oh, no. Go ahead and finish up. I'll wait."

Leading the way through the kitchen, Tyler directed her to the office. He pointed to the one chair. "You can sit in here and have a little peace and quiet if you like."

She glanced at the piles of papers on the desk skeptically. "You mean just sit here? With all this?"

"This mess really bothers you, doesn't it?"

"It would drive me insane. I've been told I inherited a certain anal-retentive gene that insists on order."

"Never heard of it, but feel free to rearrange stuff if it makes you happy."

"I will."

"Have you eaten anything yet?"

"No, have you?"

He shook his head. "I'll make us something before I turn off the grill. What do you want?"

"A great big fat burger."

"Good. I'd hate to be responsible for the after effects of the vegetarian diet." He winked at her as he left.

Serena eyed the piles of bills and rubbed her hands together in anticipation.

Now this was an area he definitely needed help with, and she wanted to help. Repay his kindness to Bobby Jack in a way. She dug through the mountain of paper and started stacking.

Within 30 minutes, she had made some good progress but still hadn't seen the top of the desk. Tyler reappeared with two steaming burgers on plates and a basket of fries for them to share. He set the food on top of her piles, and pulled over one of the boxes to sit on.

"Hey, I have a system going here." She scooted the papers to one side.

"What's that?"

"First of all, I'm putting them in order by vendor and by date."

He nodded. "Sounds like a logical system, but you really don't have to do this. My system works."

"What system?"

"I put them in order of threat." He took a huge bite.

They ate in silence for a few minutes until a screech startled them. Lydia stood in the doorway staring at them. "What you doing?"

Tyler shrugged. "Eating."

She glared at him and motioned to the desk. "You just let her take over now?"

Tyler frowned at the near-ranting woman. "What's the matter with you?"

"You no let her go through your things." Lydia flung her hands up. "She steal what you have."

"Which isn't much right now." Tyler continued to frown. "Don't worry about it, Lydia. It's late. Go home. Get some rest."

"I tell you now," Lydia wagged a finger at Serena. "If she stays, I go." She tossed her apron down with a flourish and walked out.

Serena looked at Tyler waiting on some explanation as to the woman's strange behavior. He continued to eat.

"Is she always like that?"

"Like what?" He glanced at her, then shrugged. "She's a little hot tempered, but she calms down. I don't know what got into her tonight. Probably stressed. That's the fourth time she's quit this year. She'll be back."

"Stressed?" Surely he couldn't be that blind. The woman seemed out to protect Tyler at any cost. "More like territorial."

"Territorial? About this dump?"

"I don't think it has anything to do with the restaurant. I think it has to do with you."

"Me?" he scoffed. "That's nuts."

"Oh? Were the two of you ever a thing?"

"No. Absolutely not. It's always been business with Lydia. Nothing else." He leaned forward to emphasis his point.

"Hey, I'm not the one who needs convincing."

Tyler sat back. "What does that mean?"

Serena shrugged. "I think Lydia may want more from you than just a job."

Chapter 12

Five days. Serena had resisted the temptation to call Tyler all week. So far. She'd hoped he'd call after their . . . what was it? Not a date, though he'd given her a kiss goodnight. On the cheek. Whoopee. But still, it would have been nice to hear from him, talk to him, be sure they were still on the same page.

She sat in her office waiting for her four o'clock meeting with Uncle Frank. The latest edition of "Lone Star Love Affair" hit the stands and the online edition two days ago, and she figured Frank wanted to talk it over. Again. She wasn't as concerned this time. The article had been toned down somewhat as far as passion, but it had still been highly romantic, detailing a wonderful evening spent at a family cookout getting to know all the relatives. She'd left out the twisted details of the actual events and made up an evening she would have liked very much to have with Tyler's family. It was easy, really. They seemed like such nice people.

Nolea wandered in and plopped down in one of the chairs, her pink linen suit wrinkled from a full day of sales calls. "So is this where we're meeting?"

"I guess. You know what's up?"

Nolea made a zipper motion across her lips. "I'm not saying a word." She grinned.

"It must be good, then?"

"Very good."

Will entered and took the other chair. "Y'all talking about me again? You know, being very good and all."

Nolea snorted. "Hardly, Skippy."

"Hey, I object to you calling me Skippy all the time. I want another name."

Serena smiled. "Like what?"

"From now on I want to be called," he stood and used his deepest tone of voice, "Zeus, Almighty God of Thunder."

The two women glanced at each other and dissolved into laughter.

"You've got to be kidding," Serena said.

Nolea held her stomach. "It's more like Sparky Almighty God of Static Electricity."

She pointed to the bottom of Will's pants that clung stubbornly to his ankles.

"Hey, I like that." Serena agreed. "Sparky, it is."

Frowning, Will plopped down as they continued to laugh. "I think I liked Skippy better."

"Oh good, you're all here." Frank hurried in and shut the door. He held up the Tuesday edition of "Lone Star Love Affair." "This, ladies and gentleman, was our biggestselling Tuesday edition of the *Cranfield Reporter-Star* – ever."

They all cheered and clapped. Serena couldn't believe her ears. The biggestselling edition ever?

Nolea squealed. "See, I told you it was good. In fact we've had an avalanche of calls from businesses wanting to offer their goods and services to these lovebirds for free! I mean everything from romantic dinners to weekend getaways. Our advertising dollars have gone through the roof!"

Frank leaned on Serena's desk. "You should be very proud of yourself, young lady. Not only have you almost singlehandedly increased our cash flow, you've found yourself a wonderful man."

Serena gave a weak smile, her stomach sinking. "Oh yeah, he's wonderful." Not to mention completely uninterested in anything approaching a real romance.

Frank went on, oblivious to her distress. "I see this getting bigger and bigger. I want this to be the first reality series in print. We're expanding the section, and next week I want pictures, lots of them." Frank paced as he talked. "A whole photo layout of the happy couple dining by candlelight, walking in the park, having a backyard picnic. He stopped and glanced at Serena. "You didn't happen to snap any pictures of the cookout with his family did you?"

She shook her head no. Wouldn't that have been a sight? The cowboy and the hooker.

"Well, you can always plan another one, and take pictures there," he said. "I'm thinking about running this for the entire summer. Twelve, maybe fourteen issues."

A noose tightened around Serena's neck, slowly squeezing the breath out of her. Another dinner with Tyler's family? They'd never go for that. She could fake a romance, but not an entire family dinner. She'd been determined to play this out, but had no idea it would get this big. And involve so many people. If anybody found out that the romance of the century wasn't real, her career would sink right into the toilet.

Frank walked to the door and winked. "I have one other surprise for you."

Oh God. She couldn't take any more surprises.

He flung open the door and revealed Mary Jo, her arms loaded with letters right up to her chin. She walked in and dumped the pile on Serena's desk.

Serena tried to catch several envelopes as they dashed to the floor. "What are these?"

Mary Jo smiled. "Why, they're your fan letters."

Will laughed. "Everybody in town must be reading this."

Everyone? And now there would be pictures. No more hiding. But could she really keep lying to them all? Imagining her friendship with Tyler was a passionate romance was easy, but was she willing to keep up the charade for several months? Then what?

A tiny woman with gray-blonde hair stood at her door next to Mary Jo. "I am so excited and happy for you." She extended her arms and hurried toward Serena's chair, engulfing her in hug.

"Thanks, Aunt Macy." Serena half-smiled.

"I came by to pick up Frank and wanted to tell you how pleased I am that you've finally found someone. You never know how short life can be, and you don't want to waste one minute." Tears formed in the corners of Macy's eyes.

Serena frowned and glanced at Frank. He gave nothing away but took Macy's arm and directed her to the hallway. He looked back at Serena. "We'll discuss the plans for the layout later."

"Later?"

"I'm going to the doctor with Macy, but I'll be back."

Frank never went to the numerous appointments Aunt Macy had with the dermatologist, gastroenterologist, cardiologist, and any other ologist she could find. The doctors all chatted with her politely and told her she was fine, but she visited them religiously anyway.

Concern refocused her train of thought. Which doctor? And why? What was that comment Macy made about not knowing how long you had? Did it mean something, or was it just Macy's dramatic flair? Serena rolled the questions through her mind. Macy may have said something or hinted to Serena last week that there was a problem, but she'd been so wrapped up in her own life she easily could have missed it. After all, Macy always had some medical crisis that amounted to nothing, and Serena had learned to tune it out.

"So what's the plan for the next article?" Will asked. "Do you have any idea when and where we'll be taking all these pictures?"

Serena ignored him, lost in her thoughts.

Nolea motioned Will to the door. "Can you give us a second, Sparky?" She turned back to Serena. "So what's on your mind? And I know it's more than Macy."

Serena blew out a long breath and leaned her head back against her chair. "This is getting out of hand."

"What? The articles? Are you kidding? They're really taking off."

"That's the problem."

Nolea held up her hands. "Okay, wait, and back up. What am I missing here?"

Serena needed to get this off her chest, had to tell someone, and Nolea might even offer some kind of solution. At this point, the fear of what she might lose outweighed her fear of telling Nolea. "It's all a lie."

"What?"

"Everything. The romance, the family loving me, all of it."

"I knew it! You haven't been yourself since this whole thing started. So Tyler's a figment of your imagination?" Nolea leaned forward, thrilled to be in the loop again.

"Oh no, he's very real."

"Meaning?" Nolea raised a brow.

"His sister ran a personal ad for his birthday, and he wanted me to help scare her off."

"And the romance?"

"There's not one. He's helping me with the story, and I'm helping him keep his family off his back. That simple." Serena shifted in her chair, Nolea's intense gaze slicing through her.

"I don't think it's near that simple. I think you like this guy."

"No, I don't. I mean, I do, but that's not the issue. It's a business arrangement."

"Oh, I think it *is* the issue. You're getting attached to him."

"I'm trying to keep my career out of the dumper just long enough to get my son in school. Then I'm on the first plane to New York. But now Frank wants to make "Lone Star Love Affair" a whole event and drag it out forever. I don't think I can keep faking it. What am I going to do?"

Nolea stood and paced back and forth, a perfect imitation of Frank. "Let's work through this logically. We can keep this thing going as long as we're very careful. No one." She stopped and stared at Serena. "And I mean no one can know it's a fake. Then we have to convince Tyler to get on board with the plan."

"What plan?"

"I'm working on that." Nolea's brow furrowed. "Let's start with the facts. You have had a date with him, and you *did* meet his family, right?"

Serena moaned. "They hate me."

"But that's what he wanted, and you held up your end of the bargain, right?"

She nodded.

"Then he owes you, right?"

"Right, that was the deal, but what can he do? The entire city, as well as most of our advertisers, think this is for real. I told him it would be a short little series that ran a few weeks. Not some media circus with him as the starring attraction."

Nolea narrowed her eyes. "I think you should have a good long talk with Tyler, and see how far he's willing to take this. You might get lucky and get him to agree to more than the original deal. Until then, don't panic."

"Easy to say. I'm way past panic and halfway to scared witless."

Nolea ignored her comment. "We need to sit down and map out this whole love affair step by step as far as the articles go, and I think Will can help with the pictures. You know, make it be you and not really *look* like you. That would give us more time if we have to ditch Tyler and find a replacement." Nolea stilled for a moment, then jerked the door open. Will almost fell in.

"Were you listening?" Nolea glared.

"Only to the good parts." Will smiled at Serena and lowered his voice. "So, I hear you need to fake a romance?"

Serena nodded, not at all secure with the idea that her secret was out. Not to one, but two people, even if it was Nolea and Will. They might empathize and want to help, but they could also make her life a living hell. "Look, you two, I have everything riding on this. *Everything.*"

Will winked. "Don't sweat it, Red, the Cavalry's here."

They looked more like the princess and the Shetland pony, but they were all she had. Serena stood up and put her hands on her hips. "Okay then, let's make me a love affair." She picked up the phone and dialed. A deep voice answered. "Tyler?" She glanced at Will and Nolea. "We need to talk."

Chapter 13

Tyler hung up and smiled to himself. He'd thought about calling for days, but hadn't. Serena had done everything he'd asked of her and more. It was her move, and now she made it. He had a sudden urge to high five someone. Anyone. They were to meet at her place in less than an hour. He'd bring the food, she'd have the beer.

Excitement coursed through his chest. She'd been a good sport, jumped in and helped him out of a tight spot with the restaurant, too. Not many of Tyler's friends would have done that and certainly no women he knew. A quick change of clothes, and he was out the door, pulling up to her house as the sun dipped in the sky.

"Hey there." Serena met him with a big smile. She wore a white tank top and jeans. A very casual and ordinary outfit for most women, but it looked great on her. The air between them crackled with electricity.

"Hey there yourself." He followed her into the house and moved aside a large stack of letters on the table. She handed him two plates, and he pulled sandwiches from the sack. "What's all this?" he motioned to the pile.

"Part of our project for the evening." She filled glasses with water and joined him at the table. "They're fan letters people sent to the paper, as well as offers from some of our advertisers for the mystery couple I made up."

He raised an eyebrow. "We got fan letters? Wow. Your articles have been great, by the way."

"You read them?" She seemed surprised.

"Sure I did. I wanted to know if I was going to get more than a kiss." He smiled at her. "Can't wait to find out." Her cheeks turned a pretty shade of pink. "The family cookout you made up almost made me wish it had happened that way."

"Yeah, me too."

The disappointment in her voice caught his attention. Like she wished the same thing he did. That this was real and not some act.

"Have you heard from your sister?"

"Nope. I'm guessing she isn't talking to me."

"I'm sorry."

"I'm not. That was the whole point. In a few weeks, she'll be right back to annoying me every day again."

Serena didn't look pleased with that answer. He wondered how Chelsie would like the woman that sat across from him now. The real Serena. Single mom, educated professional, great actress.

He already knew the answer. Serena would be put on a pedestal so high by his family he'd never feel worthy of her. And maybe that was where she belonged. Serena could have her pick of men. Guys with a fancy education, a home on each coast, and money in the bank. None of which he had. He didn't have any right to expect more than to spend a few evenings with her, but it was sure nice to think about. They finished their sandwiches in silence and put the plates in the sink. They both stared at the huge piles on the table.

"So where do we start?" he asked.

"Anywhere."

He pulled a mound of letters toward him and started opening. "What are we looking for?"

"Romantic ideas, outlandish suggestions, something fun for my imaginary couple to do. I want to tie in the reader's suggestions with whatever activity we decide on. Uncle Frank wants pictures, so we need to find things to do in low light to keep our identities as much of a mystery as possible."

"In the dark?" He flashed a grin.

"In low light," she insisted

"What's the difference?"

"A camera."

"Oh yeah." *Too bad.* He ripped open one letter after another.

"We should make piles according to the letters' contents." Serena sorted out several and arranged them in a long row.

"Do you organize everything?"

She looked at him like he'd grown another head. "Of course, why wouldn't you?"

He shrugged and made three piles of his own. They sorted and stacked for more than 30 minutes, commenting on the content of several letters and laughing outright at several others.

Tyler paused, surveying the work they'd done so far. "This is a lot for one or two articles."

Serena scrunched her nose and hesitated. "That's one of the things we need to talk about. Frank wants to keep it going through the summer." She held up a hand. "But don't worry, we can take enough pictures and hopefully put together enough activities in a weekend or two to fill most of the articles. Would you have a problem with that?"

She looked unsure, like he might say no. "Why would I?"

"Our original deal was pretty short term, and I want to give you the opportunity not to participate if you feel you're getting in too deep."

He was getting in deep all right, but he wasn't about to say no to spending more time with her. "I appreciate that, but we can adjust the deal as we go along can't we?"

"Yes, we can." She gave him a relieved smile.

Serena pointed to his piles. "Why do you only have three stacks?"

"The first one is the good stuff, the second is the okay stuff, and the third one is crazy people."

"Crazy people?"

He picked up a letter from stack number three and read: "Dear Lone Star Lovers, I am writing to ask if you could help with a business I'm trying to start. It's called 'Luv On A Dime' and will be a nonprofit organization that provides sexual aids to underprivileged women."

She held up her hand. "That's enough."

"Oh no, it has pictures." He handed the photo to her and smiled as her jaw dropped.

"Oh my god!" She flicked the photo across the table at him. "Okay, I understand the crazy pile. What's the good stuff?"

Tyler picked up a letter from the first pile and read: "My name is Harvey Rollins, and my wife and I married forty-three years ago. Reading your story today reminded me of the day we met in Oceanside, California. I was in the Navy and Jeanne worked in a small taffy shop close to the beach. She was the prettiest thing I'd ever seen.

"After a week, I finally got the nerve to buy some taffy from her, and when she handed me a bag, our fingers touched, and I knew. It was an electric spark that lit up my whole body. I knew right then I'd love her my whole life. And I have.

"I lost her to cancer three years ago, but that love hasn't faded. When I read your story, it brought back the best memories of my life. Thank you." He glanced up, surprised to see Serena's eyes filled with tears. "Sorry, I didn't mean to upset you."

"Oh no," she smiled. "I just can't imagine having someone love me like that." Her attention returned to sorting letters.

Tyler frowned. *Why not?* He could imagine a number of men who might jump at the chance to love her, including him. She had so much to offer.

"Why don't we take a break?" Serena grabbed a couple of beers from the refrigerator, and he followed her outside. The backyard was walled and private, and long trails of honeysuckle ran along the top of the fence. They stood on a large wooden deck, and Tyler inhaled the sweet scent. She handed him a bottle and motioned to a large metal swing on the corner of the deck with two puffy green cushions. "I sit out here and watch the sun set almost every evening."

He nodded. "My kind of activity."

"Yeah, I'm pretty easily entertained." She grinned. "Not to mention a real cheap date."

"My kind of girl." He laughed.

They sat and rocked slowly back and forth. A large oak tree arched over the swing, and a squirrel scurried up and down, ignoring their presence. A calm settled over Tyler. This was nice, real nice. He couldn't remember the last time he'd watched the sun set.

It struck him as ironic that he had worked hard for years chasing some kind of financial security, so he would have the kind of life where he could do anything he wanted, and this was exactly it. Just sit and watch the sun dip below the horizon. This simple, this easy.

"What are you thinking?" she asked.

"Hmm?" She dragged him from his thoughts.

"You were smiling."

"Was I?" He shrugged. "I was thinking how nice this is."

"Yes, it is. Justin and I have lived in this house for almost ten years, and I love it here."

He hadn't meant the house. He'd meant being with her. "So where's Justin's father? I mean, if you don't mind me asking?"

"No idea."

"How long have you been divorced?"

"I was never married." She said it quietly, and he got the idea it wasn't something she wanted to discuss.

"Well, it ain't all it's cracked up to be; let me tell you."

She laughed. "Oh really? And how were your four weeks of marital bliss?"

"Hellacious."

"Then why did you get married?"

"We were young. I wanted something to hang on to, and she wanted to get away from her dad. It was a disaster. You never know someone until you live with them."

"I've never lived with anyone either."

"Really? Never?"

"I had a son to raise, and I didn't want him getting attached to someone who wasn't permanent."

He looked at her. How many people would put their own wants aside like that? Not many. Lots of women ran men through their lives like they had a revolving door, without any concern about how it affected their kids. The last rays of light splashed an orange glow across Serena's face. "You're really something, you know that?"

She arched a skeptical brow at him. "At least I have you fooled. But don't worry, I only use my powers for good, not evil, and I keep all my horrible secrets wellhidden. You want another beer?"

He nodded. "Yeah, but that's it. I have a two beer limit."

Serena disappeared into the house.

Horrible secrets? She had no idea how bad some secrets could be, and he had no business getting close to her. She had enough to handle without him dumping any of his problems on her. If she knew the real person he was, she'd run as far and fast as she could. Maybe. Probably. He should keep his distance, though he couldn't quite help himself.

Serena handed him a bottle, and they sat together for a few minutes in silence. The stars twinkled to life one by one in the growing darkness. The air took on a slight chill. Serena scooted closer to him.

"You cold?" He put his arm around her and rubbed her shoulder.

She gave him a playful look. "How do I know what you're after, mister?"

Tyler wiggled his eyebrows and gave a sinister laugh. "Come, Little Red Riding Hood, come closer and tell the Big Bad Wolf all your secrets." He pulled her tight against his side as she laughed.

"No offense, but you don't seem the wolf type. I can't imagine you eating my grandmother."

"Oh, I don't know. You might be shocked at the things I've done." He hadn't intended for it to sound so serious, but it did. She gazed up at him almost like she wanted to say something, but hesitated.

"What? So you think you can shock me with some skeleton in your closet?" she asked.

"I know it."

"Would you like to bet on it?"

"What kind of bet?"

"Wait here." She got up and went inside.

He drew a quick breath and took a big swig of beer. Was he really ready? He realized his pulse had stepped up in rhythm and he moved to keep his shirt from clinging to the moisture in his armpits. Nerves knotted his stomach. To prepare himself, Tyler tried to imagine her reaction. The disbelief, then contempt, followed by disgust. He'd seen people look at him that way years ago and didn't imagine it had changed much. He lived with the memory every day.

He could feel himself being drawn closer to her, could even imagine himself sitting out here with her every evening. This would be a good reason for her to keep distance between them; if it were up to him, there wouldn't even be daylight between them.

Little twinkle lights strung around the deck flicked on, and Serena walked outside with several letters in her hand. She stood in front of Tyler. "I bet you one of these that my skeleton is worse than yours."

"One of what?"

"Some letters from the good stuff pile." She gave him a saucy grin. "Most involving a hot tub. Winner picks which one we do."

"You're on."

"Okay." Serena sat next to him on the swing. "Shoot."

Tyler couldn't quite figure out where to start.

"Well?" she asked.

He looked into her eyes for a moment then focused his gaze straight ahead. Might as well start at the end. They'd get there eventually anyway. Tyler cleared his throat. "I'm a convicted murderer."

Chapter 14

"What?" Serena leaned away and frowned. Of all the things she'd expected him to say, convicted murderer wasn't one of them. "You're kidding?" she hoped.

Tyler shook his head no.

A nervous chill went through her. She was sitting on her deck watching the sun set with a convicted murderer she met through a personal ad online. And here she had thought her taste in men was improving.

Serena looked at him. How could he have killed someone? He seemed a pretty solid kind of guy from what she'd seen. Fun loving and adventurous. She'd had a great time with him. He owned a business and had the respect of his employees, and his family obviously loved him. She got the impression he'd never hurt a flea. It didn't add up.

Tyler sat in silence, as if waiting for her to say something. Finally she found her voice. "What happened?"

"Matt and I were seniors in high school."

"Matt?"

"My best friend. We'd been friends since grade school. Did everything together. Then in high school we started rodeoing."

"I bet you were good." She wanted him to look at her, but he didn't. "What event?"

"Team roping. He was the header; I was the heeler. We were pretty good, I guess."

Tyler paused, and she waited. This seemed very difficult for him. He obviously didn't talk about it much. She remembered the photo on Chelsie's wall of him as a kid. The other little cowboy in the picture must have been Matt. She watched memories of emotions play across his expression as he searched for the words.

"We won our division that year, and after the last rodeo that cinched us a regional spot, we celebrated. One of the college guys bought us a case of beer, and we went out to the country and drank. Matt had a few, and I had the rest." He raked his fingers through his hair, still staring into the darkness.

"Matt tried to take the keys away from me, but the truck was new, and I insisted on driving. The road was gravel." He shook his head and clenched his teeth together. "I took a turn too fast."

Serena saw the muscles in his cheek flex, but he kept his emotions in check. Her heart ached to comfort him, but she didn't trust her voice to speak. After a few minutes, Tyler continued.

"I could hear him screaming, trapped under the truck. I was thrown out. One leg was broken and my ankles were torn up. I couldn't get to him. Couldn't move. I just lay there and listened to him scream. The whole time I kept thinking that as long as he was screaming he'd be okay, we'd both be okay. Then the screaming stopped."

Tears rolled down Serena's cheeks. She couldn't imagine the horror and helplessness he'd endured. Tyler glanced over at her.

He brushed her tears away with one finger. "Wish I could do that." Putting his arm around her, he pulled her close to his side. "They released me from the hospital in time for the funeral, which was almost worse."

"How could it be worse?"

"Matt's little brother was about thirteen at the time, and after the service, they led out the family first. Most didn't even look my way, but he stopped right in front of my wheelchair." Tyler took a big breath. "He said I killed his brother and that he'd never forgive me. And that one day he'd pay me back if it was the last thing he ever did."

"What did you say?" she whispered.

"Nothing. What could I say? He was right. I was stupid and reckless, and it cost my best friend his life. There's no undoing that, and nothing anyone ever says will make it better. So I sat there and took it. Every time I saw him after that, the accusation was there, even though we didn't speak. I felt his hate without him saying a word."

"Did he ever pay you back?"

"In a way I guess." Tyler smiled. "He married my sister."

"Jim?" Serena asked. He seemed to have as easy a time being around Jim as he did his own brother. She hadn't sensed any tension at all between them at the cookout. "So I guess you worked things out?"

"Had to. Chelsie insisted that me and Jim talk and clear the air before the wedding."

"How did the talk go?"

He shook his head and chuckled, his good humor returning. "It went about twelve rounds and took out the wedding cake."

Serena laughed with him. "Oh no."

"You'll have to ask Chelsie to show you the pictures sometime."

"So did you have to go to jail after the accident?"

"They gave me ten years probation on the manslaughter charge and took away my driver's license for a year on the drunk driving." He squeezed her arm one last time and then pulled his arm from around her. "Are you shocked now?"

She nodded. "You win." She slapped the letters into his hand and got up.

"I see how you are, don't want to sit on the deck now with a criminal?" He tried to make his tone light and teasing, but he couldn't quite pull it off.

Serena knew he needed to know she understood, yet still thought enough of him to be his friend. Which she did. She couldn't imagine the emotional hurt he'd suffered, and if she could lessen the pain for him, somehow she would.

She flashed him a smile. "Like I'd let you off that easy. I need a lover, and you're it, buddy." She held the back door open. "So which one of those letters are we doing?"

He grinned wide and walked toward her, then stopped and brushed a kiss across her lips. "All of them."

Chapter 15

The next morning Tyler climbed his condo's outside stairs trying to avoid the Rat Patrol, who would be up and about by now. The bright April sun glared off the light colored stucco of the building. With the temperature already 75 degrees, the Texas sun beat down, making it a harder climb than usual. Tyler stopped at the landing to catch his breath. Serena's perfume rose from his shirt, tickling his memory.

She'd had fallen asleep next to him on the couch last night. He'd lain there for hours listening to her breathe, holding her close. He was comfortable with her. No pretense, no trying to impress each other. He'd never been that kind of comfortable with a woman. Not constantly wondering what she thought about him or when she'd figure out she didn't want him around.

Tyler had never told anyone about the accident until he'd known them a long, long time. But he told Serena, and she passed the acid test. The reaction he expected included condemnation, revulsion, suspicion. But she surprised him again, offering sympathy and understanding.

Someone told him once that damaged people gravitate toward each other. Maybe that was it.

He guessed Serena had been through some major hurt too, but he had no idea what. Somehow it fit that they understood each other. Serena was interesting, funny, and stand-offish at the same time—a challenge he couldn't resist.

Tyler reached the third floor and opened the door to a beehive of activity, which seemed to be concentrated around his front door. His couch sat in the hallway piled with the TV and several garbage bags full of clothes. Shadow's bark rang out from the condo. Tyler rushed over to one of the men moving furniture. "Hey, what are you doing?" Before the man could open his mouth, Mrs. Lathem's door swung open.

"Oh, there you are, Mr. Cooper." She gave him a smug sneer. "You're being evicted. What a shame."

"Evicted?"

"Yes. Dick's niece is back and no longer wants you around." She gave his disheveled appearance a once over, then turned up her nose. "Though who could blame her with you out catting around until all hours." Rat dog appeared near her ankle and growled at him.

Tyler's temper flared, but one phrase flashed through his mind, like a bright warning beacon. "Krista's back?"

"Yes. Krista is out at the moment, but you can talk to me."

Tyler turned to see a man in a dark suit emerge from the condo. "And you are?"

The man smiled as if patiently speaking to a child. "Mark Ricca. Krista's friend and attorney."

Tyler gritted his teeth. Great. Krista's latest guy would have to be a lawyer. She must have finished with John and went looking for a man who could really save her ass. Tyler resigned himself immediately to the fact that the condo was a lost cause. He knew even without calling his brother for the specific legal clauses that he didn't have a chance.

"You had to know your time here was temporary," Ricca continued. "I hope we can avoid any ugliness." He exuded arrogance and confidence, and Tyler barely resisted the urge to pop him one right in the mouth.

Ugliness? That would only happen if Krista showed, and Tyler was relieved she wasn't here now. He didn't look forward to any confrontation with her after she'd left him to mop up all her financial mess. He might strangle her on sight. Tyler half listened to the guy as he tried to formulate the next step toward getting a roof over his head.

"Your things will be here until five sharp. Whatever's left will be hauled off. Any questions?"

"Where's my dog?"

Mark disappeared and returned with Shadow. The dog ran to Tyler, who picked up two of the trash bags full of clothes, grabbed her leash and headed back down the stairs. He sat in his Jeep for a few minutes thinking, and then dialed his sister's number.

"Hello?"

"Chelsie I need a place to…" The line went dead. Not that he blamed her, but this was important. He redialed and she picked up.

"Chelsie this is…" She hung up again. Tyler glanced at his watch. Almost 10. He had to dump his stuff somewhere and get to work before the lunch rush. It would get stolen if he left it in the Jeep. He looked over his shoulder at the two bags. Not that there was much to steal.

Why was it that every time things went south with a woman, he ended up with less stuff? One more rotten romance and he'd be down to a toothbrush. Shadow licked the side of his face, and he rubbed her ears. "I'd take you to work, but the way my luck's running, today the health department would pull a surprise inspection."

That left one option—Serena. Tyler dialed her cell and waited until voice mail picked up. As he listened to her message, he tried to figure out what to say. A loud tone sounded in his ear. "Serena, this is Tyler. I've had a little emergency and need a small favor. Call me when you get this." Actually, it was a huge emergency and a big favor, but he didn't have time for specifics right now. He hung up and steered the Jeep to her house.

The neighborhood appeared calm and quiet. It was a working day, after all, and most of the houses on Serena's street were dark and silent. He braked to a stop, hoping no one noticed his matching luggage, courtesy of Hefty. Grabbing both trash bags, Tyler climbed out, and Shadow followed behind him. He rang the bell but knew no one was home. Leading Shadow around to the side gate, he turned her loose in the backyard. He set the garbage bags on the deck and hurried to his vehicle.

Serena had already proven she had an understanding heart, and he and Shadow would be out of her hair as soon as he got off work. And found a hotel. That he could afford. That took dogs, too. His head pounded as he drove to the restaurant. There was no such thing as a small storm in his life. Everything turned into a hurricane eventually.

The parking lot to the side of the restaurant and the street in front were full of cars. A good sign, but he knew they were short-handed. He glanced at his watch again. The noon rush was in full swing.

Tyler hurried inside, washed up, and took his customary place beside Tony at the grill. The cook frowned at him. "Where you been?"

"Getting evicted."

Tony shook his head. "Then your day's not going to get any better."

Tyler squinted at one order sheet and tossed two thick steaks on the grill. "Why's that?"

"She's waiting for you out front."

Tyler met Tony's eyes and immediately knew. "Can you handle this a minute?" He untied his apron, dread creeping into his mind.

"Yep. Funny how your women always want a showdown in the middle of lunch rush."

Tyler shrugged. "Well it is high noon and she *does* have an audience." He winked at the cook. "Clint's never lost a gunfight yet."

"Ride 'em cowboy!" Tony's laughter followed him until he pushed through the swinging doors to the seating area. The humor didn't do much to quell his nerves. Tyler scanned the room until he saw her.

Krista sat looking out one of the front windows, sipping a glass of iced tea. She hadn't changed. Long blonde hair and smooth bronze skin set off by blue eyes and overly white teeth. Beautiful by most anyone's standard, except for his. He knew what lay underneath the surface.

To get what she wanted, the woman would sell herself to the devil or at least sleep with him. Anger and resentment coiled inside Tyler like a tight spring. This person had tried to ruin his life the past two years and still was apparently.

Krista turned and waved him over with a big smile. Like nothing had happened. Like they were friends. Like he'd forgive and forget. Not hardly. He stood for a minute and thought about how this would play out.

Tyler had practiced his lines for months after she left. What he'd say, how he'd say it, how he'd feel afterwards. Not good probably, but satisfied. He'd held his anger in check for a long time, and she deserved every bit of hate he could dish out.

He walked over and stood next to the table.

"Hi, Ty, how have you been?" She flashed her sexiest smile, expecting it to work its magic on him. It didn't.

"What do you want, Krista?"

"I thought we could talk." She motioned to the chair next to her, the multiple bracelets on her wrists clinking together. He knew the sound. Expensive. "Aren't you going to sit down?"

"No. I have a business to run. I'd like you to leave."

"That's what I want to talk about. *Our* business." She motioned to the restaurant.

Tyler gritted his teeth and growled. "It's *my* business, and I'll thank you to leave."

Krista unfolded a piece of paper and handed it to him. "John signed his half over to me before we . . ." She lowered her voice, "parted ways. So I guess that makes us partners." She stood and put a hand on his arm. "We were good partners at one time, weren't we, Ty?"

He jerked away from her touch and tried to focus on the paper in front of him. The words ran together in legal mumbo jumbo but he got the general idea. John had sold his half of the partnership to Krista. Tyler couldn't believe it. And maybe he didn't have to. "You expect me to think this is real?" Tyler observed her for any sign of uncertainty.

She gave a smug smile. "Absolutely. John and I decided it was the least he could do for me before we split up, so he gave it to me."

Tyler grunted. John figured out what Krista was a lot faster than he had. Giving her half ownership of a worthless restaurant would have gotten him off the hook fast and easy. He pictured John sitting on a beach somewhere, grateful to be rid of JT's and Krista. As usual, Tyler was left to deal with the crap, which in this case, meant a barbecue joint with negative cash flow and Barbi the bimbo with attorney in tow.

The document looked real, as far he could tell, and given the way things were going today, it probably was. *Now what?* He tossed the paper on the table. "I don't know what you're after, but if you expect to come in here and take over, it's not going to happen."

Surprise flashed across her face, and he pressed his point, putting in his best bluff. "In fact, if that's what you want, I'll sign my half over, and you can have the whole damn thing," though he had no intention of giving up JT's. It was all he had left, but he had to see how serious she was.

"Well, that's not really what I had in mind. You know I don't know anything about running a restaurant." She trailed a finger up and down his arm making his flesh crawl. "I thought maybe we could come to an arrangement. You could buy my half and then keep running the place like you always have."

"What?" Tyler knew it would come down to money. It always did with her. He shook his head and kept his voice steady. "You have more balls than anyone I've ever known. You think you can walk in here with some fake piece of paper and have me write you a check? Have you lost your mind?" His voice rose drawing the attention of people at the surrounding tables. "Did you ever have one in the first place?"

Krista teared up, going into her victim act. "I thought you'd be reasonable. I only want what is rightly mine."

Tyler wasn't falling for it. "No you don't. You want what is rightly *mine*. Like I'm some guy you can charm back into your bed and have your way with. I've seen what you are, and I don't want any part of it."

Her eyes narrowed at him. "I'd hoped it wouldn't come to this, but I guess you leave me no choice." She grabbed her purse off the table. "I will be suing you for running my investment into the ground over the last two years. Expect to hear from my attorney. I believe you've already met." She leaned closer. "You will either pay up or go under, it's your choice." She brushed past him.

Tyler's hands shook. He gripped the back of a chair to keep from wrapping them around her traitorous neck. "I'll burn this place to the ground before I give you one cent," he shouted.

Krista ignored him and strutted out the door, her braided belt swung in rhythm over her jeans, accentuating the sway of her hips. Several men glanced their appreciation and Tyler almost laughed. If they only knew. Desiring Krista was like standing on a highway with a semi-truck barreling toward you. And he wasn't about to get run over—again.

He stood a minute trying to gather his thoughts. Talking to his brother seemed the next logical step to know exactly what he might be dealing with on the legal side. Jeff's specialty was business law, and he'd know in a heartbeat how bad this was or wasn't. Nothing Tyler could do about any of it right this second. The restaurant was full, and he needed to get back to work. Turning, he noticed the quiet. Every customer, as well as all the employees, stared at him in stunned silence.

"Sorry for the interruption, folks." As he made his way back to the grill, he tried to focus on the task at hand. Meanwhile, his mind worked overtime. Had the document been real? Probably. Would her threat stand up in court? Maybe. Would she really go that far and completely ruin him? Absolutely.

Shortly after two o'clock, things slowed down enough for him to break away. He closed the door to his office and dialed Jeff's number.

A female voice came on the line. "Law office."

"Jeff Cooper, please."

"May I ask who is calling?"

"His brother Tyler."

After a few seconds, Jeff came on the line. "Hey, Ty. What's up?"

"I've got a problem."

"Yeah, I heard. Chelsie's called me four times already, trying to get me to talk some sense into you about Sherry or Sheila or whoever she is."

"Serena, and that's not why I'm calling. I've got a real problem. A legal one."

"Involving?" The change in Jeff's tone to serious business was immediate.

"JT's." Tyler took a deep breath and plowed through the details. "Krista's back. She has some papers that say John signed over his part of the restaurant to her. She says if I don't give her cash, she will sue. Can she do that?"

"Whoa. One thing at a time. What did the paperwork say?"

"It looked like a bill of sale of some kind."

"Did it look official, notarized?"

"Yeah."

"Hmm."

Tyler's anxiety mounted as several seconds of silence ticked by. "Well? What am I looking at?"

"Worst case scenario, if John really did sign over his share, you're stuck with her unless you buy her out."

"The place is barely staying afloat now."

"If that's the case, you could let her have it and walk away as long as she agreed to take everything, including the debt."

Tony stuck his head in the door. "Hey, boss, we need you out here." The noisy din of the kitchen invaded the sanctuary of the office.

Tyler held up a hand. "Yeah, one more minute."

Tony nodded and disappeared.

Tyler returned his attention to Jeff. "She'd never go for that. Krista doesn't want a job; she's after money."

"That could work to your advantage. If she decides to sue, she'd have to hire an attorney, and let me tell you, we aren't cheap."

"She already has one, and I think he's her boy toy."

"I guess some of us are cheaper than others."

Cheap is right and easy too. Not more than two years ago, Tyler was that same guy getting taken without even realizing it. "Can she really sue me?"

"Anyone can sue anyone for any reason. Even if the case turns out to be bogus, it would still cost you an arm and a leg. People use the threat of lawsuits everyday as a kind of legal blackmail. It's cheaper and easier to settle than to let a judge figure out who is right or wrong."

Tyler sat back, the first warning signs of defeat settling in. "So, I'm screwed either way?"

"Not necessarily. The best thing we can do is anticipate their next move and be ready for it. Most lawyers recognize an opponent who won't fight. They try to intimidate them and usually end up with a fat settlement. On the other hand, if we come back at them prepared and swinging, this guy may back off and rethink things."

Lydia opened the office door. "Did he tell you Debbie is stuck in the walkin? We try to open it, but it's closed tight."

Tyler nodded and waved her away, trying not to show his annoyance, though his entire life hung on this phone conversation. Could he not get one frickin' minute of peace? Lydia closed the door.

He blew out a breath, "What's our first move?"

"You can bet they are going to ask for the business records for the last two years. You'll need to be sure those are in order, and all the money and expenses are accounted for."

Tyler's gaze scanned the invoices scattered across his desk. What a disaster. He had no idea where to start, let alone how to get this mess lawyer-ready.

Jeff's voice broke through his thoughts. "Ty? You still there?"

"Yeah."

"That's not a problem is it?"

"No. No problem. Just need to catch up on a few things." A few thousand things.

"Do it quick. Does she have access to the building?"

"Not unless John gave her his key."

"Just to be safe, I'd take all the records out of there as quick as you can. You don't want her getting her hands on them until we're ready. Got it?"

"Got it."

"Start there for now. I'll make a list as I think of things and call you at home tonight.

"Make that my cell. She had me evicted from the condo."

"Where are you staying?"

"Working on that."

"Jesus, little brother, when it rains on you, it pours."

"No kidding."

"Don't let it get to you." Jeff's confidence came through loud and clear. "We'll work through this and figure something out."

Tony popped the door open again. "The girl is nearly a Deb-sickle." He lowered his voice to an awkward whisper. "I think she's crying."

He nodded. "I'm on my way."

"What?" Jeff asked.

"Not you, just stuff I have to take care of here," Tyler said. "Thanks, bro. I appreciate it."

"No problem."

The dial tone hummed in Tyler's ear. He dropped the receiver and leaned his elbows on the paper-strewn desk. He rubbed his temples with both hands. Somehow in the space of eight hours, his life had become a mess. An absolute fucking mess.

Chapter 16

Serena sorted through hundreds of emails. She'd come in to the office early to try and catch up, but the response to "Lone Star Love Affair" had the entire staff working overtime. The good wishes and positive response overwhelmed them all, but reading heartfelt letters from fans left her empty. She'd created the imaginary couple and their experiences from hopes and dreams she'd had herself: about finding the perfect fit, the one you were meant to be with. It was a dream she'd given up long ago, but seeing it in print made her want to believe—that it was real, that it could happen, that Tyler could be the one.

The phone rang as Nolea stuck her head in. Serena motioned her to a chair and picked up the receiver. "Serena Finley."

"Good morning, Miss Finley. This is Deborah Blackwell with *American Woman* magazine."

The name didn't ring a bell, but the publication did. *American Woman* was one of the top 10 magazines in the country and one she'd sent an application to more than a year ago. She hadn't been surprised that they didn't respond. They were the big leagues.

"I'm wondering if you might be interested in getting together sometime?"

"Getting together? For what?"

"An interview."

Serena stared at Nolea. *An interview?* One of the top 10 magazines wanted to interview her? What for? It's not like she was a leader in her field, or had any expertise in a specific area. The articles *American Woman* ran were serious and thought provoking. A far cry from the fluffy crap that Uncle Frank favored. "An interview for what?"

"A job."

The air left Serena's lungs. A job? "Are you sure?" She couldn't believe it. Did they not know she worked at a little tiny paper in the middle of nowhere? Surely they had more qualified people to choose from.

The woman laughed. "Very sure. I have family in that area of Texas, and they have been sending me the *Cranfield Reporter-Star* for years. I've read some of your work, and you have a fresh voice. One we're looking for in a new assistant editor. Are you interested in discussing it further?"

"Absolutely." This was it. The call she'd dreamed about. The chance she'd worked for the last 15 years. She'd imagined herself starting in New York and working her way up the ladder to this kind of publication.

Now she had the chance to skip over the ladder completely. She jotted the date and time down, as her mind whirled. Clicking the receiver, Serena sat for a minute, stunned, still not believing what she'd heard.

"What?" Nolea quizzed. "Somebody die or something?"

"Yes. I mean, no. I mean I might." Serena jumped up and grinned, doing a little happy dance around the office.

"Who was that?" Nolea laughed at her antics.

Serena shut the door and whispered, "*American Woman* magazine."

"Oh my god!" Nolea leaned toward her.

"They want to interview me for a job as assistant editor."

Nolea's jaw dropped; then she jumped up joining Serena in her excitement. "No kidding? This is the big time."

Serena grabbed Nolea's hands. "You have to promise me not a word to anyone. It's only an interview. Got it?"

"Got it." Nolea gave Serena a big hug. "I'm so happy for you. This will give you the chance to put this cowtown in your rearview mirror for good. And what great timing! With Justin leaving for college, there won't be anything or anyone to hold you back."

Serena sat back in her chair and frowned. Nothing to hold her back? "It's rotten timing. Why couldn't this have happened two months ago? Before this whole "Lone Star Love Affair" thing started?"

"That's a fantasy. As in fake." Nolea gestured with her hands. "As in *not real*."

Yeah, it was fake. That's what she meant, but not what she hoped. It figures this would happen now, right when she'd let herself believe there was a glimmer of a chance with Tyler.

"What's that look?" Nolea frowned.

"What look?"

"That undecided look. You *are* going to the interview aren't you?"

"Of course. Why wouldn't I?"

"Good. I wouldn't want you to let something or *someone* get in your way." Nolea softened her tone. "You know I want the best for you. This thing with Tyler hasn't really even happened yet. I don't think he is what is making you hesitate. It's the idea of a *possibility* of a relationship."

"Like a long shot of a long shot?" Like this job offer?

Nolea shook her head. "I'm just saying step back and take at look at this for what it really is. Have you even had sex with him yet?"

"No. Absolutely not." But she'd thought of him nonstop since that first kiss. And she definitely liked the idea of waking up in his arms.

"Wanting to doesn't count." Nolea peered at Serena reading her thoughts. "Besides, do you really want a life with a guy that started out as a lie?"

"No. You're right; that wouldn't make sense." And it almost sounded like she meant it, but Serena knew better. Deep down she wanted to be with Tyler, but not because he exhibited any qualities that she usually looked for in a guy. He had little education, no financial security, and couldn't smooth talk his way out of a wet paper bag. But the way he treated her, looked at her, confided in her. Not like a woman he was trying to get into bed, but like a friend. A friend she'd never had, but wanted so badly. Now that was worth something.

"There will be other guys."

Mary Lou swung the door wide and rushed into the office. "You have to see this. It's on the news."

The women all ran to the break room where a crowd gathered around a small television.

"Our calls to the *Cranfield Reporter-Star* were not returned, so this reporter must conclude that there is some basis of fact in the rumors that "Lone Star Love Affair" is a false ploy created to fool readers and dupe advertisers." The woman's dark eyes sparkled with barely concealed glee. "Back to you, Carl."

Nolea frowned. "Don't we know her?"

"You certainly do," Mary Lou huffed. "She was that flirty intern we had here a few years ago, Jackie Landess. Thought she should be editor after three months. She's still full of it." Mary Lou flicked off the set and the crowd dispersed.

Nolea lowered her voice. "Word is, the manager at the TV station went ballistic when they got their sales figures this morning." She glanced at Serena. "Looks like they're on the warpath."

Serena nodded as her chest tightened. Nolea knew what this meant, and so did she. There would be reporters crawling all over the story now, and if they smelled a skunk, "Lone Star Love Affair" was through.

Serena wasn't about to let that happen. She wanted to leave this paper with a successful track record, not a big black mark against her name. She had to talk to Frank. Spinning on her heels, she headed straight for his office.

She gave a short rap on the door and then peered inside. The lights were off, but she could see Frank sitting at his desk, his silhouette enhanced by the light peeking under the blinds. "Uncle Frank? Are you okay?"

"Yeah, I'm fine."

Serena could tell by his voice that he wasn't. Slipping into the office, she sat in a chair in front of his desk. "What's wrong?" He couldn't have heard about the broadcast yet, but something bothered him. Something big.

"It's Macy. They found something."

"What?"

"They think its cancer. Uterine. They're doing a biopsy next week, but the doctor already warned us that this type is usually malignant."

Malignant. A horrible word synonymous with death in Serena's mind. But Macy virtually lived at the doctor's office. Surely anything they found would be in the early stages. "What kind of treatment are they looking at?"

Frank shrugged. "The doctor won't talk about treatment until we know for sure what we're dealing with. But Macy looked it up on the Internet. It's not good. Fast moving, difficult to treat. Less than twenty percent survive more than six months after diagnosis."

His statement hung in the air between them as the clock on his desk ticked. Fear filled Serena's heart only to be pushed aside by guilt. Macy had talked to Serena about her various imaginary medical problems so often, she'd never considered the possibility something might really be wrong.

"You know I never really took her illnesses seriously," Frank echoed Serena's thoughts. "She's complained for years about this or that, and it always turned out to be nothing. I figured this was the same. And now. . ." He shook his head.

And now it could be over. Serena stared at the clock. Odd how things came into perspective when the stakes were life and death. She couldn't imagine the hurt and guilt Frank felt. And what about Macy? A small vivacious woman, she had an energy that nothing tempered, but this might overwhelm her completely. Macy's paranoia of contracting some dread disease had finally come true. How would she cope with that? How would any of them deal with that harsh reality?

Frank cleared his throat. "Your mother is coming into town."

Arlene Ganz was coming here? More bad news. Serena stiffened. The tension between them had only worsened during the years since Serena had been sent away to have Justin. She'd come to think of the woman as "Arlene" rather than "Mother." It was easier to imagine a stranger had chosen to send her away out of shame, rather than her own flesh and blood.

"Like Macy said, you two need to talk about things and come to some kind of understanding. You never know when it will be too late." Frank's chair squeaked as he turned around to her.

Heat crawled up Serena's face, and she forced the memories aside, searching for a way to change the subject. "Channel 7 ran a piece at noon that "Lone Star Love Affair" is a sham."

Frank leaned back. "I knew they were rooting around for something on us. You worry too much. Channel 7 has been sliding for some time. It's desperation on their part, that's all. They might even get a backlash from people who love the articles. If you acknowledge the attack, you give it life. Ignore it, and it dies a quiet death. In the meantime, it's more free publicity for us. Can't beat that with a stick."

"I hope you're right." They sat in silence for a few minutes. Both consumed by their own worries.

"I figure I'll be away from work quite a bit," Frank said. "I'll need to hand things here off to someone."

"For how long?"

He shrugged. "Maybe weeks, maybe months. I don't know."

"Oh, of course." Serena nodded. The other editors would gladly pick up the slack and do whatever they could to help Frank, as would she.

"I know you're ready. You have been for some time. And if things go well with you as interim editor-in-chief, and Macy gets through this, I may look at retiring soon."

Editor-in-chief? Serena stifled a groan. When she started at the paper, she was only 22, and being editor-in-chief had been her goal. To learn all she could and follow Frank in the business, taking over after he retired.

But now? Things had changed; she had changed. She finally had the chance to go to New York. To get a shot at a national magazine and have a real career that she earned, instead of a job that was given to her by family. Not that she wasn't grateful, but it wasn't the same.

"What do you say?" Frank waited on an answer. "Can I count on you?"

Everything in her being wanted to scream "no." She'd seen the possibility of achieving her dream, only to have it threatened less than an hour later. How could life be that cruel? To her? To Macy?

Macy had taken Serena in 18 years ago and had given her the chance to become more than a statistic. The future for many single teenage moms was a life of welfare and food stamps. If not for Frank and Macy, she'd have never had the encouragement to go to college or even the confidence to raise her son alone. She owed them. She owed them both.

Serena took a deep breath. "Sure, Uncle Frank. You know you can count on me."

Chapter 17

Tyler arrived at Serena's a little past five in the afternoon. He'd rescued the TV and most of his clothes, as well as the recliner, which now perched upside down strapped to the roll bar of the Jeep. By the time he'd gotten to the condo, the rest of his belongings had already been hauled off. Several members of his staff had generously volunteered to work double shifts, so he could try to get his life back in order. Not that he had any chance of that. He'd settle for mildly chaotic and a roof over his head at this point. Any roof.

Knocking gingerly on the door, Tyler half hoped that no one was home. Then he could take his stuff and go, and Serena would never know how precarious his life had become.

Justin swung the door wide and grinned. "Hey, Ty." He dried his hands on the dishtowel he carried and shook Tyler's hand. "You need help with that?" Justin pointed to the upended recliner.

"No, it's fine."

The boy raised a skeptical eyebrow.

Tyler shrugged. "Kind of having a bad day."

Justin smiled and nodded. "Must be going around. C'mon in." He led the way to the kitchen and resumed stirring a skillet full of meat and beans. The aroma drew Tyler across the room. "What're you cooking?"

"Chili."

"Smells good." Tyler spotted his garbage bags and box in a corner. Had Justin brought them in? Hopefully the boy hadn't told Serena. Tyler tried to keep the talk from turning to him. "Your mom teach you to cook?"

"Are you kidding?" Justin scoffed. "It's not really her thing."

"So, where'd you learn?"

Justin tilted his head. "I don't know. I just kind of tried stuff until it tasted good. Want some?"

"Sure. Where's your mom?"

Justin jerked his head toward the back door. "On the deck, but I'd leave her alone if I were you."

Tyler gave a nod of resignation and hoped she wasn't too mad. He couldn't imagine coming home to find a guy's junk *and* his dog dumped in the backyard. He needed to do some explaining. Fast.

"She had a bad day at work. Said she wanted to be alone."

"Why? What happened?" A tingle of concern and apprehension ran up his neck. Figures he would pick the worst time to unload his problems on her. Had something happened with the articles? Or with her uncle?

Justin dished up two bowls of the chili and set them on the table. "Don't know, but she's real upset."

Pulling up a chair, Tyler sat opposite the boy. "Real upset? As in crying?"

"No. Mom never cries." He shook his head. "Never."

That was a foreign concept to Tyler. He'd never been around a woman that didn't have a built in sprinkler system she turned on and off at will.

But then, he'd never been around anyone like Serena. Actually, he'd seen her cry the other night on the deck.

He glanced at Justin. Maybe she didn't cry in front of her kid. That sounded like her. He'd already seen that tough front she put up for everyone.

Tyler scooped a big spoonful of chili and shoveled it into his mouth. Stopping a moment, he savored the taste. Fresh herbs, garlic, onions. Spicy, but not too hot. Perfect in fact. He watched Justin, who ate so fast you'd think it was his last meal. If he'd come up with this on his own, then the boy had a gift. "How do you know she's upset if she never cries?"

"She's quiet. I mean, when she's a little upset, she yells. Medium upset, she screams. But quiet, now that's bigtime upset."

"She that way very often?"

"No." He shook his head and stared toward the back door. "Hardly ever." Worry creased the boy's brow heightening Tyler's concern. He should go talk to her, see if he could help. Shadow jumped on the back door and looked at him through the window.

"Shadow's a great dog." Justin took his empty bowl to the sink. "I set her out some water and Mom got her the dog food. She wasn't sure what kind to get, so she got a little bit of everything." He pointed to a small table by the back door.

A large bag of premium dog food and several varieties of canned food filled the surface, as well as a couple of bags of doggie treats and one or two rawhide chews. Tyler stared. Serena must have spent a fortune. Guilt gnawed at his conscience. "She didn't have to do that."

Justin smiled. "Mom's a sucker for a furry face."

Tyler ran a hand across his cheek. Then maybe he should let his beard grow. The good part of this was that if Serena liked Shadow, then she might keep the dog for a little bit while he set himself up in another place. It seemed a lot to ask right now, but he didn't have many options.

Justin pointed to the box and the garbage bags. "So are you homeless or what?"

Tyler almost choked on the chili. The kid cut right to the point. "You could say that."

"Where you planning to go?"

"Not sure, but I'll figure something out."

Justin frowned. Tyler hated to imagine what went through the boy's mind. What kind of man, and business owner to boot, was homeless at his age? Other than maybe Bobby Jack. The image of himself at 70 hobbling down an alleyway begging for a sandwich, turned Tyler's stomach. The way things were headed right now, it could happen. Easily.

"What kind of place you looking for?"

The question halted Tyler's depressing train of thought. "Don't know, haven't had much time to think about it."

A roof would work for now. He glanced at the door as Shadow whimpered. She knew he was here; Serena probably did too but hadn't come in yet. She must be really upset. The dog leaped up to look in again. "Be nice to have a yard. Shadow's never had a real yard."

Justin frowned again. What could the kid be thinking now? And why all the questions? Was he worried about his mom? Or afraid that Tyler would take advantage of her? It sure might appear that way if he started asking for favors.

Justin heaved a sigh. "I have an idea if you're interested."

An idea? He couldn't imagine what kind of suggestion he'd get from a kid, but at this point, but he'd listen to anything. "What's that?"

"Well, you know Mom has been trying to rent out Jacie's old room. Ran an ad and everything."

"Yeah?"

"And you know I'm going off to college this fall, right?"

"Right."

"Well, I wondered if you might want to rent the room. I mean, I don't want her to be all alone without anyone to look after her. You know?"

Dumbfounded, Tyler stared at Justin. Surely the kid had no idea what he was saying, and Tyler knew that Serena had no inkling of the turn this discussion had taken, or she would be in here in a heartbeat. "Your mom seems plenty able to take care of herself."

"She acts tough and all, but she doesn't like being alone. I mean, I know it's a lot to ask, but it's not like you have anywhere to go right now."

Okay, so he had a point. And the solution seemed so simple to hear Justin tell it.

"You might even like her once you get used to her." Justin shrugged. "You seem like someone I could trust."

Like her? Was he kidding? Tyler'd had fantasized about Serena every night since he'd kissed her and held her in his arms. He couldn't even image what it would be like to be around her everyday.

He had to seriously question the boy's judgment on the trust issue, though. You don't hand a homeless fox the key to the hen house and expect him to keep his paws to himself. Not with Serena. He looked up at Justin. The kid had no idea how fabulous his mother was and how incredible this offer would be for any guy. Let alone him, given the situation.

"Will you at least consider it?" Justin's eyes bored into his.

"Don't you think your mom should have something to say about it?" Serena would never agree, which was too bad. The idea provided a perfect solution for both of them in the long run. Not to mention giving Tyler the chance to hang around and prove to her he wasn't a complete loser.

Justin waved his hand with a smile. "You know she likes a sob story. So do me a favor and give her one."

"That's the easy part." His whole entire life was a sob story. Tyler put his bowl in the sink and gazed out the kitchen window. Serena sat in the swing with her back to him, slowly rocking back and forth. She scratched Shadow's ears, and the dog sat at her feet eating up the attention. Well, at least she liked his dog. That was a start.

"I gotta get to work. Will you tell her I'll be home by eleven?"

Tyler nodded. "You don't have any idea why she's upset?"

"No, but I do know that the message on the answering machine isn't going to make it any better."

"What's the message?"

"Grandma's coming to town."

Chapter 18

Serena pushed the swing slowly back and forth. Shadow trotted between her and the backdoor. Tyler must be here. Her life had hit one of its lowest points today. It lifted her sagging spirits a little knowing he was close by. Not that he could do anything to help, but she needed to talk to someone. Her head hurt from trying to process the events of the day, let alone deal with them.

She hadn't called Aunt Macy yet to see how she was feeling, so now she had a whopping load of guilt on top of everything else. Serena feared she'd end up blubbering the second she saw Macy, knowing her aunt might have very little time left.

Her chest hurt every time she thought of the job offer with *American Woman*. She'd tried to push it from her mind, but it refused to give her any peace. The dream of what life might be like in New York brought images of excitement, the constant motion of the city mixed with the thrill of working on important articles and projects that could really make a difference. She imagined herself in an office high up with a view of the Empire State Building or Central Park. Serena heaved a sigh; New York wasn't an option at this point. Torturing herself wouldn't change the facts. Her family needed her, and she couldn't disappoint them.

Family. A sense of dread filled her as she thought about Arlene's arrival. The woman conveyed disapproval and disappointment with every glance. Her daughter's pregnancy had been a huge embarrassment to Arlene, and she had never let go of that emotion. Somehow being around the woman turned Serena into a rebellious 16-year-old all over again. Every old hurt, argument, and past conflict tainted any conversation they tried to have. Not that there had been that many in the past 19 years.

If Arlene said black, Serena said white. It had always been that way. But not this time. Her mother may not be over it, but she was, and it was time they related to each other as adults no matter how Arlene felt about things. She would not let it get to her. Besides, Arlene was coming for Macy, not for her. Never for her, never for Justin.

Serena could count on one hand the number of times Arlene had visited since Justin was a baby. Each and every visit defined disaster in its own way, driving them further apart, which was fine as far as she was concerned.

From arguments over her lack of motherly skill, to her taste in men, nothing was ever good enough for Arlene. Nothing ever erased the past, and Serena refused to dwell on it. It was time to let it go, and if Arlene insisted on replaying the old hurts, she was through trying.

The sun sank below the horizon, and she stood to go inside. Shadow circled her legs and stepped everywhere Serena did almost causing her to fall. Reaching down she pushed the dog out of the way, but Shadow immediately circled her legs again, rubbing against them. Tyler opened the door and smiled.

"This dog will not let me take one step without her." She finally made it to the door. "Is she that lonely?"

"No, she does that to people she likes."

The dog followed Serena inside and circled her legs again. "It's like she's glued to me. Like she's . . ."

"Your shadow? It's not an original name, but it suits her." He stood at the sink and washed two bowls and two glasses.

"Where's Justin?"

"Work. He said he'd be back after eleven." Tyler glanced at her. "He fed me some great chili."

"Yeah, he loves to cook."

"I was thinking about offering him a job."

Serena stared at Tyler's back. He'd already helped her so much, doing everything she'd asked of him and more. No one could ever say he hadn't gone the extra mile, and here he was doing it again. But she and Justin had made it this far on their own, and she certainly didn't want Tyler feeling sorry for them. "You don't have to do that."

The muscles in Tyler's back flexed with every move. Remembering his kiss as she watched him, Serena's tongue traced the inside of her lips. She'd let herself hope he cared for her beyond the normal friendship. Even spent the evenings fantasizing about what it would be like to be with Tyler, instead of just being around him. Serena pressed her lips together in frustration. Good grief she was starting to believe her own press, that the "Lone Star Love Affair" actually had love in it—or at least an affair. That idea sent a chill up her spine and her gaze to his firm butt.

"I want to. He's a good worker and a great cook. Who knows, he could be a famous chef someday." He smiled over his shoulder at her.

She forced her attention to his face as a sad, almost apologetic expression passed across his features. "I won't ask him if it's not okay with you. I'd understand if you don't want him to work for me."

Serena frowned. Why would he say that? Did Tyler think she was that controlling where her son was concerned? "I don't mind at all." In fact it would give her a much better idea of what was going on in her son's life if he were working alongside Tyler everyday. Serena hesitated a moment. Okay, maybe she was a little nosey, but not controlling.

"You hungry?" He asked. "There's some left."

She shook her head. "Not really."

He turned and leaned against the sink, drying his hands. "I hear you had a bad day."

"The worst."

"Don't be so sure; mine sucked pretty bad, too."

"Is that why I inherited a dog and some dirty clothes?"

"Yeah, sorry about that." He carefully draped the towel over the oven handle to dry. "I was in a hurry and couldn't think of anywhere to leave her that had a fence."

Serena leaned down and patted Shadow. "I didn't mind. I enjoyed having her around. So what made your day so bad?"

She pulled out a kitchen chair and sat. Tyler joined her. "It started off okay," he flashed a grin.

Serena recalled waking up in his arms less than 12 hours ago. It seemed like days had past since then. She smiled back as the heat rose to her cheeks.

"But then, I got kicked out of my home, threatened by a scum sucking attorney, and almost blackmailed out of business."

Serena's eyes widened. "Wow. That's some day."

"Oh, that was all before noon."

"Who's blackmailing you? And why?"

"My former business partner sold his half to a very ruthless person who basically wants cash, which I don't have. So they said I will either come up with it or be run out of business."

"Can they do that?"

"Maybe." He shrugged. "I'm hoping my brother Jeff can come up with something. He's a lawyer in Dallas."

"Why were you kicked out of your condo?"

"My name was never on the lease. It was owned by the uncle of my old girlfriend. I knew it could happen someday, and it finally did."

"Where are you going to stay?"

He hesitated. "Well, I got a really interesting offer a while ago."

"From who?"

"Your son."

"Justin? What kind of offer?"

"He wanted me to consider staying here and renting out your extra room. Said he wants me to keep an eye on you."

"What? Why would he say that?"

Tyler shrugged. "He doesn't want you to be alone when he leaves for school. I told him that I didn't think you would go for it, but you have to admit the idea has some merit."

"How so?" Serena's mind whirled, and her heart pounded. She loved the idea, despite Justin's faulty reasoning. She did, however, want to know Tyler's thought process. Did he see her as a sympathy case and a convenient answer to his problems? Or did he really want to be with her? Right here, in her house, 24/7.

"Well, you need to rent out the room, and I need a place to stay. Shadow likes you and would have a yard. You have to admit putting an ad in the paper for someone to live with you can be dangerous. You already know me pretty well, and we seem to get along alright."

Serena frowned. *Shadow likes you?* Was that some kind of Freudian man-speak for "I'm scared of my feelings," or did he really not have any for her? She and Tyler certainly did get along; there was no denying that, and Serena would love for them to get along even better. Not that she'd ever admit it, but she had had nightmares about some of the people that had come by to look at the room. Borderline ax murders at best. She'd never have been able to sleep with any of them in the house. Not that she'd be able to sleep with Tyler in the house either, but for completely different reasons.

How perfect was this? Not to mention the fact that it could take "Lone Star Love Affair" to a whole new level—both in fantasy and reality. She could hardly wait to see that little reporter's disappointment when she found out they were living together.

"So what do you think?"

Serena looked at him and nodded. "Okay."

"Okay?" He seemed shocked. "As in, I can stay?"

She nodded.

"For how long?"

"As long as you want."

He looked at her as if she needed to explain.

Serena shrugged. "You're right, it's a good plan. For everyone." She got up and went to the front door. "Where's the rest of your stuff?"

They spent the next few hours shuffling furniture in the spare bedroom and arranging his things. What few there were. They worked out a rental agreement and division of chores. Tyler offered to do laundry and cook on the days he was off. Justin would be thrilled, and so was she. As he got busy sorting the clothes from his garbage bags, Serena decided to take a long bath.

Sitting in the steaming water, she smiled to herself. Who would have thought such a rotten day could have turned out so well? At least Tyler had taken her mind off her own problems for a few hours and solved a number of other worries that had weighed her down. She now had the room rented, was living with her "lover" from "Lone Star Love Affair," and though New York would have to be put off; as difficult as that was to think about, it would still be there when she was ready. All in all, things could have been worse, much worse.

Shadow whined and scratched at the bathroom door. Serena reached up and turned the knob, and the dog poked her head in first, then pushed through the door. Serena scratched Shadow's ears.

Tyler's footsteps echoed, then slowed in the hallway. "Is she bothering you?"

Serena could tell he stood well away from the door and was impressed by the gentlemanly gesture. "No, she's fine."

"Okay." He left her to her bath, and Serena reached over and closed the door.

Shadow sat on the green rug and leaned her jaws on the edge of the tub. How could the animal have become so attached to her so quickly? She smiled and dripped water on the dog's nose. Shadow shook her head then resumed her position. As annoying as it was to have an animal worship the ground you walked on, Serena liked it. Funny how she could have this effect on a dog, but not its owner.

Serena soaked in the tub until her fingers turned pruney. Dressing in silk PJs and a white chenille robe, she made her way to her bedroom, which was next to Tyler's. She'd hoped to say goodnight, but the door was closed. Disappointed, she went to her room, Shadow on her heels. Serena tossed the robe aside and climbed into the large four-poster bed. She looked at the white coverlet and frowned at the dog. Surely she didn't expect to sleep up here with Serena.

"Stay." Serena held up her hand. Shadow stayed perfectly still. Hopefully, the animal understood. Serena turned off the lamp and snuggled down into the covers. An occasional thump resounded through the wall as Tyler continued to arrange his room. Serena squinted through the darkness at the space between them. Ten, maybe 12 feet. That and a wall.

She huffed a sigh and flopped over, trying to clear her mind. She glanced at the digital display on the clock. It flashed 10:30, then 10:45, then 11. Serena heard Justin's truck pull up in the drive. Hushed voices drew her attention, and she sat up, trying to pick up pieces of conversation. What did he think about Tyler being here? She strained but couldn't hear anything and flopped back down on the pillows.

Sexual frustration was a bitch, as Nolea would say. And that was the root of this problem. She needed some relief and soon. Serena stilled for a moment. It had been a while, but if the batteries were still good, then she was in business.

She yanked open the drawer of the nightstand and felt around in the dark. Her hand brushed against cold rubber and she pulled the object out of the drawer. She held it for a moment then felt for the switch. It leapt to life, vibrating for all it was worth. A single woman's best friend.

Shadow let out a whine that quickly turned into a tiny howl. Serena flicked the button off and glared at the dog in the dark. "Shhhh." After a minute, Shadow settled back onto the rug. Serena tried again, and the dog went into an allout howl.

A knock sounded at the door.

Serena jammed the device under her pillow, trying to locate the off button as her heart pounded. "Come in."

Tyler poked his head in. "Everything okay?"

"Yes, fine. Why?"

"What was she howling at?" The light in the hallway illuminated Tyler's silhouette. He was wearing boxer shorts and no shirt.

"Who?"

"Shadow. You know, the dog." He spoke to her like she was slow-witted, which was true right now. Nothing could make a woman sound more foolish than sex on the brain.

"She's fine. I'm fine. No problem here." Serena knew she babbled.

He stood for a minute, looking at her. "Okay, if you say so."

He started to pull the door closed, leaving only a sliver of light and then turned around. "Um. Do you have a cat?"

"No, why?"

"Your pillow is purring."

As soon as Tyler was out of sight, Serena slammed a hand down on the quaking pillow next to her. Oh, heaven forbid that she be purring tonight, but the pillow? Why not? She grabbed the now silent vibrator and tossed it into the drawer. So much for getting any relief. What kind of dog howls at a vibrator? She glared at Shadow. "How cruel can you be? Are you *trying* to push me over the edge?"

The door popped open again. "Talking to yourself?"

She heard the smile in Tyler's voice. "I was talking to Shadow for your information."

"Oh, that's so much better."

She started to argue as he held up his hands. "Just trying to figure out what kind of woman I'm living with."

What kind of woman? If he had any idea he'd probably take his garbage bags, ratty recliner, and vibrator-hating dog and run for the hills.

Tyler pulled the door. "Goodnight, Mary Ellen."

She smiled at him, "Goodni-"

"Goodnight already, John Boy." Justin's voice boomed down the hall. "Don't you people sleep?"

Serena stared at the sliver of light, where Tyler had stood a moment earlier and felt a small ache. No, at least for her anyway, there'd be no sleep tonight.

Chapter 19

"Do you think it's too much?" Serena gazed at the morning paper, her eyes scanning the newest installment of "Lone Star Love Affair" for the 10th time. The newsroom buzzed in the background, but she forced herself to focus.

"Absolutely not. It's like we talked about, going through the perfect relationship step by step." Nolea held a copy, rereading as she talked. "This part about the deepening respect and friendship is great. Just the kind of drivel our advertisers love." She tossed her paper on the desk. "If I didn't know better, I'd say you were really in love with the guy." She raised a questioning brow at Serena. "So? Are you?"

"It's like I said, we're just friends."

"I'm not so sure. I think the less you see of him the better, this is no time for things to get sticky."

"Well, " Serena hesitated. "There has been a development."

"A development? I knew it!" Nolea's voice climbed an octave. "You slept with him!"

"No, I did *not* sleep with him."

Nolea leaned back, relieved. "Then what?"

"He kind of moved in last night."

"Moved in? As in made a move, made a pass, put the make on you, right?"

Serena cringed, anticipating Nolea's reaction. "As in moved into the spare room with his dog, a recliner, and two garbage bags of dirty clothes."

"What in the hell are you thinking?" Nolea stood up, disgusted. "How are you going to walk away from this when you leave? The more you let this guy worm his way into your life, the harder it will be."

"Now, think about it a minute." Serena held up her hands hoping to minimize the lecture. "I need someone to rent the spare room, and he needs a place to stay."

"Are there no homeless shelters? No more YMCA? They take bums from all walks, even penniless restaurant owners. He can go there." She plopped down in the chair. "You said yourself he's not the kind of guy you would ever have dated for real. Why expose yourself to getting hurt by a man who's totally not worth it?"

Serena frowned, fighting the urge to defend Tyler. He wasn't worthless. Not in the ways that really mattered. Granted, he didn't have much in the way of material assets. And Nolea was all about guys with assets. "This is only temporary. Besides, that snotty reporter keeps turning up, trying to prove we're faking "Lone Star Love Affair." As soon as she finds out Tyler and I are living together, she'll have no story, and we can move on."

"If that's all it is."

"That's all it is."

A few seconds of silence passed.

"So did you tell Frank about the job offer?"

Serena sighed. "No."

"Chicken."

"It's not that." Serena lowered her voice. "Macy has cancer."

"Oh my god!" Nolea leaned forward in her chair, her mouth open.

"Yeah. So before I could even talk to him about the job, he drops the news on me and then asks me to stand in for him as editor-in-chief."

"What did you say?"

Serena closed her eyes and rubbed her temple with two fingers. "What could I say?"

"You could've said no."

"I could *not*. I owe them everything. It's a job *interview*, not a job. I'll get my chance later."

"Later?" Nolea stood and started pacing. "Like I have? You want to look back in ten years and still be sitting right here out of some sense of obligation, family honor or martyrdom? If you had told Frank about the offer before he asked you to stand in for him, he would have worked out something else, and you know it."

Serena gave her an exasperated wave.

"You know I'm right. There are plenty of people here to pick up right where Frank left off. If either Frank or Macy knew you were putting aside the biggest opportunity you ever got to babysit the paper, they'd go ballistic."

Serena pointed a finger at Nolea. "I want your promise that you won't breathe a word of this to them."

Both women glared, neither blinking. A silent war of wills. Nolea flinched first. "Fine. I won't say a word to them, but you know what I really think?"

"Would it matter if I said no?"

Nolea paced around the office, her cheeks glowing red. "I think this had nothing to do with Frank or Macy or this paper. This has to with the fact that you are in love with some fantasy man you keep writing about who doesn't exist."

"That's not true."

"Is too. And you know what else?"

Serena clamped her lips shut not even bothering to try to stop the tirade.

"I think you're scared of going to New York. This gave you a chance to wimp out, and you took it." Nolea started toward the door. "I'm not letting this happen."

"You promised." Serena's face radiated heat. Nolea knew her so well. She had been scared. Scared she'd get all excited, and then the magazine wouldn't want her. Scared she wouldn't be able to produce the level of work they were used to. Scared of leaving the security of her boring life.

Nolea paused, her hand on the knob. "Well, congratulations. Now you can always say you got the chance of a lifetime, but didn't have the balls to take it." Nolea yanked open the office door and stormed out. The door slammed against the wall, then vibrated away leaving a noticeable divot.

Will stopped short in the doorway, watching Nolea march down the hall. "What did you do to piss her off?"

"What makes you think it was me?" Serena growled.

"She's jealous 'cause you have a hot lover boy and she doesn't." He grinned. "Not that I haven't offered."

"No, I don't have a hot lover boy." Why did everyone keep saying that?

"Do too."

"Don't." Serena grabbed several paperclips and flung them at him.

Will ducked as the tiny metal objects bounced harmlessly off the door jam. "Well, somebody's lying and it ain't me."

Serena dropped her head in her hands. "Shut up, Skippy."

Chapter 20

Tyler rolled the Jeep to a stop in front of Serena's house. The sun had barely set, and he could see the lights on, though Serena's car was gone. He'd left money for his part of the groceries this morning. With any luck she'd remember laundry soap. He'd had to hunt for something clean to wear before work, and the socks he'd found were definitely in the questionable category.

Grabbing the sack of barbecue sandwiches from the restaurant, he hurried up the walk and unlocked the door with the shiny new key Serena had given him. Tyler walked through the house straight to the kitchen. Shadow's high-pitched yelps greeted his arrival. He set the sack on the table and let her in, grinning as she rubbed his legs and tried to force his hand along her head. He bent down and rubbed her ears. "Miss me, girl?" She wagged her body playfully, and she ran off down the hall.

Tyler stood and breathed deeply, reveling in the quiet after the chaos of the restaurant. It was great to be home. And oddly enough, even after only a few weeks, this felt more like home than anyplace he'd been the past several years. His gaze fell on the beatup cardboard box next to the back door. He'd pointedly ignored it lately, but papers and invoices poked out the top demanding for his attention. Jeff would be asking about it soon.

He'd come home early to try and get a start on the mountainous mess of paperwork, and while not looking forward to it, he was more determined than ever to get rid of Krista. Especially after today. She'd hung around talking to customers and telling everyone she owned the place. Like she actually belonged there and had any kind of hand in making it run. Every time he'd turned around today, there she'd been with that plastic smile and fake "help me help you" attitude. The only person she'd ever wanted to help was herself and she'd helped herself to every dime he'd had a year ago. It now gave him the motivation to dig through the financial hell of his business no matter how bad it might be. And this had to be the only time he hoped it was bad. Really bad. Once she realized how broke he really was, maybe she'd give up this stupidity and move on.

Shadow streaked through the kitchen and into the living room, hopping up onto the sofa. Tyler caught a flash of blue and pink shiny material in the dog's mouth as she ran. He frowned. He needed Serena in a good enough mood to help him with the bookwork, and he'd bet a chewed up night gown would not help matters. He walked up and leaned over the back of the couch, snatching the piece of fabric from Shadow's mouth.

He held it up and grimaced. The garment looked like something his grandmother used to wear. Long, shapeless, and covered with some kind of tiny pink flowers, it was definitely not what he'd pictured Serena wearing to bed—ever. He glanced at the dog. "Where'd you get this?" Shadow took off down the hall and disappeared into Tyler's room. The light was on. Tyler followed and stopped short in the doorway. A suitcase full of clothes lay open on the bed. Shadow scratched at the closed bathroom door. Tyler crept across the floor straining to hear any noise.

Just as he leaned an ear to the wood, the toilet flushed and the door swung open. Tyler stood face to face with a woman in her 60s. They stared for a moment, and then the woman screamed. Tyler flinched from the sound, then ducked as the woman threw an extra roll of toilet tissue at him.

"I'm calling the police right now, so don't you try anything."

Tyler looked back to see the woman brandishing a plunger like a Samurai warrior. She walked toward him as he backed up.

"I've heard of sickos like you that think they can take advantage of single women. Give me that." She snatched the nightgown from his grasp.

He held up his hands. "Hey, lady, I live here."

"You get out of my daughter's house right now, mister." Arlene chased him to the living room then swung and missed, though he knew it wouldn't have hurt even if she'd connected. When she tried again, he caught the wood handle and they struggled back and forth a few minutes. Shadow barked and circled the pair, jumping on and off the couch. The dog tipped over a large vase of flowers on the coffee table, spilling water all over the couch.

"Now see what you've done!" Arlene struggled harder apparently determined to bash his skull in.

The front door opened, and Serena stared at the two of them caught in a tug of war over the plunger.

"What is going on in here?"

"Call the police, honey, this man is some kind of sex pervert."

Tyler saw a twitch of a smile at the corner of Serena's mouth.

The woman kept talking. "I caught him going through my unmentionables."

Serena couldn't hide her smile anymore as she raised a brow at Tyler. "A sex fiend? Wow. I might have to let her plunge you to death."

They all stood in silence a minute, and finally Serena set the bag down. "Arlene, this is Tyler."

Arlene relaxed her grip, and Tyler twisted the offending weapon from her hands.

"Oh. So you know each other?"

The woman's gaze assessed him up and down as only a mother can. "He said he lives here. Is that true?"

It was more an accusation than a statement of fact. Tyler frowned. Living together wasn't a crime the last time he checked, and that's all they were doing. Living together.

Serena paused, pressing her lips together. "Yes, he does."

"Oh."

The air crackled with the electricity of unspoken thoughts. Like the dead calm before a tornado. Tyler didn't move and almost didn't breathe. He'd been caught in the crossfire between a woman and her mother several years ago and barely survived it. In the end, they'd both turned on him. He couldn't afford that here. Not that he had any fear of Arlene, but Serena had the power to make him and Shadow homeless in a heartbeat.

Arlene held up her gown. "Why is this wet?"

Both women looked at Tyler. So much for laying low. "Uh, Shadow brought it to me."

Arlene wrinkled her nose at the garment. "This is dog slobber?" She slid a relieved glance toward Tyler's zipper. "I'll be washing this."

As soon as the woman disappeared down the hall, Serena blew out a long breath. She looked tired. "I'd hope to be here when you got home."

"I wish you had been. I don't think I've ever had my life threatened with a plunger before."

"Sorry about that. We need to talk a minute." She nodded her head toward the door. "Can you help me with the rest of these groceries?"

Tyler followed her to the car and took the bags she handed out of the back seat.

"I really didn't expect her to stay here. She usually stays with Frank and Macy, but with Macy's surgery scheduled for this week, she asked if she could stay with me." Serena grabbed the last of the bags and led the way back to the house.

So where am I sleeping? Tyler set the bags on the kitchen counter and sorted through the purchases, placing the canned goods on the shelf in the pantry. "Do you need me to stay at a hotel for a while?"

"No." Serena leaned around him and rotated the cans he'd put away so the labels faced forward. He squinted at the vegetables, trying to determine if they were alphabetized, too. "I already decided that I am not shuffling my life, or yours, to suit my mother. She will have to deal with things the way they are."

"And how are they?" Arlene stood in the doorway.

I was wondering that myself. Tyler waited for Serena to respond, but she continued putting groceries away and ignored the question.

The silence grew louder by the second until Arlene finally broke it.

"Would you like me to make a good dinner for you, dear?" Arlene emptied several grocery bags on the table.

"No we've existed on my bad cooking for years now." Serena's tone suggested irritation, covered by the thinnest veil of politeness.

"That's not what I meant."

Silence descended again. Tyler's attention darted from one woman to the other. If this tension kept up, it could be a long night.

"I brought home some sandwiches," he offered.

"That sounds great." Arlene's smile seemed a bit too bright.

"Tyler owns a restaurant," Serena said, putting away the last of the groceries.

"Really?" Arlene looked at him with renewed interest. "You own your own business?"

He nodded. *And I'm damn broke.* He would have to seriously consider getting a T-shirt with that phrase. It was automatic woman repellant.

Opening the sack from JT's, Serena placed the sandwiches on a plate to heat them up. "Justin works for him," she explained. As far as this conversation went, she did the least that she could do not to leave them gawking at each other in awkward silence. Tyler had to wonder what kind of history had caused this kind of rift between the women. And when would be a good time to bring up the sleeping arrangements?

Serena looked at him as the microwave hummed. "So why are you home so early?"

"I hoped to get started on the financials that Jeff needs." He watched her gaze dart to the box and then to her mother.

"Can I help with anything?" Serena asked.

Obviously she needed something to do other than deal with Arlene tonight, which worked out perfectly for him.

"Sure, if you don't mind."

He got plates for each of them while Arlene filled glasses with water. They sat and ate around the small kitchen table. Arlene made polite conversation covering the safe topics. Weather, stuff in the news, the TV programs they'd seen lately. Anyone listening would think they were strangers chatting in a doctor's office. Serena and Arlene shared nothing of a personal nature at all, which seemed completely bizarre compared to his family. Afterward, they cleaned the table and Serena dragged the box of papers out.

Arlene peered inside. "Would you like me to help with this? You know I did the accounts payable for the church for years."

Tyler opened his mouth to accept, but Serena cut him off.

"No, I'm sure you're tired and need your rest."

Wow. It was almost like slamming a door in her face, but Arlene seemed to shrug it off. "Okay, I have a book I'm almost finished with, and then I'll probably turn in for the night."

"If you need to get anything from your room, you might want to get it now." Serena gave him a pointed stare.

"Uh, sure." He hurriedly gathered up clothes and some personal grooming items. Once back out in the hallway, he paused. Where was he going to put this stuff? He started back toward the kitchen and heard Arlene's hushed whisper.

"I don't think it's right to be living with him."

"Well, I am living with him and that's not going to change," Serena whispered back.

"What kind of effect do you think this will have on Justin?"

"They get along fine. They even work together. Justin is almost grown, Mother. I don't think he'll be damaged for life by Tyler's presence."

Tyler grimaced. Arlene was putting Serena through an emotional beating, and he couldn't figure out why. Serena was a great mom, and Justin proved it. Arlene talked as if the kid were 3 years old.

Arlene turned down the hall and almost ran into him. Serena wasn't far behind. Tyler stood with his arms full of clothes. He'd been caught eavesdropping. He looked at Serena, whose face flushed a bright pink. He shrugged an apology and nodded at the garments. "Where do you want me to… put these?" But what he wanted to ask was, "sleep?"

Arlene scooted past and gave him a small smile. "I hate that I've forced you to have to sleep on the couch."

Me too. Tyler gave her a quick smile. "It's no problem."

"He's not sleeping on the couch."

"I'm not?" A few other possibilities passed through his mind. The best of which was bunking with Serena, and he knew that would never happen. The worst was sharing a pallet with Shadow. He waited for his instructions, dreading the hard floor and furry bedmate.

"No," Serena said. "You're sleeping with me."

Chapter 21

Serena dug through the box and plopped an armload of papers on the table. She couldn't believe she'd let it happen again. Her mother pushed her into a corner, and she'd spouted off the most outrageous thing she could think of: sleeping with Tyler. What must he think?

Tyler helped empty the box, placing envelopes, papers, and manila folders in a haphazard pile. Picking up several of the envelopes, she watched him covertly. He didn't seem the least bit phased by the fencing match with Arlene or his new bedmate. Did anything bother him?

At least for a little while, Serena needed to get her mind off her mother and the possibility of sharing a bed with Tyler, not necessarily in that order. Even if it meant going cross-eyed looking at numbers all night. She glanced at the postmark on the first envelope. "Is this unopened mail?"

He nodded.

"It's from *January*." She waited for an explanation. Surely he at least opened his mail once in a while.

He continued piling, the stack now so high it threatened to slide off the table.

"How far behind are you?"

"A ways. I never can find the time for this type of thing."

"How far is 'a ways'?"

He paused. "I'm not really sure."

"Didn't you file your taxes last year?"

"I talked to the accountant and told him I could bring stuff over, but I didn't have it all together yet."

Didn't have it all together? From what she could see he didn't have anything together, least of all his finances. "What did he say?"

"Not to worry about it until August."

"So he filed an extension?"

"A what?"

Oh my god! She gazed at the files and invoices, formulating a plan of attack.

"Look, you don't have to help; I know it's a lot of work." Tyler tried to let her off the hook. "My business partner took care of this kind of stuff; I managed the people and cooked. After he left, I was so busy trying to keep things going I didn't really pay attention to all the details."

She gave him a small smile, realizing he needed her help more than he even knew. It gave her a surge of energy and brought out the cheerleader in her. "We can do it. The good thing is, we don't have to conform to what someone else has done; we can start from scratch."

"Start from scratch?" He looked overwhelmed.

"That's a good thing," Serena tried to reassure him, as she made her way to the desk in the living room.

Tyler's voice rang out from the kitchen. "Are we taking a break?"

Serena returned with her laptop and letter opener. "Absolutely not. No breaks until we get this in some kind of order."

"That could take years."

She pulled out a chair and motioned for him to sit. "We don't have years. I'm sure it's not as bad as you think." She didn't believe a word she said. It was an auditor's worst nightmare. Hopefully, they could piece enough together to get by. She handed him the envelopes and letter opener. "You start opening all the mail, and I'll stack invoices.

They worked in silence for almost half an hour. Tyler finished the last of the unopened mail and stood to help arrange it into the correct piles. His arm brushed against hers and she glanced at him. He didn't seem to notice. Serena's feminine pride took it hard.

While her thoughts strayed from the paperwork in front of her time and again, Tyler seemed to have no problem concentrating. If one little touch made her heart flutter, what would it be like tonight? In bed with him? She imagined herself lying next to him, trapped in a sleepless frenzy of sexual frustration while he snored. That would be about her luck.

Tyler shuffled papers, unaware of her perusal. He had to think she was a floozy. After all she'd told him that he'd sleep with her. Didn't ask, or politely suggest, but commanded. In front of her mother. What kind of sane woman would do that? If it struck him as odd, he hadn't said so.

In fact he hadn't commented on it at all. What did that mean? Did he think she did this everyday? That certainly wasn't the case. If Arlene hadn't shown up unexpectedly, things would be exactly as they were last night.

The conversation with her mother both irritated and disappointed Serena. Nothing had changed between them in the last 20 years. Absolutely nothing, including her own reaction to the moral indignation her mother displayed.

Arlene still treated her like a teenage floozy, and, damn it, she'd reacted like one. It didn't matter what Arlene thought about her or her parenting techniques. Serena had gotten over that long ago, but the fact that the woman still pushed her buttons added to the disappointment. It hardly seemed worth the effort to have some kind of relationship with Arlene at this point.

"What's wrong?"

Serena met his gaze, suddenly aware that she'd been staring into space. "What?"

"What's wrong?" Tyler asked. "Did you find something?"

"Uh, no. I was thinking about other stuff." She waved her hand to dismiss the subject and tried to concentrate on the invoice in front of her. It looked very familiar, like she'd read it 10 times, and probably had.

Tyler put down the papers and lowered his voice. "You know, if it's the sleeping arrangements, I don't mind sleeping on the floor in your room. She'd never know the difference."

So he *had* been thinking about it. "It's not that." He was such a nice guy, trying to give her an out and save her pride at the same time. She whispered back, "I'd hoped it might be different this time with my mother."

He nodded. "Things seem a little tense between you."

"A little?" She gave a smile and pointed to the mess on the table. "And this is a little pile of paperwork."

He laughed with her, lightening her mood. "I guess you have a point there. So why'd you tell her that we'd sleep together?"

Good question. Serena thought about Jeffery, trying to remember if he'd ever given her a good "shrinkified" excuse for this thing between her and Arlene. "Well, it was sleep with her or with you."

"So you're saying I rank barely above a sixty-year-old woman?"

Serena gave him an exasperated sigh. "I'm serious."

"So am I." His grin gave him away.

"It's not like we haven't sleep together on the couch before." Her face warmed, remembering his kiss. She tried to read his expression. "Two adults can sleep in the same bed and not have sex."

"Yes, but why would they?" He teased.

"My mother."

"Of course." His tone indicated how ridiculous her response sounded. And it was.

The stress of the day weighed heavy on Serena's shoulders. She rubbed the back of her neck.

"Why don't you go soak in the tub? I can finish organizing this stuff."

Great idea. As much as she'd been determined to jump into this paperwork, her mind refused to focus on anything. Except her mother. And Tyler.

He reached over and pulled the papers from her hand. "Go."

"Are you sure you can handle this?"

"Absolutely not, but it's my mess. I'll do the best I can, then we can try again tomorrow night. How's that?"

She nodded and left him to it. Trudging down the hall, Serena turned into her room to gather her pajamas. She paused at the dresser. Tyler's brush, toothpaste and shaving items sat on the surface in a jumbled pile. She glanced in the mirror at the bed behind her. She'd be sharing it with him soon. The idea excited and made her nervous at the same time. What would it be like lying next to him? In the same bed? For hours on end? She'd wondered exactly that last night as she lay staring at the wall that separated their rooms.

Shadow followed her to the bathroom and sat patiently observing the bath preparation. Serena lowered herself into the steaming water and the dog assumed her now familiar posture resting her head on the side of the tub. Serena rubbed Shadow's ears, while the water soothed and relaxed her tired muscles.

Sinking down to her chin, she closed her eyes, enjoying the quiet. After what seemed like only seconds, Serena realized the water had grown cool. She shook the sleepy fog from her brain and turned on the faucet with her toes, adding more heat. In only minutes, the tub engulfed her in warm pleasure once again. Her mind drifted away. Away from the stress over her job, away from her mother, away from the evening's pending sleeping arrangements.

A sharp rap on the door brought her to full sitting position. The now cold water splashed over the edge of the tub. "Just a minute," she sputtered.

"I was afraid you'd drowned in there." Tyler's muffled voice came through the door. "It's been over an hour."

"No. I'm fine." Serena grabbed for a towel. "Be right out." She stood and allowed the frigid water to drip from her body before stepping onto the rug.

Gooseflesh rippled across her skin and all her fingers and toes resembled white prunes. She must have been more tired than she thought. Pulling on her white silk PJs, Serena quickly ran a comb through her hair. She yanked open the door, running right into Tyler's chest.

"I hated to wake you, but your mother's in there." He pointed to his room.

Serena glanced around him at the closed door. Had Arlene made some awful accusation while she'd been fast asleep in the tub? She hated to think about it. "And?"

He cleared his throat. "And, I really have to . . ." he pointed at the bathroom, "You know."

She scooted out of the way, her face warming. "Of course, I'm sorry."

"No problem." He quickly shut the door.

Completely embarrassed, Serena shook her head. How long had he waited, with a full bladder, before he woke her? He was really taking this nice guy thing to the extreme.

Tyler opened the door and caught her standing in the exact same spot. "Thanks a million."

"You didn't have to wait like that. You could of . . ."

"What? Peed off the deck?" He breezed around her and turned into her room. "Thought about it, but one thing stopped me."

Convinced he was teasing, she had to ask. "What was it?"

"Mosquitoes." He shuffled through his pile of clothes. "That's not really an area you want exposed to the little critters."

She stared at his back, not quite believing him.

"I should get you one of those bug zapper things. Then you could soak in the tub as long as you want." He disappeared out the door and into the bathroom with no hint of a smile.

He was serious. Serena plopped down on the bed and dropped her head into her hands. Like she'd even consider making it easier for him to personally water her backyard, so to speak. Let alone have one of those electrical death traps that left a pile of insect corpses. She still didn't know quite what to make of him. He seemed to know what to say to ease her mind and soothe her anxieties, but he had none of the qualities she usually considered important.

She stared at his haphazard pile of clothes. She didn't think he even owned a suit and probably wouldn't know cashmere if it bit him in the butt. She didn't want to even think about what other social skills he lacked if peeing off the deck was acceptable. Then there was the whole financial mess. Her mind wanted to classify him as Mr. Wrong, not an option, in the "just friends" category. But her heart wouldn't allow it. Why? It's not like she was in love with him. That would be ridiculous. They'd known each other barely a month. She listened to the sound of water running as Tyler took a shower. Mr. Right or Mr. Wrong, it didn't matter. He was her bedmate for the night.

The front door opened, and Serena heard the flop of Justin's backpack on the living room floor. A spike of panic jammed her chest. She'd thought that she'd come up with an idea of how to explain this odd turn of sleeping arrangements to Justin before he got home, but she'd spent most of the evening snoozing in the tub. Hurrying toward the kitchen, she found him heating a take-out tray from the restaurant in the microwave.

Justin glanced at her. "Fancy jammies. What happened to the sweats? Somebody here?"

She let the comment about her attire slide. "Your grandma." Although she'd selected the white silk with Tyler in mind.

"Swell." He didn't sound pleased. "So, do I get the couch?"

"No, there was a small incident. The couch is wet."

He frowned. "Did you not take Shadow out?"

"It's water. Your grandma and Tyler kind of…"

"She tried to kill me with a plunger." Tyler rounded the corner, his wet hair slicked back.

Justin laughed. "Sounds like I missed some good stuff."

"Definitely." Smiling, Tyler filled a glass with water.

"I was about to explain the new sleeping arrangements," she said, expecting Tyler's cooperation.

The kitchen went silent.

Serena searched for the right phrasing. "Since the couch isn't really an option, Tyler will be bunking with me."

"Bunking?" Justin raised an eyebrow at her. "Is that what they called it in the wagon wheel days?"

Her hand itched to smack the smirk off his face. "For your information, two adults can sleep in the same bed and *just sleep.*"

"But why would they?" Justin gave her that fake confused look he'd used since he was 3. "You know, you could have called, and I could have stayed over at David's, and he…" He pointed to Tyler with an elbow, "…could have had my bed."

Why didn't she think of that?

"I offered to go to a hotel," Tyler chimed in.

"That would have worked too." Justin took a big bite of barbecue.

Serena glanced from her son to Tyler. Only a short time since they started to work together and they were even sounding alike. As much as she'd wanted a father figure for Justin while he was growing up, she wasn't sure Tyler was what she had in mind. And she definitely didn't like them ganging up on her.

Tyler crossed his arms and waited for her response, a grin twitching at the corners of his mouth. She glared at them both, irritated and annoyed that they pointed out the weakness in her rash decision. Like she wasn't well aware of it.

"Fine. Sleep where you want. I'm going to bed." She stalked down the hall and flipped off her bedroom light as she entered. She could still see without much trouble and left the door open, hoping to catch any conversation that floated down the hall. Yanking down the covers, she climbed into bed and pulled them up to her chin. She ground her teeth together.

She knew her idea had been impulsive without either one of them pointing it out. Especially Justin. Most of the time she loved the fact that he was growing up and had a great since of humor, but there were times, like tonight, it pissed her off to no end. Not that Tyler was any help. Nice guy just lost points on that one. Big time.

Chapter 22

Tyler sat alone in the living room watching the news. Then the late show. Then the late-late show. Serena had been angry at him for teasing her about the sleeping arrangements, and he wanted to make sure she was asleep before he turned in. Her nerves were on edge tonight, but so were his. He'd thought of nothing else but holding her close every night since he'd kissed her on his sister's porch. Now that the opportunity presented itself, he felt like a teenager on a blind date. He had numerous reservations about this situation, the main one being the fact that this wasn't exactly how he'd fantasized things would be.

He'd pictured more of a slow seduction—maybe a fabulous steak dinner by candlelight followed by soft music and slow dancing. Not a forced event, with a tense bedmate, her mother in one room and her son in the other. He'd never been the most romantic guy, but even he could see this had the potential for a bad outcome. Tyler had learned at least one thing about women in the last two decades. If the test drive was a disappointment, they never gave you another chance. He yawned.

Quiet had descended on the house several hours ago. He'd put this off long enough.

Turning out the lights as he went, he made his way down the hall. The doors to both Justin and Arlene's rooms were closed. Serena's stood wide open. He slipped inside pulling it shut behind him. If she was waiting to chew him out, there was no sense in having the entire house hear it.

He allowed a minute for his eyes to adjust to the darkness and then moved to the side of the bed. She lay on her side, facing the window with the sheet pulled up to her chin. Tyler shed his jeans and T-shirt and crawled in, hoping she was asleep. Lying back on the pillow, he exhaled a slow breath.

"What time is it?" Serena rolled over.

"Late. I didn't mean to wake you."

"You didn't."

He moved his arm and she scooted up next to his side, her silk PJs sliding against his skin. She didn't seem upset at him at all. He hugged her close, relieved. "You okay?"

"Yeah. Sorry I was a bitch."

He grinned in the dark. "You weren't that bad. I've been around worse."

He felt her smiling against his chest. "I don't know if that's good or bad."

"It's good." He laughed. "I learned to lay low and let it blow over."

"Did Justin finally go to bed?"

"About an hour ago."

"How did he seem?"

"About what?"

"Us."

"Fine, I guess. He didn't really say much."

"I don't know. This has to be a little weird. I've never had a man sleep over."

Sleep over? "The living arrangements were his idea, remember?"

"This is different."

Tyler agreed. This went beyond living arrangements and was different from any friendship, romance, or relationship he'd ever had. He hadn't quite figured out which category this one fit into yet. He rubbed her back with one hand, the silk floating over her skin. "What's the deal with you and your mother?"

Serena released a slow breath.

"You don't have to talk about it if you don't want to. Even though she did try to dent my head with a plunger."

"Fat chance of that." Her laughter vibrated against his chest. The feeling warmed him from the inside out. Some parts more than others.

"Are you sure you're interested? It's kind of a long story. You know, with lots of women yelling, holding grudges, and talking bad about each other."

He laughed. "Is there mud wrestling or bikinis involved?"

"Definitely not."

"Too bad, but I'll listen if you want to talk."

She hesitated a minute. "Well, I guess I do owe you a skeleton."

Tyler thought back to the night he told her about the wreck. She'd never shared what her big secret was. Maybe this was it. He waited, letting her collect her thoughts.

"The basic story goes that I was a wild, angry teenager."

"No way." He was shocked—and meant it. Serena could be the poster child for anal uptight adult. Wild teenagers don't grow up to alphabetize their canned vegetables. "What's your definition of wild?"

"Very. As in, partied all the time, snuck out, smoked weed by the bale."

He burst out laughing. "By the bale?"

"You could say I was one of those big hair, heavy metal chicks for whom the roach clip was not a decorative accessory."

He tried to imagine her at 16 or 17. With wild red curls and a tight mini skirt, she'd have caught his attention then as much as she did now. "Why were you angry?"

She squirmed against his side. "My dad died when I was 13."

"I'm sorry."

"So was I. We were very close, going to ball games, fishing; he even taught me to play golf out on the neighborhood putting green."

He could hear the grief in her voice. "Sounds like a nice guy."

"He was perfect."

How would life have been to have a dad like that? His old man and been hard right up until the day he died. A hard living, hard drinking hard ass. Big on working his kids as much as possible and short on understanding—let alone forgiving. The little boy in him was secretly thrilled the day the old man had the accident driving his cattle truck. At least Serena hadn't had to endure that kind of life, and he was glad for it. He hesitated to ask more, not wanting to bring up the sadness she obviously still felt.

She seemed to sense his question. "I can talk about it now."

"What happened?"

"Massive heart attack. At work. Total surprise." Her voice softened. "Anyway, I hadn't even begun to deal with it, and barely six months later, my mother married this preacher who'd hovered around the house since my dad died like a wolf sniffing around wounded animals."

"Ouch."

"He was the fundamentalist type, and we butted heads from day one. So, I made up my mind that it was him or me and started living the wild life."

"How did that go?"

"Terrible. My grades plunged through the basement, and I couldn't remember most of what I said or did for weeks on end. I was so wasted, I'd hook up with guys I didn't even know at parties and have no idea what their names were. I finally turned up pregnant. When I told them, he demanded to know who the father was. I couldn't tell him."

"You wanted to protect Justin's father?" Tyler could feel her heart race.

Serena paused. "No, because I honestly had no idea. My stepfather called me a lying whore who got what she deserved."

"God, that must have been awful for you."

"The night I told them I was pregnant, he kept screaming at me about how this was God's punishment for my sins and that he'd pray for my poor kid who had to grow up knowing his mother was a whore. It was the final straw. My mother was forced to choose."

Her voice trembled, "She chose him and sent me to live with Aunt Macy and Uncle Frank."

"What a bastard. Where is he now?"

"Dead. Six or seven years ago."

"Good. Otherwise I'd have to kill the son-of-a-bitch."

"Thanks, but I got over him a long time ago."

Tyler didn't quite believe that. Serena seemed like a woman with many pentup hurts that continued to affect her life no matter how hard she tried to hide it. "But you never came to an understanding with your mom?"

"Oh, we have an understanding all right. She thinks I'm a floozy, and I think she abandoned me when I needed her the most. End of story."

"Until now."

"Yeah. Macy's illness has thrown us together again, but I can endure it. I've worked my whole life to prove to myself that none of those things he said were true. It doesn't really matter what she thinks at this point."

He squeezed her shoulder. "You've done a hell of job, too. You're educated, professional, and a great mom. Your mom should be proud."

Serena snorted. "Sure. Now. Twenty years too late."

Tyler worked out her story in his mind. "So how did you get from wild child to fabulous career woman?"

"Just decided. I remember when I was about eight months pregnant looking in the mirror one day, and it sank in for the first time I was about to be responsible for another life. I decided right then that my life would be different. I set a few goals, like finishing high school and getting into college and worked toward them. I've been doing that ever since."

"How do you just decide something like that?" Tyler couldn't imagine sitting down and planning his life. Things had always just happened, and he dealt with them as they came.

"It wasn't easy. But I broke everything down into baby steps, and they add up over time."

"Baby steps. Why don't you use that approach with your mother?"

"Fat chance."

"You don't really want her here, do you?"

"No, I don't. All that goes through my mind is where was she when I needed her? When things were hard? She wants to weasel her way back into my life now that all the work is over and done. I can't bring myself to forgive or forget. And I'm not sure I want to."

No matter how she denied it, Tyler suspected that the hurt far outweighed the anger she felt toward her mother. "Don't blame you a bit. If I'd known this earlier tonight I would've chased her with the plunger."

They lay in companionable silence for a while, Tyler's mind working over everything Serena had revealed. He had numerous questions about her mother, but held off, not wanting to pry any more than he already had.

Serena needed to vent this pentup anger, and he was glad that she had trusted him to listen. Like he had trusted her enough to talk about the accident that killed Matt. He wondered if she'd ever shared this with anyone and why Serena seemed to prefer being alone. "So you never married?"

"No."

"Or had a live-in lover? Except for me of course." He felt her smile again.

"No."

"Why not?"

Serena shrugged. "It always seemed like a luxury I couldn't afford. I had a kid to raise. While Justin was little, I worked two jobs and went to school. We barely got by and I hated being away from him. I guess you could say I sowed all my wild oats before I was seventeen and I don't have the patience for it anymore."

"No guy ever swept you off your feet?"

"Absolutely not."

He could change that. Everything fell into place in Tyler's mind. It had been years since he'd wanted any kind of real friendship or relationship. He and Matt had been like brothers, closer in fact. They shared everything. When Matt died, so did part of Tyler. The part that wanted to feel, to laugh, to enjoy life. All the things he'd had the last few weeks with Serena.

Long ago, he'd accepted the fact his life would be a dismal

shadow of what could have been and lived that way. Not expecting much of anything. He didn't deserve Serena; he'd already told himself that. And he couldn't give her anything but problems. But he didn't want to let her go, either.

Serena slid her hand across his chest and snuggled closer. Tyler laid still, her scent swirling into his senses pushing the reason from his mind in a whirlpool of pleasure. He wanted to love her. Not once, but forever. She deserved every happiness life could offer, and he'd do anything to see she got it. Even if it meant taking a baseball bat to some holy roller's headstone.

Serena's breath grew steady as Tyler stroked her back. He rolled to her and scooted down, pulling her into his form like a missing piece to a puzzle. She fit him perfectly.

Serena nuzzled his neck. "Umm. You're in serious danger of getting raped, mister." Her hands slid around to his back.

He chuckled. "Promise?" he nipped at her ear and she met his lips with her own, their noses bumped and they laughed together, easing some of his nervous energy. Their next kiss was slow and lingering. Not like the hot gropefest they'd shared on Chelsie's porch, but deeper, stronger. Tyler's heart pounded against his ribs as his hands moved over her body. He'd dreamed of Serena in his arms like this. The sensation of her heart pounding against his fingertips sent a fiery need through his veins.

Did she want this as much as he did? Serena slid her hand down across his boxers and around to his butt. She gave a squeeze. It was all the encouragement he needed.

Tyler unbuttoned her top and trailed kisses down her chest; she arched her back in response to his touch. He moved his lips down her stomach, inching the pajama bottoms off as he went. The barrier of thin silk fell to the floor in a whisper.

Her creamy skin lay bare in the darkness as Tyler moved his hands over her body. Serena's flesh rippled with goose bumps and her nipples tightened to hard buds beneath his touch. She moaned as Tyler licked and sucked one nipple then the other. Her body writhed under his as her need grew. Tyler's heart reached a frenzied pace. Sliding off his boxers, Tyler gathered her in his arms. Intense pleasure rocked him at the feel of their bodies entwined.

Tyler knew she needed to be held, loved. And so did he. He

slid his hand down her stomach and between her legs, sliding his finger into her. She groaned, moving her hips against his hand. Wet heat almost pushed him over the edge as her need throbbed. He moved his hand in steady rhythm, bringing her closer and closer to release.

Serena tugged him on top of her, both their bodies now covered in a fine sheen of moisture. Tyler positioned himself between her legs and slid inside her. He paused allowing the intense pleasure to wash over his whole being. Serena moved under him, and he joined her in a heated rhythm. Their need built higher and higher, a passionate fervor growing between them as they strained together. Serena moaned, and Tyler's body stiffened joining hers at the peak of release. They clung together for several minutes gulping air waiting for their pounding hearts to slow.

Finally, Tyler rolled to his side, taking her with him, not wanting to let go. Within moments sleep claimed Serena, and Tyler dozed off realizing she had given him something he hadn't had in years—hope.

Chapter 23

Serena stirred. Morning light poured through the bedroom window. Tyler's arms still held her close. She refused to open her eyes. Would it be so bad to spend the whole day right here? Her palms flattened against the firm muscles of his chest, producing a primal hum in places she'd almost forgotten existed. The attraction between them vibrated, beckoning her. His scent engulfed her and she wiggled closer, reveling in his warmth.

Tyler's arms tightened around her. His body responded to hers in his sleep, and she smiled, remembering their lovemaking. She had to add "fabulous lover" to the list of his positive attributes. Serena gave a sigh of frustration. If she allowed her thoughts to keep going this direction, she'd be jumping on him again this morning. Not that the idea didn't have some appeal; it had a lot of appeal, but not with that big "just friends" speech she'd given Justin or the fact that her mother was up and about.

Arlene banged pots in the kitchen. Serena's face warmed. She hoped no one had heard the two of them last night. She disentangled herself from Tyler's embrace and scooted to the edge of the bed.

"Where're you going?" his sleepy voice whispered.

"I have to go to work."

"You have some time. Come on back to bed."

Tempting. Very tempting. "No, Arlene's already up fixing breakfast."

"So? Let her." He gently tugged at her waist. She swatted his hand playfully then slipped away into the bathroom. Splashing cold water on her face, she tried to cool the heat Tyler stirred up.

He seemed completely unaware how attractive he was, and that turned her on more than anything. With Tyler, what you saw was what you got, and that was a good thing. A big change from any other man she'd known with their little white lies and secrets kept carefully hidden behind an upwardly mobile professional façade.

Serena completed her morning routine in record time and then slipped from the room, leaving Tyler sleeping.

Arlene smiled as Serena entered the kitchen. "Good morning." She held a spatula poised over a skillet full of small pancakes. "Don't you look fabulous?"

The compliment grated across Serena's nerves. "I always look like this for work." Arlene's fake attempts at a normal mother-daughter relationship seemed almost laughable.

"I thought I'd make some pancakes. You used to love them."

Can't buy me with carbs, Arlene. "I don't usually eat breakfast."

"Oh. Then maybe Justin will like some."

"Some what?" Her son appeared, tucking in his shirt.

Arlene moved several pancakes to a plate. "Breakfast."

"Great." Justin picked up three steaming pancakes and rolled them together like a burrito, taking a big bite out of one end.

Arlene glanced at Serena as if waiting for her to say something about his manners. She refused. *This is how teenage boys are, Arlene, bottomless pits with zero manners.* At home, anyway. Not that her mother would know squat about teenagers. That thought triggered another concern. The condoms. She'd meant to talk to Justin about this the past few weeks, but the opportunity hadn't presented itself. Actually it had, several times, but she'd chickened out.

Arlene might make the same discovery she had if she decided to snoop through Justin's room. Serena could hear Arlene's voice in her head, reciting "like mother like son." Serena would not have her son repeating her mistakes, nor would she allow Arlene the chance to point out any flaws in the way she had raised her son.

"Hey." Serena poked Justin's ribs with her elbow. "We need to have a chat when you get home tonight."

Justin paused mid-bite. "About?"

She glanced at Arlene. "Some things."

For a moment Serena thought she saw a worried expression shadow his features. Or was it fear? Did he know that she'd found his little secret?

He shrugged. "Okay. I've been wanting to talk to you about something, too."

"Oh?" Maybe he did know and wanted to come clean. She'd be proud of his maturity if he did. Not that she still wouldn't give him the lecture of a lifetime. His eyes flicked toward her mother and she took the hint. "We'll talk about everything tonight, how's that?"

Justin nodded, grabbed two more pancakes and his backpack and left. "Thanks for the breakfast," he yelled as the door banged shut.

Serena picked up her purse and keys and followed him out.

"Have a nice day!" Her mother's voice trailed behind them. Things were so much harder when Arlene tried to be nice. It immediately raised Serena's suspicions. She'd sounded bitchy this morning, and she knew it, but she had to keep her guard up and not let Arlene think things between them were okay. They weren't. And never would be.

Serena barely remembered the drive to work, formulating her daily to-do list in her mind. The newspaper hummed with activity as she arrived, dragging her into its whirlwind of daily crises. Frank had already shifted some of his meetings and critical functions off to her. This morning she hadn't had time to sit down for five minutes, when Nolea poked her head into Serena's office.

"You up for lunch?"

"Lunch?" Serena glanced at the clock on her desk. "Oh God. It's noon already." Weariness pressed in on her shoulders. "I still have to write the next "Lone Star Love Affair" by two to get it into tomorrow's edition." She glanced down at the notes she'd made. It would certainly be easy to write after last night, when the whole thing turned from fantasy to reality in the space of a few short hours.

"No rest for the weary, but you still have to eat." Nolea shrugged off the mountains of paperwork on Serena's desk.

"Eating's become a luxury these days. How did Uncle Frank get all this done?"

"He had a staff, and so do you. Stop being so anal and delegate already." Nolea dug through her purse for her sunglasses.

Delegate. Serena had already encountered some resistance to her new position. She knew a few staff members felt she didn't deserve the job of editor-in-chief, even though she'd been in the newspaper business for more than a decade. It was still viewed as her uncle giving her the job rather than her earning it. Hopefully, they would adjust to the idea of her being the boss, and so would she. But the paper still had to go out on time, every single day. No excuses.

"Come on." Nolea took Serena's arm and dragged her along. "You need a break."

Serena grabbed her purse and followed Nolea down the street to Jorge's Cantina. Many of the newspaper staffers frequented Jorge's for lunch. It was close, fast, and served topnotch food. They settled into a booth in the back corner away from any interested listeners.

Ricky, Jorge's son, waited tables for the noon crowd. Recognizing Serena and Nolea, he hurried over with a big smile. "The usual, ladies?"

They nodded.

"Two taco specials," he wrote on his order pad as he talked, "light on the guacamole, heavy on the sour cream." He disappeared and returned with iced tea and a basket of fresh tortilla chips.

Nolea dipped one in salsa and munched. "So what's up with the live in?"

"Which one? Tyler or my mother?"

"Your mother showed up?"

"Yes, and it turned into a whole *thing*." Serena huffed.

"What kind of thing?"

"A circus. A huge dysfunctional circus."

Nolea's perfectly sculpted brows rose an inch.

"She started in on the living arrangements, and somehow Tyler ended up staying with me last night." Silence lingered a minute between the women.

"*Staying* with you? Did you sleep with him?"

"Yes, we were in the same bed."

"No, did you *sleep* with him?"

Serena shrugged.

"You did." Nolea gave a disappointed frown.

"So what? I needed it, and so did he. What's wrong with that?" Her cheeks warmed. "It's not like you haven't ever had a little fling."

Nolea leaned forward. "This isn't a fling. You don't fling. I fling, on occasion, but you don't." She shook her head. "We talked about this. You said he wasn't your type."

"He isn't."

"You said he didn't have any of the qualities you look for in a guy."

"He doesn't."

"You said New York was what you'd always wanted," Nolea insisted.

"It is."

"Then why are you letting yourself fall for this guy?"

"I'm not."

"You're lying to yourself, Serena, and you know it. This can't and won't work, but you're trying to convince yourself it might."

Serena nibbled another chip. "Why are you trying so hard to convince me it won't?" Nolea had been her best friend for years, and in all that time she'd never been so determined to break up a relationship. Could she be jealous? Serena immediately tossed out that idea. Jealous of what? Tyler had numerous strikes against him as Nolea had just pointed out, but he also had some fabulous qualities that her friend knew nothing about. Was Nolea convinced that she had no sense at all when it came to men? That irritated Serena. She was a grown woman, after all, not some teenager in the throws of puppy love.

Steaming plates of tacos, refried beans, and rice were set before them. Nolea jabbed the rice with her fork. "I don't want to see you give up your dream for some loser."

"Tyler isn't a loser. Haven't you ever wanted to jump in and see if things might work?"

"Yes. And I have. Jumped in and jumped right back out. It was a disaster every time. I was even stupid enough to marry a few of them."

"Then you understand."

"I understand that I gave up what I wanted. I understand that instead of being sales manager at a large market newspaper, I'm a little account executive in Podunk Holler. I understand your heart will reach for a dream that reality will stomp on."

They ate in silence a few minutes as Serena tried to gather her thoughts to explain her feelings for Tyler. Only she wasn't sure exactly what they were. Last night they had moved way past friends. But exchanging "I love you" seemed a long ways off too.

Nolea pushed away her plate. "Look, I'm trying to save you from making the same mistakes I did and giving up your dream for a man that is everything you don't want."

Serena's back stiffened. "What if he is everything I want? What if he's the guy I've been waiting for my whole life? What if I want to sail off into the sunset with Tyler and damn the consequences?" *Oh my god.* Serena took a deep breath. Did she mean what she just said? She wasn't sure, but the idea had tumbled out of her mouth so easily it scared her to death. "Why should you care anyway?"

Nolea softened. "Because you're my friend. Because I've traveled this same road. Because this guy's the Titanic and no matter how great you convince yourself he is, the ship's still going down."

Chapter 24

Tyler pushed the sheet and comforter off his body. The house had been quiet for more than an hour, but he'd lain in Serena's bed catnapping, half-remembering, half-dreaming of the night before. He smiled. There was no way he'd ever get his fill of making love to Serena. His body responded to the mere thought of her full breasts pressing into his chest. He still hadn't figured it all out, her past hurts, her dreams, her fears, but every discovery added to the delicious mystery. All no nonsense on the outside, she had a soft inner core that drew him in like a whirlpool and refused to let go. Rolling over, he buried his face in her pillow. Her scent still lingered teasing his imagination.

Tyler raised his head and glanced at the clock. He needed to be at the restaurant by 10 to meet the delivery truck. Reluctantly, he dragged himself out of bed, showered and dressed.

All was quiet as he hurried to the kitchen. Arlene sat at the table rearranging the stacks of invoices. What did she think she was doing going through his records? Irritated at her forwardness, he cleared his throat.

She smiled at him over her halfglasses. "Good morning, Tyler. I made some pancakes, if you're hungry."

"Thanks." He went to the refrigerator and pulled out a pitcher of orange juice and waited to see if she offered an explanation. She didn't. "Serena and I are planning to get to those tonight, Arlene. You don't have to bother with them."

"Oh, I don't mind. Macy's treatment isn't until two this afternoon so I have some time." She moved several papers into another stack. "You have them sorted by date instead of company."

"Serena asked me to do it that way."

"Oh, no. That will never work. You have to arrange them by company and then by date to see who is paid and who isn't. I did the books for the church for years, and it could be a real mess sometimes."

Tyler knew he should be annoyed by Arlene's insinuation that they had no clue what they were doing but instead squashed a smile. No wonder the two women never got along. There's no two right ways to do anything and no convincing either one to give an inch. He leaned back against the counter and watched her as he drank his juice.

She seemed like a nice lady. A little bossy maybe and a tad on the nosy side but determined and unafraid if the plunger incident was any gauge. In other words, like Serena. He remembered his conversation with Serena and the hurt she'd encountered after her father's death. Arlene didn't seem like the type to abandon Serena, but apparently she had. "Why did you come here?"

Arlene put down an invoice and looked up at him. "Macy's cancer treatments. Not that Frank isn't great, but he has a lot of responsibilities, and she needs someone to hold her hand on occasion and tell her everything is okay."

"No, I mean why are you *here*?" He motioned to Serena's house. He knew for a fact it would have been easier for her to stay with her sister rather than inconvenience Serena.

Arlene laid her reading glasses on a pile of invoices and gave him a small smile. "I'm sure you've heard some awful things about me and my daughter."

He nodded.

"I hoped things would be different this time, but," she shook her head, "since she went to live with Macy, I've kept my distance, hoping she would make the first move and we'd come to an understanding at some point. But it hasn't happened. Not in all these years."

"So you thought you'd help things along?"

Arlene smiled. "It's pretty obvious I guess. But I've run out of ideas of how to get my daughter to have a relationship with me, and I'm tired of waiting."

"She's still angry."

"That's my fault. It was horrible, the tension between Serena and my second husband. I thought I was giving her a better life by marrying him. I couldn't support us, and her father's life insurance barely covered the funeral and hospital bills. I was about to lose the house, everything we'd struggled so hard for, and I didn't see any other option." Arlene shook her head. "Turned out to be a big mistake."

"Did you ever tell her that?"

"No. She was so upset after her father died, she wouldn't listen to anything, and I was at my wits end worrying where she was and what she was doing all the time."

"The two of you should sit down and talk."

"Have you ever tried to make Serena do anything she doesn't want to?"

He grinned. "No."

"Good, because you would have failed miserably like I have. She's stubborn and hardheaded, but so am I, and I'm not giving up."

"Good for you." He set the glass in the sink and glanced out at Shadow lying on the deck in the morning sun. The dog had adapted to their new home remarkably well in the past few weeks. And so had he.

"Are you off to work?" Arlene's glasses were once again perched on her nose.

He nodded. "I appreciate you helping with all this paperwork."

"You're welcome. You know, you might want to order copies of all your checks from the bank."

"Why's that?"

"Just a precaution. Some of these things look like they may have been paid twice, and some not at all."

"Will do."

Tyler stopped by the bank and requested the copies on his way to work. He had seen the financial side of his business as a waste of his time this past year, but now he was determined to fix the mess and make JT's something to be proud of. He wanted to belong with Serena and not feel embarrassed by his lack of success.

He'd taken the restaurant for granted this past year, but the idea of losing the place or having to sell stabbed at his soul. This dream had been his from the beginning, and now he'd make it work no matter what obstacles lay in his path. Tyler had never cared before if anyone thought him successful. Until Serena. Until last night.

The truck driver waited as Tyler pulled up and unlocked the restaurant door. Tony arrived shortly after the first stack of boxes was wheeled into the kitchen.

"We get everything this time?"

Tyler glanced up from the lengthy invoice. "Looks like it."

"Good. I was afraid we'd have to start shooting squirrels if they shorted us on chicken again." Tony stared out the back door. "Jake's back."

Tyler leaned around the boxes and glanced into the alley. No one had seen Jake for days. They had all speculated on what might have happened to the old guy. He'd shown up several times a week ever since they opened, until last week. Tyler motioned to Tony. "Can you get me a couple of sandwiches and some potato salad?"

Tony nodded. "Jake loves the potato salad."

Tyler stood by the truck waiting for the old man to make his way to them. Jake looked up, saw Tyler, and hesitated.

"Hey, Jake." Tyler moved toward him and the man took a step back. Jake had never been scared of him before. "We've been wondering where you've been lately."

"I'm just passin' through, wasn't gonna bother you none." Jake's voice was a horse whisper.

Tony hurried over to them and held out the bag of food.

The old man shook his head and stepped back again. "I can't take that from you."

"Why not?" The men asked in unison.

"The new owner said he'd have me arrested if I came around anymore." Jake's hands shook. "I don't want no trouble."

"What new owner?" Tyler took the food from Tony and stepped closer to Jake.

The old man glanced around as if waiting for the devil himself to hop out from behind the dumpster. "The guy in the suit with that real pretty lady. Said they was the new owners and I'd better skedaddle if I knew what was good for me."

Tyler clenched his teeth. So now Krista's lawyer boy was pretending to own the place too and threatening someone as harmless as Jake? He laid a hand on the man's shoulder feeling sharp bone barely covered by skin. "I'm still the owner, Jake. You're welcome here anytime." He looked into the man's eyes. "I mean that. If anyone tells you any different you let me know, okay?" Tyler handed the bag to the man.

He took it and nodded. "I sure do thank ya, Ty." He grinned. "That soup down at the shelter don't hold a candle to your barbecue and tater salad." Tyler watched Jake hobble to the street and disappear around the side of the building.

"Can you believe that?" Tony sidled up to Tyler.

"It's time to put a stop to this right now." Tyler marched toward the back door.

Tony laughed. "If we're whoopin' ass, count me in."

Tyler jumped into lunch preparations with a vengeance, trying to keep his temper in check. The rest of the staff arrived one by one. No matter what Jeff had said, he couldn't tolerate Krista for one more second. Not to mention her boyfriend. What kind of cruel bastard would run off someone like Jake?

If Krista kept to her usual schedule she'd show up right as the lunch rush went into overdrive. She loved to flit around the dining room, putting on a big show as "owner" and generally making a damn nuisance of herself. Somehow he had to get a grip on his emotions and bide his time until most of the customers left. Then he'd confront her.

As people streamed in the front door, Tyler concentrated on cooking and filling orders. Sure enough, Krista made her grand entrance right in the middle of the mayhem that was lunch at JT's. Tyler heard her chilly laughter long before she made an appearance in the kitchen. He saw her scoot by the prep tables so as not to get a drop of barbecue sauce on her designer jeans or pink leather jacket.

She gave him her best smile. "Don't forget that Jackie Landess will be here this afternoon."

"Who?" The name rang a bell, but he really didn't give a damn right now. "You and I need to talk as soon as lunch is over."

She ignored him. "You know who she is. That reporter who wanted to do a story on us."

"Us?" His head pounded like a jackhammer. He growled, "There is no us. In fact there was never an us. There was you and that's it." The pentup anger he'd had toward this woman for the past year rolled out unhindered. "And it's over, you hear me?" He shouted.

She looked annoyed but otherwise ignored his tirade like he was a gnat she could flick off her hand. "Not that us, the restaurant us. She'll be here at one." Krista looked him over and wrinkled her nose. "You should think about cleaning yourself up before she gets here."

Tyler turned to the grill and tossed on two more hamburgers. If he spent one more second looking at her face, he knew he'd smack her with his spatula. Later, he promised himself, later.

Seventy-five sandwiches and 12 steaks later, Tyler glanced at the clock. One fifteen. What had Krista said? The reporter would be here at one?

A cold chill passed through him as he thought about Krista talking to the woman alone. He had no idea why this reporter had a sudden interest in his business but was determined to find out. It smelled like some kind of ploy by Krista's lawyer, and if that were the case, he'd stop it right now. Jerking off his apron, Tyler rushed into the dining room and paused.

Krista sat in a booth, in the far corner with a dark-haired woman he assumed to be the reporter. They chatted and laughed like old friends. Were they?

Someone walked up and stood next to him at the counter. Anger rolled toward him like a silent storm. Turning, he looked straight into Nolea's glare.

"So what's up with Jackie, Tyler? And who's the blonde?"

"Nothing." Tyler shifted his focus from Nolea back to Krista. "And nobody."

Nolea narrowed her eyes. "Right."

Will slipped out of the booth behind the women and walked across the dining room to them. He sneered at Tyler with disgust. "She's asking all kinds of questions about him." He nodded in Tyler's direction. "Apparently he and Barbi both own this place and are a hot item."

Nolea turned on Tyler. "You bastard."

"We are not." Tyler rose to his own defense. "She's my ex and showed up one day trying to take this place away from me. Not that it's any of your business." He tried to keep his voice down and his eye on Krista.

"It is my business where Serena's involved. That reporter has been chasing her around for two weeks trying to prove "Lone Star Love Affair" is a fake, and here you are helping the enemy." She paused. "Make that, you and your honey helping the enemy."

Now Tyler remembered where he'd heard the reporter's name. Serena had complained about her some time ago. He couldn't believe he didn't put it together. This had to look bad.

Will stepped in front of him and poked a finger in Tyler's chest. "What kind of game are you playing here?"

Tyler glared at the little man, desperately wanting to break that finger in two. He didn't have time for this. He had to get Krista out of here and explain this mess to Serena before Nolea beat him to it. He had a good idea that Nolea's version of the current circumstances would ruin any chance of him having another night, or anything else, with Serena.

Nolea pushed Will away from Tyler. "Down, Skippy. It's not like it matters anyway. Serena will be gone soon and you," she pointed at Tyler, "will be history."

"Gone where?"

"New York. She has a job offer, and I'm here to see she doesn't blow it by staying behind with some loser."

A job offer? Serena had never even hinted that she had plans to leave. Nolea could be lying. He watched her closely. "What makes you think she'll take the job? She's editor-in-chief at the paper now and "Lone Star Love Affair" is going great."

Nolea glanced at the reporter again. "No thanks to you apparently. She finally got the opportunity she's been waiting for her whole life. Do you really think she'd give that up to be head of some podunky little paper in Texas?"

Tyler didn't have an answer. In fact, he was speechless. Had Serena been stringing him along all this time? If that was the case, then what was last night about? His gaze went back to Krista. He had to deal with the reporter and get rid of Nolea and Will so he could sort things out. And talk to Serena. "Are you done?"

Nolea gave a satisfied smile. "No, but you are. You know, a real man would step out of the picture, don't you think, Will?"

"I sure do." He started to give Tyler one last poke, but the look from Tyler made him think better of it.

Tyler watched the pair leave, then realized the reporter had slipped out too.

Krista gathered her things and flashed a grin. "Don't look so worried, I handled everything." She gave him a quick wave and almost ran toward the door.

He beat her there, knocking over two chairs in the process. Jerking the door shut, he saw something that almost looked like fear cross her face. "I don't know what exactly you and your little lawyer are up to, but I'm warning you," he leaned in. "You step foot in this place again and they will never find your body."

Krista hesitated, the smile gone. She believed him, he could see it. Shit, he almost believed it himself.

Tyler leaned back as she scrambled out the door and ran to her little sports car. He watched her speed away from the curb. He'd allowed women to push him and push him, and today, one had almost pushed him to physical violence. Problem was, he didn't know which one.

Krista made no secret that she was out to steal his business, then disappear, and he had every intention of protecting himself. But Serena threatened to steal his heart, and he had no idea how to stop her.

Chapter 25

"He's been flat out lying to you." Nolea's stare dared Serena to deny it.

"You don't know that." A cold chill raced through Serena. She didn't believe Tyler could be involved with someone else. He'd never given any hint to that effect. Had he?

"I saw her. So did Will."

"He told me an old business partner resurfaced. We didn't get into details." Serena watched the message light on the phone blink. Her mounting work load was stressful enough without worrying about what Tyler was doing or with whom. Why did this have to come up right now? "I'm sure it's no big deal. Just an oversight."

"He *hid* it from you, Serena. That's the same as lying." Nolea yanked her feet off the edge of Serena's desk and banged her green spiked heels into the floor. They coordinated perfectly with the green silk suit and white blouse, although Nolea's red face did nothing for her outfit. "When are you going to get a clue that this guy is taking you for a ride? What about that reporter? What business could she possibly have there except to blow the lid off

"Lone Star Love Affair?" Nolea leaned against the desk. "How humiliated do you need to be to call it quits?"

Serena's temper coiled like a snake ready to strike. "I can take care of myself, thank you very much."

"I'm trying to help you," Nolea insisted.

"Help me what? End up alone?" Serena lowered her voice. "I've tried to figure out why you hate Tyler so much. The only thing that I can come up with is that you don't believe there is a 'right guy' out there for anyone, including you."

"That is not it." The atmosphere in Serena's office electrified as Nolea fumed.

Serena knew she'd hit a nerve. Did Nolea really believe that no man was good enough, or was she afraid to find out? Maybe that was the one thing the two women had in common all these years.

Nolea glared. "My point is, that you wouldn't know the right guy if you tripped over him."

"Well you've tripped over plenty and don't seem to have done any better." Serena grabbed the receiver from its base and pushed the voicemail button, eager to end this conversation. "I have work to do, and so do you."

"Yes, ma'am, Miss Finley." Nolea gave a sarcastic salute. "Right away, Miss Finley." She marched from the office.

Serena slammed the receiver back on the hook and blew out a long breath. She hated arguing with Nolea; they'd been best friends for years and close allies in the political jungle of the newspaper business. But, damn it, Serena was tired of defending herself and angry at the thought that Nolea might be right about Tyler. How could he lie to her like that? Well, maybe not lie, but leave out certain very pertinent details. Was she ignoring Tyler's obvious faults and hoping for the best? Or was she allowing every comment and innuendo to be blown out of proportion?

Serena hated feeling insecure. Normally it wasn't an issue. But lately every relationship she had seemed to be shifting, changing into something new and different before she had a chance to catch her breath and figure it all out.

The job of acting editor-in-chief threatened to overwhelm her these days. She feared her feelings for Tyler already had. What if he disappeared from her life without a word? How would she handle it? Could she handle it? And for God's sake, *when* would she handle it?

Glancing at the clock, Serena grabbed her purse and headed past the newsroom desks to the back door. Tessa, her new assistant, tagged behind, a pile of messages in her hand. "These are the urgent ones, and these . . ."

Serena stopped and held up a hand. "I'm sorry, Tessa, something's come up." She glanced at the small stack of paper. "Pass those out to the senior staff and have them return the calls. I have something to take care of."

The girl's eyes widened. "How will I know which ones to give to which staff member?"

"Use your own judgment. I trust you." She left, refusing even to worry about it for once. Nolea had been right about one thing. It was time to delegate.

Serena arrived home at four o'clock. Tyler's Jeep sat by the curb. She wasn't ready to talk to him. Fearing she'd come across like a screaming banshee, Serena had hoped for a few more hours to get her thoughts together before confronting him. Justin's truck pulled in the drive as she opened the front door. Their conversation from this morning flashed through her thoughts. She'd planned to talk to Justin this afternoon, but given her state of mind, and having no idea where her relationship with Tyler stood, it was probably a good idea to wait.

"Hey." She smiled at his ruffled hair and half tucked T-shirt. It looked like his day had gone about as well as hers. "How was school?"

"People suck," he grumbled.

She laughed as they walked in together. "Why's that?"

"Lots of crap to do. Mrs. Miller gave me this big attitude speech."

"Did you deserve it?" She raised a brow as he plopped down on the couch, his backpack hitting the wood floor with a thud.

"Probably. Just ready to be done and gone from there."

She nodded. Senoritis at its worst. Not that she blamed him. It was early May already, only a few more weeks until graduation. "So what did you want to talk to me about?" she asked.

He sat up a little straighter. "What did you want to talk to me about?"

"I asked first."

"I asked second."

"I'm the mom." Serena grinned forcing herself to relax, hoping to keep the conversation casual and not confrontational.

Justin squirmed on the couch. "Well, I've been thinking about this for a long time, but I didn't know how to bring it up." He met her gaze, then looked at the floor. "Promise you won't freak out."

Serena clenched her teeth and tried to remain calm, fearing the worst. Had she waited too long? Was the damage already done? She mentally kicked herself for not talking to him the first day she found the condoms. She watched him closely and tried not to convey her dread. Maybe it was something else altogether. Maybe he wanted to join the Army. Backpack across Europe. Or get a motorcycle. *Oh my god!* Didn't he know that the only way to get her to panic was to insist she not freak out? She gave him a small smile. "Okay, shoot."

"I've been thinking about the college thing."

"Good." And it was. College? Was that all he wanted to talk about? Surely not. Maybe he wanted to ease into the discussion with a positive subject.

"No, not good."

"Why not?"

He tapped a toe against the backpack, stalling for a few seconds. "I've decided to go to culinary school instead."

Serena stared at him, stunned. Culinary school? Was this a joke? She hoped for a sign to that effect, but he seemed serious. Her heart pounded in her chest. After all the years of saving, planning, and working toward college, he'd decided to learn to chop veggies and flip burgers? An angry surge of emotion rose within her.

"Now, just hear me out." He scooted to the edge of the couch.

She forced herself to listen, trying desperately not to panic.

"I really like the restaurant business, and I think I'd make a great chef." He glanced up at her, "Tyler says he can help me get into one of the top schools and…"

"Tyler says?" That did it. Panic moved to all outrage. "Why are you all of the sudden listening to what he says? He shows up for a few weeks, and you're his disciple now? What about the plans we made?" She stood and paced. Tyler was responsible for this. That figured. Justin had elevated the man to some kind of hero status. She should have seen this coming. "What about all the hard work you put into getting good grades? How do you expect to make a living without an education?"

"I will have an education. These schools give out fouryear degrees. It's not some six-month cooking course."

"And then what?"

He grinned at her. "Then I'll get a job just like I would if I got an accounting degree. I'll work my way up and get experience and maybe someday have my own business."

"You don't get it, Justin." She shook her head. "Your education will affect the rest of your life. This restaurant thing may only be a phase you're going through."

Justin refused to look at her. He didn't even seem upset. Certainly not as upset as she was, anyway. "What if you decide you hate it? What then?"

"I won't hate it. And I thought the goal was for me to become independent, own a business or something, and make my own mark on the world."

She gave an exasperated huff. "Like that's going to happen with a restaurant. You won't get anything but long hours, low pay, and no life. Not to mention having to deal with rotten customers day in and day out."

"But Tyler says…"

"Let's talk about Tyler for a minute. Do you want to end up at forty with no money, no family, no life, and a business that's not worth dirt, just like he has?"

Justin clamped his teeth together. His face glowed red.

"Is that the kind of life you always dreamed about?"

"I thought you loved him."

"Love doesn't pay the bills, Justin." Serena's breath caught in her throat. When had she become so heartless and jaded?

"You don't know beans about being in love anyway. Writing a pretend column doesn't mean you know what it feels like."

Justin knew her better than anyone. He'd attacked the only area that would hurt. She didn't know beans about being in love.

"I've thought about this a long time, and it's what I want to do." He stood and grabbed one strap of the backpack.

"Well you're just now springing it on me, and I don't agree with it one bit. I did not work and save for almost twenty years so you could blow your college money learning to flip burgers." Serena followed him to the door. She only had his best interest at heart. Couldn't he see that?

"It's what I want." He turned a sad expression toward her. "And you can keep your money. If you won't help me, I'll figure out a way to do it myself." The front door slammed behind him.

Serena stood paralyzed. Why was he doing this? Justin was never the type of kid to wake up one day and turn their lives upside down. She watched his truck speed off, and the idea came to her he might not come back. They'd had shouting matches before, but Justin got over it very quickly. This felt different. The sadness in his face, the resignation in his voice, the determination to go it alone if he had too. All signs that she was losing him. That fear reverberated through her mind. She was losing her son.

Arlene cleared her throat.

Serena's head snapped around at the sound.

"It's none of my business," Arlene started.

Serena cut her off. "No, it's not." She went to the kitchen and grabbed a glass from the cabinet, then banged it shut. She needed time to think, not get her mother's two cents worth of critique on her parenting skills. Not that Arlene even had two cents worth.

"But," Arlene's voice rose a notch.

Movement on the deck caught Serena's attention. Tyler sat in the swing right next to the open kitchen window. Had he heard everything? Guilt slammed through her heart. Probably. He brought it on himself, convincing Justin to turn away from his college dreams and throw his life into the restaurant business. What did he expect? That she'd be thrilled? After all the evenings Tyler sat in that very swing telling her how hard it was to run a restaurant? Why would she want that for her son? Why would anyone? Serena tried to convince her heart, but it stubbornly refused to listen. She'd sounded bitter and mean. Just like Nolea.

Arlene cleared her throat again. Serena turned and faced the woman whose face now glowed a bright cherry red.

"You are handling this all wrong."

"As if you're any kind of expert." Serena'd had enough of keeping her mouth shut and trying to endure her mother. "Stay out of it."

"I think you're trying to make him into something he's not. Like I did you. We both know from experience that's a dangerous path."

Emotions tumbled through Serena's chest. "How dare you compare me to *you*. I love my son."

"Not enough to let him try to do what he really wants. Not enough to let him go. That's the real problem isn't it, Serena?"

"You have no idea what you're talking about, and I really don't care to listen." She walked to the hall. Where did this woman get off? Serena had worked very hard to make sure she was nothing like Arlene. The thought that she may have failed burned like acid tossed onto her heart.

"Tough snot."

Tough snot? Serena stopped in her tracks. That was as close to a curse word as she'd ever heard Arlene utter.

"Serena, I'm tired of this anger and resentment. I have endured your cold shoulder and sorry attitude for years now. I've tried to make the best of it and keep my distance. But I *will not* stand by and let you ruin your relationship with your son, no matter how badly you've treated me."

"How I've treated you?" Serena spoke through clenched teeth. "You abandoned your child when things got tough. That's not how I do things. As far as I'm concerned, you could never suffer enough."

Arlene's jaw dropped. "Serena, is that what you think?" Her eyes watered. "What you've thought all this time?"

"It's what I know. I'm a better parent than you ever were, so save your advice." Serena took a deep breath.

"Don't you remember the cross I sent you? With the inscription?"

How could she forget, the only object that remained from the idyllic life she'd once known. "I remember, you couldn't wait to get rid of anything that reminded you of me or my father." She'd dreamed about doing this, but hadn't worked up the nerve. Now was the time. "I'd like you gone from my house before dark."

Arlene struggled to regain control of her emotions. After a few minutes, she spoke, her voice strong and unwavering. "I'll go, Serena, but I want you to know you were never abandoned. I knew you could never have any kind of life and raise your son with all the small town rumors and innuendo." She paused, allowing her words to penetrate Serena's anger. "I loved you enough to let you go. It was the hardest thing I have ever done, and I refuse to apologize for it anymore. I hope one day you can love your child enough to give him his freedom, too."

Arlene walked past and softly closed the door to her room as hot tears flowed down Serena's cheeks.

Chapter 26

"Are you sure you're okay?" Tyler glanced over at Arlene. She'd accepted his offer of a ride to Macy's house, but sat stoically in the passenger seat most of the way without saying a word.

"I'm fine," she stared out the window. Her voice softened. "Just fine."

More silence. Tyler didn't really know what to say. Serena had laid out her accusations and true feelings for them both in the space of 10 minutes. Not that anything she'd said about him wasn't accurate. It was. And as they say, the truth hurts. He needed a break and some time to think.

"Are you going to be all right?" Arlene asked.

No. Tyler had finally seen who and what he was from Serena's point of view, and right now, Bobby Jack looked like a better catch than he did. It went so far beyond depressing, he couldn't put it into words. Not that he wanted to.

"She was upset, she didn't mean it."

He gave her a skeptical look.

"Well, not all of it."

At least Arlene tried to put a good spin on the afternoon's events. Serena may not have meant all of it, but he was afraid to think about which parts she did mean. "I thought you were going to stick it out, no matter what?" He pulled to a stop at the curb in front of Frank and Macy's.

Arlene blew out a breath. "I'm thinking of this as a tactical retreat." She gave him a small smile. "I have to think about things. You know, regroup and try another angle." She leaned over and patted his arm. "Maybe you should do the same."

Tyler helped Arlene with her bags, then waved good-bye. He replayed her words in his head as he drove to Chelsie's. *Tactical retreat.* He liked that. And it sounded much better than skulking away to lick his wounds.

Chelsie sat at the kitchen table and barely looked up from her newspaper when Tyler knocked. She waved him in. Though they hadn't talked much, at least she was speaking to him again.

Tyler's nose picked up the distinct smell of chicken and dumplings bubbling away on the stove. Lifting the lid, he frowned. "It's almost ninety degrees today, Sis. What are you thinking?"

She glanced over at him. "Had a craving for it, now shhh. Let me finish this."

He sat down at the table beside her, noticing how much bigger her stomach had grown in the past few weeks. When was that due date again?

Chelsie sniffed, her eyes filling with tears.

"Are you all right?" Tyler asked.

She put down the paper. "Yes. That is just so, so beautiful." She grabbed a paper towel and wiped her nose.

"What?"

"That "Lone Star Love Affair" that's been running in the paper. It gets me every time. Those people are so lucky to be so much in love."

Tyler gave her a disgusted look. Lucky wasn't the word he'd have chosen, especially after today.

"Don't look at me that way. Love can be a beautiful thing. And stop staring at my stomach. I know I look like a whale."

Great. He'd come over here for some peace and quiet. Now had to deal with another emotional woman. "So when's the…"

"Three weeks, which I've only told you ten thousand times."

Tyler raised his brows. What a time for her to have a breakdown when he needed some advice. Today was obviously not a good day for either one of them. He stood to leave.

"Oh, don't go. I could use the company." She motioned for him to sit, and he did. "I'm sorry I'm such a witch today." She sniffed again. "The doctor said this morning it could be any time, and I don't think I'm ready. They hand you the baby and you're supposed to know what to do. Have all the answers, or at least some of them."

"Didn't you go and buy all those baby books? Didn't Jeff send that *What to Do When You're Knocked Up* book?"

She glared at him. "It's called, *What to Expect When You're Expecting.*"

"So, didn't it give you some answers?"

"Well, yes, but what if I still screw it up? What if I panic, and my poor kid has to suffer for it his whole life?" She stood and paced, her arms folded over her stomach. "What if I'm not cut out to be a mom?"

Tyler tried his best not to stare. The fabric of her shirt stood almost straight out. She looked like she could pop any second. What would he do if something happened? Like right now, this very minute?

A nervous chill crawled up his neck. He suddenly felt very alone. With a *very* pregnant person. "It's a little late to be wondering that, don't you think, Sis? Besides, you love kids, and so does Jim. You're getting all worked up for nothing." He reached for her hand. "Now, why don't you sit down and take it easy." Very easy. Think relaxed thoughts. Please. "Isn't Jim coming home soon?" At least Jim was a vet and could handle the basics of reproduction if need be. He hoped.

"No. He's tied up at work this evening. I'm glad you're here, though." She frowned at him. "Why are you here? It's not like you to show up in the middle of the day. What gives?"

"Nothing. Just needed a break."

"A break? From what?"

More like, from whom. He didn't even know where to start, and now felt a little guilty about unloading any of his problems

Liar's Fire

on Chelsie, given her questionable mental state and precarious physical condition.

She grinned. "It's Serena the Wonder Ho, isn't it?" She giggled with glee. "I *knew* you would come to your senses eventually."

"It's not like that." Tyler jumped to Serena's defense.

"So, it's not her?"

Chelsie's disappointment irritated him even more. "Yes it's her, but she's not like that. Where did you come up with Wonder Ho, anyway? Was that Sam's doing?"

"I saw her for myself, Tyler."

"What you saw that night wasn't *her*. I mean, it was her, but it wasn't her."

"Whatever." Chelsie waved a hand dismissing his explanation as ridiculous. She got up and stirred the dumplings, turning off the heat.

He watched her trying to figure out how to explain about Serena. The only thing he hadn't tried was the truth, and at this point it didn't seem he had anything to lose. "What if I told you that what you saw was an act that we came up with?"

She ignored him and went about gathering bowls and silverware to serve dinner.

Tyler glanced at the newspaper on the table and tried another angle. "What if I told you that she is really a newspaper editor and single mom with a teenage son named Justin?"

Chelsie glanced back at him, one brow raised. Then she turned her back to him again.

Okay. She didn't believe him, but at least he had her attention. "What if I told you that she's the author of "Lone Star Love Affair," and the guy she's writing about is me?"

Chelsie smacked the bowls on the table. "Oh really, Ty, you should leave the tall tales to Sam. You're a terrible liar and your initials aren't..."

"LRS?"

Chelsie turned slowly toward him. "Right"

"We made those up to. Hers are COM, Captain Old Maid. Mine are LRS, Lieutenant Rolling Stone." He glanced at Chelsie's stunned face. "She's also a great actress, which is why I asked her to help me throw you off the trail."

"What trail?"

"To find me a woman. Her uncle wanted her to answer some online personal ads and write about them in the paper, and I needed to get you off my back, so we came to a little arrangement."

Chelsie narrowed her eyes as if peering into his soul. "Arrangement? So you're living with her as some kind of farce just to prove a point to me?" She tossed the silverware on the table. "I don't buy it. It's not like you put up with a woman for five seconds unless you're in love with her."

Tyler squirmed. It made him more than a little nervous the way Chelsie threw the word *love* around so much. Like it was that simple. He could barely grasp the concept of what love is, let alone deal with it.

"That's it isn't it?" Chelsie gave him a strange look. "You're in love, aren't you?"

Tyler hated being put on the spot like this. He still wasn't sure what he felt for Serena, but he knew he was neck deep in it.

"Aren't you?"

He shrugged. "Maybe."

Chelsie burst into a fit of giggles. "I can't believe it! Ty's in love! With the Wonder Ho!"

"Stop calling her that. I told you it was an act."

"Of course." She gave him a disbelieving look as she dished up two bowls of food. She placed them on the table as Tyler poured two glasses of iced tea from the refrigerator.

Tyler scooped a dumpling into his mouth and stopped in mid-chew. The thing was so rubbery it could have been a hunk of Silly Putty. Chelsie didn't notice. Tyler could almost see the wheels in her mind spinning. Finally she looked up at him.

"So, let's assume for a minute that what you're telling me is true. That Serena is this fabulous career woman with a son, and you're madly in love with her."

Tyler cringed at the word *madly*. She tried her best to annoy the crap out of him and succeeded as usual.

"Then what's the problem? Why are you here?"

He swallowed another dumpling and took a long swig of tea. "Lots of reasons." Satisfied he'd eaten enough not to raise any questions, he pushed the bowl away.

"Like?"

"Like, I'm incredibly in debt and about to lose my business."

"Yes, I know. Jeff told me."

Apparently the attorney-client privilege didn't extend to family. She stared at him, expecting more.

"I don't own anything but a ratty recliner and a dog."

She still waited.

"Serena has a job offer in New York that I found out about."

"And?"

"And what?"

Chelsie dropped her spoon in the bowl and concentrated on him. "And you wouldn't be over here telling me this unless you felt guilty about something. What did you do?"

Tyler twirled his thumbs. "I kind of convinced her son to go to culinary school instead of business college."

Chelsie's eyes bulged in amazement.

"He's a natural, Sis, and he really loves the restaurant business. He'd make a world-class chef."

Her jaw dropped.

"I mean, if it was your kid," he motioned to her stomach, "wouldn't you be grateful if someone helped him find what he really wanted to do with his life?"

Chelsie clamped her teeth together. "If you try that with *my* child, I will shoot you on sight."

She grabbed both bowls from the table and stood at the sink attacking them with a sponge. "I mean really, Ty, what were you thinking?"

"I was trying to help. Justin was going to go off and get some accounting degree or something. I may have saved him years of unhappiness before he figured out what he really wanted to do."

Chelsie scrubbed harder, splashing water on the counter.

"Why am I the bad guy?"

She turned on him, her face red. "Because you're a dumbass man, I guess. Did you talk to Serena before you did this to her son?"

"No."

"How did she find out?"

"Justin told her."

"So you're a coward, too? Who are you to butt in like that?" Chelsie tapped her foot and shook her head. "I'm guessing she's upset."

"A little." Okay, a lot. "It's not like it matters now; she's leaving for New York."

"She told you that?"

"No, I found out from a friend of hers that she'd been offered a job at a magazine."

"Offered, huh? But she hasn't said anything to you?"

"No." Now maybe Chelsie would at least feel a little sorry for him. He was tired of always being the one who was wrong.

"Interesting."

"Interesting in what way?" He found it downright depressing.

Chelsie sat and thought for a minute. "Well, it doesn't mean she is taking the job."

"Why wouldn't she? It's what she's wanted her whole life."

She gave him that strange look again.

"What do I do?"

"You can start by groveling and begging her to forgive you."

That thought had already occurred to him. "What if she leaves?"

Chelsie thought for a minute. "You let her go."

"Let her go? Just like that?" He shook his head. This wasn't helping at all.

"Yes." Chelsie leaned forward. "Don't you get it?"

"Get what?"

"If I'd been offered my dream job when Jim and I were dating, he would have insisted I take it."

"Why?"

"He loves me enough to let me do what I want to do."

Where had he heard that before? "But then you wouldn't have married."

"Sure we would."

"How's that?"

Chelsie smiled. "Because I love him enough to always come back."

"What if she doesn't come back?"

"Then it wasn't meant to be."

"Just like that?"

"Just like that." Chelsie excused herself for a minute.

Tyler pulled the newspaper over and scanned the latest edition of "Lone Star Love Affair." If he had to guess, the woman who wrote it loved someone. But was it him? Was it real? Did Serena really feel this way? He read the last few lines.

Our relationship has grown far beyond what my skepticism would ever allow. I have to wonder if I've stopped myself from finding the right person all these years because of fear. Fear of failure, fear of what others might think, fear of losing myself in a relationship. Honesty seems to be the key for us. As long as you have that, everything else can be worked out.

Tyler was more confused now than he'd been an hour ago. He and Serena had started this whole thing as pretend lovers, lying to everyone they knew and the general public at large. But where did they stand now, after last night?

She'd kept her job offer in New York from him. What did that really mean? Was it a good thing, like Chelsie thought, or proof she'd leave the minute she got the chance? And how would he explain keeping Krista's identity from her, not to mention the reporter's little fact-finding tour this afternoon.

He glanced back at the article. Honesty? That seemed to be the only thing he and Serena *didn't* have.

Chapter 27

Serena perched on the edge of her bed listening to cars roll down the street in front of the house. She held her breath when one neared, then gave a sigh as it passed. She hadn't heard from Justin in hours, and he wasn't answering his cell phone.

Fear played tag with reason as the house grew quiet and darkness settled in. What if he didn't come back? What if he headed down the highway and kept going? Serena paced about the room trying to shake off her dread.

She told herself it was silly to think an argument about college would create a rift between them so deep or complete that he might leave.

Justin wasn't the foolish type. He had to know she meant the best for him.

Serena's breath caught in her throat. Arlene had used those same words. She only meant the best for Serena when she sent her away. And look at how that turned out. Serena couldn't bear the thought that this might have a similar outcome. Justin had been her whole life.

The last argument with Arlene played through Serena's mind, the yelling, the tears, the cross. It stirred painful memories and opened old wounds. She went to the old desk in the living room and unlocked it. The rolltop rumbled up with a nudge, and she pulled open the tiny drawer above the writing surface. Red and green stones embedded in the sliver glistened up at her. Serena picked up the cross and laid it in her palm. Just more than three inches long and heavy for its size; Serena hadn't remembered it being so pretty. She turned it over, the long chain dangling between her fingers. Squinting at the inscription, she tried to read the strange words.

Tá mo chroí istigh ionat. The cross had been handed down from Serena's great-grandmother who came from Ireland on the boat. She vaguely remembered the stories her father told her but had no idea what the words inscribed on the cross might mean.

A car slowed to a stop in front of the house. She shoved the cross into her pants pocket and quickly locked the desk. Serena yanked back the curtains in time to see Tyler grab a bag from the Jeep and stride up the walk. She dropped the fabric and let her shoulders droop.

Did she have to face Tyler right now? After all the things she'd said about him? He must think she was the worst bitch on the face of the earth. She didn't want to have to deal with his feelings or her guilt about the things she'd said. She wanted her son back.

Her teeth clamped together. Why was she so worried about what Tyler thought, anyway? He could have mentioned that Justin wanted to go to cooking school, maybe given her time to formulate a decent response rather than blow up at everyone. If she believed the story Nolea told her about his blonde girlfriend, he wasn't to be trusted anyway. But did she believe it?

The front door closed quietly. After a few minutes Serena heard him rummaging through the kitchen. She crept down the hall and poked her head around the doorway.

"I thought you might be hungry." Tyler didn't turn around as he unloaded the bag. "I stopped by the restaurant and picked up some food."

Serena cringed. His thoughtfulness made her feel even worse about the rotten comments she'd made. True or not. "Thanks."

Tyler put two plates and two glasses of water on the table. He sat, motioning for her to join him. She picked at her sandwich while he consumed his. An awkward tension settled between them compelling Serena to say something. Anything.

"Was the restaurant busy?"

He shrugged. "So-so."

What now? She was horrified that he'd overheard the conversation with Justin, but what could she do about it? She certainly didn't feel like apologizing. Not after Tyler convinced Justin to throw away his future. And he'd been less than honest with her about his own life. "Thanks for taking Arlene to Macy's."

He glanced up, finally making eye contact. "No problem. She's a nice lady."

Of course. She's a nice lady, and I'm the wicked bitch of the west. Serena cleared her throat. "I'm sorry you had to get caught up in all that."

"It was my fault, remember?" He gave her a little smile.

Serena couldn't help but smile back, relieving some of the tension. At least Tyler recognized he caused part of the problem. She watched him munch on french fries. Nolea had said Tyler's girlfriend was pretty. How pretty? Was something going on between them? Serena's "cheating man" radar was usually pretty good, but Tyler hadn't given any indication that he'd been distracted lately. He didn't avoid being with her and generally looked her right in the eye. Either he was honest or the best liar she'd ever come across. "Nolea said she saw you today."

"Yeah. She did, but jumped to the wrong conclusion about some things."

He seemed awfully eager to talk about it. "Like what?"

"My old girlfriend is the business partner I told you about."

"Why didn't just say so?"

He shook his head. "I don't know. I guess I hoped she'd give up and disappear."

"But that's not happening?"

"No. Her new guy is a lawyer, and he's convinced I've got some cash stashed somewhere."

Serena grasped onto a thread of hope. "She has a boyfriend?" Her mind raced for an explanation of why he might hide the woman if she were with someone else. He wouldn't, unless it bothered him. Maybe that was it. Maybe he still had feelings for his ex. "Does it bother you that she's with someone else?"

He dipped a french fry in ketchup and frowned. "Good God, no. It's humiliating, though. This woman took my money, ran off with my best friend, conned him out of his half of the business, and now she's back to run my life into the ground. She's a parasite I can't seem to get rid of. Like a bad case of financial diarrhea."

Serena relaxed. Good answer, Cowboy. Her stomach growled and she stole a few of his fries. "What does your brother say about your legal options?"

"He's working on it. Truth is, you were right about me being broke. And my business isn't worth dirt. But in this case, that may work to my advantage."

Did he have to bring up every comment she'd made? Serena felt even worse now that he'd explained what a fix he was in, and better because she knew Nolea had blown things completely out of proportion.

Tyler pushed aside his plate. "You know, I'm really sorry I messed things up for Justin. I was trying to help."

Serena's gut instinct about Tyler had been right. He was exactly what he appeared to be. A nice guy. Stupidly well-meaning, perhaps, but a good one, nonetheless. She was convinced of it now. "I know, and I can't say that I handled it very well."

Tyler reached over and squeezed her hand. "Don't worry about it. You can talk it out when he gets home."

Her throat constricted. "*If* he comes home."

Tyler took her hand and pulled her to her feet, wrapping her in his arms. Serena clung to him, as the small stream of tears became a torrent. He held her as she cried, asking nothing in return. She didn't deserve this after what she'd said about him, how cruel she'd been, but she couldn't let go either.

Crying even harder, Serena allowed her heart to release all the pentup emotion that had simmered inside her for so long, the mistrust, the insecurity, the fear. She let it out, all of it. Tyler accepted it, but more than that, he accepted her. They clung to one another for how long she didn't know. She only knew that she didn't want to let go.

"Of course he'll come home," Tyler finally said. "He's blowing off a little teenage steam, that's all."

"I don't know."

"He's supposed to be working tonight. Would you like me to check and see if he came in?"

She raised her head from his shoulder. "Would you?"

He nodded.

While he made the call, she stayed huddled to his chest. The deep vibrating tone of his voice comforted her as he spoke.

"Hey Tony, did Justin come in?" He listened and nodded. "No, no problem, checking up on things is all." Tyler flipped the phone shut and squeezed her close. "He's there. I'm sure he'll be home as soon as the shift is over."

"I hope so." Serena breathed a big sigh of relief. "Now I have to figure out what to say to him."

"Why don't you relax for a couple of hours?" He rubbed the back of her neck. "Maybe take a hot bath or something."

She nuzzled his earlobe. "That sounds great. Would you like to join me?"

He groaned and clasped her tighter. Their lips met in a soft kiss that soon deepened into a tangle of frustrated need. They clung to one another as if starved for some kind of confirmation of their bond. Tyler pushed her tank top up and over her head then made quick work of the hooks on her bra. Serena arched her back, straining upward in anticipation. His mouth clamped down tight on her breast and she gasped with pleasure as he massaged her nipple with his tongue. He moved from one breast to the other, sucking and licking with a passionate fervor.

Serena's hands fumbled struggling with the large belt buckle Tyler wore. *Why in the hell did cowboys wear these things, anyway?* She tugged in frustration then gave up and unzipped his pants, forcing her hand inside.

Tyler paused and popped open the buckle and top button, giving her more access. He discarded his shirt, never taking his gaze off Serena's naked breasts. Excitement surged through her at the hunger she saw in his eyes. Sliding her hands into the top of his underwear she wrapped her hand around him, firmly holding his throbbing penis. His pulse pounded inside her palm so hard, the vibration traveled up her arm. His groan of sheer pleasure filled her ears.

Yanking at the top of her jeans and underwear, Tyler slid them to her knees. She hadn't even noticed him unbuttoning them. Tyler stopped and gazed at her taking in every detail of her body. He put his hands on both sides of her face, kissing her deeply.

When he finally raised his head and looked at her face, Serena's legs turn to jelly. She stared into his blue eyes and saw a universe of raw, swirling emotion. Tyler bent and picked her up, holding her gaze captive as he carried her to bed. Swinging the door shut with his heel, he placed her on the comforter.

Serena lay watching as Tyler removed the last of his clothing, his firm muscles rippled as he worked. Her fingers ached to touch his skin, but she lay still, allowing him to see her. She loved the way he looked at her, as if she were something precious, something treasured, something loved.

Serena smiled at him. No one had ever made her feel this way—ever. Crawling onto the bed, he straddled her legs and leaned down, brushing her lips with his mouth. He teased and nipped the most tempting places, until she writhed beneath him with pent-up need.

She slithered down underneath him until her head lay between his outstretched legs, then licked his balls gently sucking one into her mouth. His groan encouraged her to do the same to the other as she watched his erection pulse with intensity. She nipped and teased, torturing him with pleasure until he dragged her back up to meet his mouth.

His ragged breath rasped in her ear. "Jesus, where did you learn that?"

She chuckled. "Cowgirl school."

He grinned, sweat glistening off his forehead.

"Want to see what else I learned?"

"Oh, yes ma'am."

Serena pushed him over onto his back and straddled him. "I learned this in bronc riding class." She grabbed his throbbing flesh and pushed him deep inside her.

He smiled and closed his eyes, grasping her hips with both hands. "You gotta go the full ride, baby."

She bucked and writhed on top of him for all she was worth working them both into a blinding passion. Their bodies glistened with a fine mist as her scent merged into his, a blend of sweet vanilla and thick musk. Serena's hands tingled signaling the onset of her climax. She gasped with pleasure as Tyler stiffened, bursting inside her. Leaning her forehead against his chest, she gasped for breath. Tyler kissed the top of her head, and she slid off trying to cool their bodies.

Serena lay back on the pillows, her breathing labored. She relaxed into a warm sensation of complete physical satisfaction. Tyler rolled over next to her, pulling her to him and cupping her entire body with his own. Serena recognized the steady pattern of his breathing as sleep claimed him. She reached back, running her fingers along the long lean warmth of this thigh.

They fit together perfectly. Ying and Yang. Her organization and his laidback style. Her fascination with the future and his focus on the present. Her insecurities and his confidence.

Emotion welled inside her threatening to burst from her chest. She loved this man. The idea both shocked and thrilled her. She would have never picked him if she'd been seriously looking, might have walked by him on the street and never given him a second thought. It frightened her that she might have missed the chance to love Tyler.

She wrapped her arms over his and hugged them to her chest. What now? Why did she have to fall in love when her dream seemed within her grasp? If Fate were standing in the room right now, she'd seriously have to think about kicking its ass. What kind of cruel joke forced her to choose between a career she'd always wanted and a love she'd thought she'd never have?

Other people fell in love and lived happily ever after, didn't they? Serena knew she could figure this out. She'd prided herself on seeing things from different angles, looking at all the options, coming up with solutions to impossible problems. If two people loved each other, they could work out the details. But did Tyler love her? She felt like he did, but he'd never said it. And even if he did love her, was that love strong enough? Serena's eyelids drooped as she made mental notes, all of which came back to the same question. Did he love her enough to hold on?

Chapter 28

A distant ringing roused Tyler from sleep. His arm still circled Serena's waist, her soft skin beckoning his touch. The noise sounded again, and Serena nudged him.

"Your phone," she whispered. "I think it's in the kitchen."

Tyler shook the sleep from his mind and sat up on the edge of the bed and pulled his briefs on.

The house was dark, and the ringing drew him to where his jeans lay in a heap, the cell phone still in one pocket. He grabbed it on the next ring and glanced at the number. Not one he recognized. With any luck, it was a wrong number, and he'd be able to crawl back under the covers.

"This is Tyler."

Tony's voice crackled through the connection. "You gotta get down here; the whole place is on fire."

"What?" Clamping the phone between his cheek and shoulder, Tyler jabbed one leg into the jeans. Tony had never been one to panic, and the strain in his voice conveyed that was a real emergency. A big one.

"The fire department is on the way, and we're trying to make sure everyone is out."

"I'll be there in five minutes." Tyler snapped the phone shut. Adrenalin pumped through his veins making his breathing short and shallow. Fire. A nightmare he'd never wanted to think about, but had on many occasions. The wiring in the building had always been a cause for concern. Grease in the large fryers could go up at a moment's notice. If a fire wasn't caught quickly, the whole place would go up. Had he paid the last insurance bill? Tyler didn't even remember seeing one. He could lose everything tonight. Gathering up his boots, Tyler swung open the bedroom door.

Serena sat up. "What's the matter?"

"Restaurant's on fire."

She scrambled out of bed and scooped up her clothes, her face lined with panic as she tugged on her clothes. "Is Justin okay?"

"They're making sure everyone is out now. I'm sure he's fine." He pulled on his boots and found his keys as Serena dressed quickly.

Grabbing her purse, Serena ran out the door behind him and piled into the Jeep. They sped along the highway. Faint sirens grew louder as they approached the historical district. Thick black smoke billowed from the entire area, and sparks sprayed into the night sky. The air took on a mystic quality, like pictures he'd seen on the news that happened to someone else, somewhere else, far away. Tyler slammed the Jeep to a stop a block away. He and Serena ran to the restaurant. Police and firemen swarmed the area, preventing them from getting close.

Flames leaped from the broken windows, and the roof had a large hole where it had partially collapsed. Tyler stared at the orange tongues that licked the old red bricks turning them black. He could hardly comprehend what he saw. Three years of his life had gone into the place. Three hard years, with lots of disappointment and struggle. To come to this? Just when things seemed to be coming together to make it viable, fate had one more cruel twist in store. Heartsick, Tyler focused his gaze on the pavement. He couldn't watch his life burn to the ground.

Serena tugged on his arm, her voice desperate. "I can't find him. I can't find Justin."

Tyler scanned the faces around him. "He has to be here." A surge of energy rushed through him as he located Tony across the crowd. Cupping his hands to his mouth, he yelled, "Tony, where's Justin?"

The big man glanced around, shrugged, and shook his head.

"Oh my god. Oh my god." Serena stared into the flames.

"We'll find him," Tyler tried to reassure her. "He's probably in the crowd somewhere. Call his cell."

Fumbling through her purse, Serena located her phone and dialed the number with shaking hands. She waited. No answer. She dialed again, paused, and then smiled at Tyler. "Justin? Where are you? Are you okay?"

Tyler breathed a sigh of relief. Losing the restaurant was one thing, but losing a life, Justin's life, would be more than he could bear. He motioned one of the firemen over, intent on making sure there was no one else left inside.

Serena dashed past him, ducked under the barrier and grabbed the first fireman she saw. "My son's in there!" she screamed.

Tyler grabbed her shoulders. "You just talked to him."

Serena gasped for air. "He's trapped in the walk-in. He can't breathe."

The fireman shouted to his crew, "Chief Clark, we have someone in the building." Another fireman rushed over. "Where?"

"The walk-in refrigerator. Right inside the back door to the left."

"Does it bring in outside air?" the chief asked.

"Only when the compressor is running."

The man glanced back at the building. "We cut off all the electricity more than thirty minutes ago. That may buy him some time."

"It locks on its own sometimes," Tyler added. "From the outside."

Chief Clark nodded. "We can break through if we have to."

Tyler watched the men scramble for equipment. A strong sense of urgency and blame pulsed with each heartbeat. Your fault, your fault, your fault. Why hadn't he had that damn latch fixed? The men still gathered things from their truck.

"They have to hurry!" Serena cried.

He held her close as he watched. This was taking too long. How much time did Justin have? Five minutes? Ten? Tyler could be in and out in five seconds, less if he got lucky. He was the only one who knew how to pop that stubborn door open. He'd done it many times. Firemen busting through the three inch metal door didn't even seem feasible with Justin's life on the line. He grabbed Serena and forced her to look at him. "I'll find him, stay here."

She nodded, his panic reflected in her eyes.

Running around to the back of the restaurant, Tyler looked for an opportunity. The fire didn't seem as bad here with more firemen aiming hoses on the roof. Orange flames glowed in the kitchen through the back door. He took a deep breath. *This is it.*

Racing through the shower of water coming off the large jets that sprayed the top of the building, he slipped inside amid shouts from the firemen. Thick black smoke billowed up the walls and across the ceiling. Covering his mouth and nose with the collar of his shirt, Tyler held his breath. The door to the walk-in stood five feet away. He reached for the metal handle, and the flesh of his fingers sizzled as he tried to grip it. He jerked back, the pain racing up his arms. He choked on the thick smoke, the acrid air burning his lungs and nose. This was the boy's only chance.

Summoning all his strength, Tyler grabbed the handle again and yanked hard. The door opened a few inches, stopped by debris from the roof. Water poured on him from above, cooling the metal slightly. He could see someone lying on the floor of the walk-in. Face down. Not moving. Tyler wedged through the opening.

Smoke had filled the small space but the air next to the floor was breathable. Tyler crawled over and shook the boy. "Justin?" No response. Tyler rolled him to his back. "Justin?" he yelled. Still no response. Soot ringed the boy's mouth and nose. Was he too late? Trying to find a heartbeat, he laid a hand on Justin's chest. The burns on his palms and fingers prevented the detection of a pulse. What was he supposed to do? He wasn't a paramedic and didn't know how to help. The only thing he could think of was to get the kid out of here. Now. The walk-in quickly filled with smoke. He grasped Justin's armpits and dragged the boy to the door.

The firemen reached them as Tyler tried to drag the body through the opening. Leveraging the door open with their equipment, they carried Justin out. Tyler followed.

Serena stood motionless, staring at the paramedics that worked on Justin. They put tubes in his arm and pushed on his chest in rhythm. Tyler watched, but what could he say to her? How would he make up for the loss of her son? The seconds ticked into minutes, each taking another year from Tyler's life. Why couldn't it have been him on that stretcher? Why?

After a few minutes, the boy moaned. Tears of relief spilled down Serena's checks as Justin open his eyes and coughed.

Tyler breathed deep, the pain in his hands throbbing. An angry Chief Clark stood beside him. "That was the dumbest thing I've ever seen any damn fool do."

Tyler gave a half grin. "Oh, trust me, Chief, I've done much dumber things."

Serena ran to Tyler and wrapped her arms around his neck. "Thank you so much. You saved his life and mine too." She looked back at her son being loaded him into the ambulance. "He's all I have."

She gave Tyler another quick hug and ran for the ambulance door.

Tyler watched the flashing lights speed off. *No*, he thought, *you have me too.*

Chapter 29

Serena sat by the hospital bed and held Justin's hand. He slept soundly, the crisis now passed, but they still wanted to keep him overnight for observation. The beep of hospital machines amplified the quiet in the room. Reaching up, she rubbed a smudge from Justin's cheek. The soot on his face provided a stark contrast to the white sheets. She almost lost him tonight.

Serena laid her hand on his chest. It rose and fell with each breath. How often had she done this when he was little? She couldn't even count the times. As a baby, there were many days he'd nap a little longer than usual, and a nervous chill would run up her spine, and she'd rush into his room and do this exact same thing. Lay her hand on his tiny chest and make sure he was breathing. It didn't seem that long ago. She gazed at his strong angular chin now covered with a crop of thin whiskers. He'd changed so much, grown up right before her eyes.

Serena cringed at the thought of their last conversation. Did it really matter where or even *if* he went to college? Compared with the thought of losing him, it seemed trivial. As long as he was happy, and alive, what difference did it make? She pulled out the cross that was still jammed into her pocket and stared at the strange inscription again.

Macy rushed into the room then stopped, proceeding on tiptoe as if her slight footsteps would wake Justin. "How is he?" she whispered.

"He's fine. They'll release him in the morning if all goes well." She smiled at the jaunty handkerchief wrapped around Macy's head, hiding her lack of hair. The woman wore it like a badge of honor. "How are you?" Serena asked, knowing Macy looked better than she had in years.

"The chemo is done. They'll start a round of radiation in a few weeks. I thought I'd be on death's doorstep by now, but, you know, I feel really good." She smiled. "It's funny, I'd prepared myself for years to have some horrible disease, and now that it's happened, it hasn't been that big a deal. Certainly nothing like I'd imagined."

Serena hoped Macy's hypochondriac days were over.

Macy shook her head. "What a waste of time it is to worry about the future."

Serena glanced at Justin. "I agree." For years, she'd worried that he'd mess up his life. She'd planned out his future in great detail, never giving him a chance to make his own decisions, his own mistakes. Somehow he'd managed to become his own man with his own dreams. That was all she'd ever wanted for him. He hadn't disappointed her one bit, but her reaction to his plans had disappointed him. Thank God she'd have the chance to make it up to him.

Macy pulled up a chair next to Serena's and pointed to the cross. "I haven't seen that in years."

Serena handed it to her, and Macy squinted at the object turning it over. She smiled at the inscription.

"Your father gave this to your mother on their wedding day. Arlene wore it day in, day out, for years." She gave the cross back to Serena. "When you father died, she swore she'd never part with it."

Serena turned it over, rubbing a finger on the engraved words. "What does this say?"

Macy patted her shoulder as she stood. "My heart lies within you."

Macy leaned over Justin and rubbed his cheek with a frail hand. "He seems to have come through this fine. It's amazing; the boy must have nine lives."

"I certainly hope so." Serena hugged Macy goodbye and resumed her place next to Justin. She rubbed a finger across the cross again. *My heart lies within you.* Is that what Arlene had been trying to say? Serena had seen the cross as a symbol of her mother's rejection and abandonment all these years. Had she been wrong?

Her cell phone rang, and she slid the cross into her purse. She hoped the call was from Tyler. He'd never shown up at the hospital as she'd expected. He was probably still at the restaurant waiting for the last of the embers to be put out. Her heart ached to comfort him and longed for his strength to soothe her ragged emotions.

"Hello?"

Nolea's voice greeted her. "How is Justin?"

"Fine. He's sleeping. Tyler ran into the building to save him." Tears threatened again. Tyler had risked his life to save what was most precious to her. He was a better man than she deserved.

"I'm glad to hear he's okay. Now for the bad news."

Serena sat up straight in her chair. "What bad news?" She'd had enough close calls for one day. Her stomach gurgled with what had to be the beginnings of an ulcer.

"Turn on the TV. Jackie the bimbette just screwed us."

Serena grabbed the TV remote and pointed it toward the set hanging from the wall in front of Justin's bed. It blared to life. Quickly finding the channel, she listened in stunned silence.

Jackie's jet black hair and too-white teeth gleamed in a satisfied sneer. "To recap, this reporter has discovered that the "Lone Star Love Affair" series appearing in the *Cranfield Reporter-Star* is a sham, a deception developed and perpetrated by several staff members and written by the acting editor-in-chief, Serena Finley."

"Oh, shit," Serena whispered into her phone.

"To say the least. It gets worse," Nolea said.

The camera pulled back showing the remnants of the still smoking restaurant in the background. "Sources have named Tyler Copper, owner of JT's restaurant, as a participant in the "Lone Star Farce" as well."

"Lone Star Farce?" Serena squeaked.

"Catchy isn't it? I'd damn sure like to know their sources of information, if there are any." Nolea paused. "Hey, do you see that guy on the far left of the screen?"

"What guy?" Serena asked. This was a potential career-ending crisis. How could she pick out a guy in the crowd?

"The one that ducked away from the camera."

"No, I don . . ." The words died in her throat as the reporter continued.

"Tyler Cooper is being held for questioning by authorities this evening in connection with a suspicious fire that destroyed his business only hours ago. We'll bring you more details as they become available."

"I hate that woman," Nolea growled.

"Tyler's in jail?"

"Held for questioning. That doesn't mean he's been arrested. It's pretty standard with these type of deals from what I understand. I used to date a cop, you know."

Standard? Nothing about this situation could be called standard, and Serena didn't see any reason to take chances. "Nolea, I have to make some calls. Would you mind going down to the paper? We have to come up with some kind of statement by tomorrow. I'll be there as soon as I can."

"Will do. I'll deal with Jackie. But if that witch tries to get a comment out of me, I'm using her as a speed bump."

"Then you'll be in jail, too."

"Some things are worth doing time for."

Serena hung up and sat for a moment, her hands shaking. Tyler needed help. Right now. His brother that lived in Dallas. What was his name? The lawyer. Jerry? John? Jeff? That was it! Jeff Cooper. She dialed information only to be told there were six Jeff Coopers in Dallas proper. Starting with the first number, she went down the list. The first one connected her to an answering machine. A female voice recited, "You have reached the Cooper family." She hung up. Jeff wasn't married. The next produced an elderly man.

"I think I have the wrong number. Are you the Jeff Cooper who is an attorney in Dallas."

"No, I'm sorry."

Serena let out a sigh of frustration; then her old newspaper skills kicked in. A little help from someone who knew the area is what she needed. "All I have is a list of Jeff Coopers and I'm trying to find him. There's been a family emergency."

"Well, if I can help you, I will."

Great. She tried to sound as sweet and helpless as possible. Which she was right now, except for the sweet part, but she could fake that. "I know he lives in a condo."

"Hmm. A condo?" The old man paused a minute. "Read me the addresses."

Serena read the first one.

"No, that's an assisted living building. Have a friend up there. You can see Cowboy stadium over in Irving from his living room window."

They went through two more addresses. One in a slum area and one in an older residential section. Frustration mounting, Serena read off the next to last address, desperately hoping Tyler's brother didn't have an unlisted number.

"That one might be it. It's not too far from Stevens Golf course. Was just a creek over there when I was kid. But I figure it's a good area for condos."

Serena quickly thanked him, hung up, then dialed the number. Within minutes, she was connected to what she hoped was Jeff Cooper's condo.

"Hello?"

She hesitated a moment. The man sounded so much like Tyler it interrupted her train of thought.

"Hello?" he repeated.

"Uh. Hello. Is this Jeff Cooper, Tyler's brother?"

"Yes."

"Fabulous." Relief washed over her. Taking a deep breath she plowed into her story. "Tyler's in trouble. How fast can you be here?"

"Who is this?"

"Serena."

"Serena the Wonder Ho?" He laughed. "This is one of Tyler's pranks, isn't it?"

She jammed the scrap of paper into her purse. "Listen to me," she said in short staccato bursts. "Your brother's restaurant burned to the ground tonight, and the police are questioning him now."

Hesitation lingered on the line. "Who did you say you are?"

She could tell from his tone that she had his attention. "It doesn't matter. I didn't think he could have called you yet, and I didn't want to upset Chelsie in case she doesn't know." Serena paused. "Although it was on the news tonight, so the whole town will know by morning."

"What happened? Is everyone all right?"

"Yes. Justin's in the hospital, but he'll be fine. I don't think there were any other injuries."

"Who's Justin?"

"My son. Can you come right now?"

He hesitated. "I'll need to call Chelsie and verify this."

Serena stood, her patience at an end. "You just do that, buddy. You call and upset a very pregnant person with the news that her brother is in the slammer."

"I, uh . . ." Jeff stammered at her tirade.

"And by the way, the next Cooper that calls me the 'Wonder Ho' will have his nuts knocked into his throat. Now you get your ass up here, got it?"

"Got it. I'll be there by morning."

Chapter 30

Tyler sat in a wooden chair at a table in the center of the interrogation room. How long had he been here? One hour? Two? The cinder block walls, painted a pale green, shimmered with the flicker of florescent light.

He stood and paced. Peeking out of the tiny vertical window on the door revealed nothing but one empty desk and the long hallway the police had escorted him down. Maybe they'd forgotten him.

He strolled the four steps to another small window covered with wire mesh. A full moon greeted him from the world of freedom. He hadn't thought about it in those terms in years. Not since the accident. Not since Matt's death. That was his only other time behind bars and, though the circumstances were different, this felt very much the same. Back then he'd lost his future, what might have been, if not for that tragic mistake. Convinced he'd spend his whole life behind bars, Tyler had ceased to care anymore. His best friend gone. The guilt that plagued him every waking hour of the day. He'd wrestled with his own will to live.

Why was his life spared and Matt's taken? He'd have gladly traded places with his friend as he would have traded places with Justin this evening.

Thank God the boy had survived. JT's, though, was a total loss. Gone, just like that. Tyler's future, his dream, the only hope of having a decent life with Serena now lay in ashes. He had no insurance that he knew of, no miracle that would come along and save him.

He'd always expected the worst from every situation; for a time it worked, kept him grounded, living within his means, not chasing dreams that would never come true.

Serena had made him think he could achieve more. She had believed in him even when he didn't believe in himself. What in the hell was he supposed to do now? Work as a cook until he got his debts paid off and could start again? It had taken 10 years of scraping and saving to start JT's. He couldn't go through that again, and he couldn't ask Serena to stand by and wait. She deserved better.

Two detectives entered the room. The older one, short and balding, held out a hand to Tyler. "I'm Detective Rossnagle, and this is Detective Hammond." The bandages on Tyler's hands prevented a handshake. Detective Rossnagle motioned him to a chair. Hammond sat opposite Tyler and opened a manila folder. His bushy mustache twitched. "We need to ask you a few questions about the fire, Mr. Cooper." His booming voice echoed off the cinderblock walls. "Nothing formal, mind you. We're just gathering some facts. Are you okay with that?"

"Sure." Tyler nodded ready to end this so he could get some sleep.

"We show you and Krista Langford to be the owners of JT's Restaurant. Is that correct?"

Tyler frowned. "My attorney is still looking into her claim."

"What claim?"

"My former partner signed over his half to her, but I don't know if it's legal or not."

The detectives exchanged a glance. Hammond continued, "Weren't you and Miss Langford involved romantically at one point?"

Tyler sighed. Might as well air out all the dirty laundry. The restaurant was gone anyway. What good would it do now to fight Krista for the ashes? "Yes. But my partner, John Suther, ran off with her over a year ago. I didn't hear from either one of them until a couple of months back when she showed up trying to get me to pay her off."

"Pay her off?"

"She showed me the paperwork giving her half ownership and said if I didn't pay up she'd drag me through the courts."

"Blackmail?'

"I wouldn't call it blackmail." But that's exactly what it was.

"So, there were problems between you and Miss Langford?"

"Yes." Of course there were problems. What were they getting at?

"One of your employees stated that they overheard you threaten to burn your restaurant to the ground before letting Miss Langford have half. Did you say that?"

A chill went through Tyler. This conversation seemed to be taking a turn for the worse. This sounded bad. Really bad. "Well, yes, I said it, but I was angry at the time. I didn't mean it literally."

Rossnagle scribbled something on a legal pad. "We've been told that your business has had recent financial difficulties. Is that correct?"

"Yes, but it was turning the corner."

The detective nodded. "Was it insured?"

"Not that I know of. I'm not the best bookkeeper."

Rossnagle nodded again, then glanced up at Tyler. "Were you at the restaurant when the fire started?"

"No, I was at home."

He scribbled some more. "We'd like for you to write a statement of the series of events this evening. Can you do that?"

"I think so." Tyler flexed his fingers, ignoring the pain.

The detectives left him alone with a legal pad. He stared at the yellow paper. Did they think he burned his restaurant to the ground? He'd seen enough Crime TV to know that's exactly what they thought. And why wouldn't they? The ex-girlfriend shows up and tries to blackmail him, he threatens her, and the place burns to the ground. It could be a movie of the week with Tyler as the fall guy. He needed to talk to Jeff. Right now.

Tyler printed his statement on the paper as best he could with bandaged hands. After about 20 minutes, Detective Rossnagle returned and looked it over. "We appreciate talking with you, Mr. Cooper. We'll be in touch if we have any more questions." The detective's glare pierced him. "You will be in town, won't you?"

"I'm not going anywhere."

"Make sure you don't."

As the sun peeked over the horizon, Tyler hurried out the station's revolving door. Footsteps followed behind him.

"Hey!"

Tyler froze and turned. Jeff caught up, and relief flooded through Tyler. "Man, am I glad to see you."

Jeff smiled at him. "I bet. I heard you had a rough night."

"You have no idea."

"You okay?" He pointed to Tyler's bandages.

"Yeah. It's pretty sore, though. Did Chelsie call you?"

"Not exactly." Jeff shook his head. "Why don't I drive you home and have someone pick up the Jeep?"

Tyler nodded, grateful he wouldn't have to shift gears with sore hands.

They climbed into Jeff's Mercedes. The car's leather seats and top-of-the-line appointments made Tyler all the more aware of how far his life had fallen. This is what Serena needed. A professional guy who could give her everything. Not some loser who couldn't even drive himself home from jail. The motor hummed like a lion's purr as they flew down the street. Maybe Serena's friend was right. There came a time when a man had to step out of the picture. The last thing he wanted to do was hold her back.

"I talked to a few of the cops. Seems the fire looks suspicious, and they consider you a strong suspect," Jeff said.

"So would I, except that I wasn't there."

"Do you think Krista's capable of setting you up?"

"If she could get some cash out of it, yeah, but there's nothing to get."

"Nothing? No insurance?"

"Not that I know of."

"And I suppose all the paperwork you had went up in the fire?"

Tyler sat up straighter. "No. It's all at Serena's. I cleaned out the office like you told me to."

"Great. Maybe we can find something."

Tyler flipped open his cell phone. By now, Serena had to be wondering where he was.

She picked up on the first ring. "Tyler? Are you all right?" Her voice sounded worried and tired.

"Yeah. How's Justin?"

"He's fine. They should release him later this morning. Are you sure you're all right?"

"Jeff's here. We're heading to the house."

"Great. We should be there soon."

Tyler said goodbye and hung up. She didn't seem the least bit surprised that Jeff had arrived. He glanced at his brother. "Did Serena call you?"

"No. She threatened me." He grinned. "That's some lady you got there."

Tyler nodded, the smile fading from his face. He loved Serena, but had nothing to offer, not even a way to support himself. She was quite a lady.

And one he'd never forget.

Chapter 31

Serena glanced over at her son as they drove out of the hospital parking lot. "You still with me?"

Justin turned droopy eyes toward her. "Yeah. That stuff they gave me hasn't worn off yet."

They drove in silence a minute. Serena had thought about what she wanted to say to him all night. "I'm sorry I got so upset about the college thing."

Justin smiled. "I guess I kind of dropped it on you, didn't I. It's not that big a deal anyway."

"Yes it is. If this is what you want, then that's fine with me."

"Really?"

She could tell he tried to temper his excitement, but failed. His heart was set on it. "Really."

"That's awesome." He grinned. "I should have a near death experience more often."

"Don't even think about it." Serena felt the tension between them slip away, back into the comfortable relationship she'd always had with her son.

"I have a little confession to make." Justin squirmed a little. "I planted those condoms."

"You what?" Serena glared at the road. "Why would you do that?"

"See if you were paying attention, I guess." He shrugged. "And you were."

"How did you know I found them?"

"One day a couple of weeks ago, I was talking to Debbie at the restaurant, and Tyler pulled me aside and gave me this big responsibility speech. When I went home, I noticed the box had been put in the drawer backwards from how I had it. It didn't take much to figure out."

A weight lifted from Serena's shoulders. Tyler knew she'd chickened out numerous times about having this discussion with Justin. But Tyler treated him like his own son, and this time she was grateful for his concern and intervention. "So there is no girlfriend?"

"Not yet, but I'm hopeful. You gotta be prepared you know." He gave a wide yawn and scooted down in the seat to doze. "Mom?"

"Yes."

"Thanks."

She smiled. "You can go back to bed as soon as we get home, Romeo."

They rode in silence a while. Finally Serena cleared her throat. "There's something else."

Justin glanced over at her. "What?"

"That whole 'whose my dad' thing."

His brows arched in attention.

"Well," she took a deep breath. "The real reason I haven't told you who he is, is because I don't exactly know."

"What does that mean?"

"I was pretty wild when I was your age, and I did a lot of things that I'm not real proud of—and more that I don't even remember."

Justin chuckled, "Now that's funny, my mom, the Wonder Ho."

"Well, yeah, sort of." She smiled.

"No sweat, Mom, no one is perfect."

"No we're not," she reached over and squeezed his hand, "but I think it turned out well."

"Me too."

The relief of letting go of that burden flooded through her. Justin hadn't even cared, yet she'd stewed about what he might think for years. It seemed so silly now. Home beckoned like paradise. Serena's neck still hurt from the few hours' sleep gained sitting in the hospital chair. A long hot bath, maybe a short nap, and she'd be good to go. The fact that Jeff had shown up relieved some of the stress. He'd know what to do to help Tyler.

She clicked off a list in her mind as she drove. There would be meetings to schedule at work Monday. They'd have to decide on a statement concerning "Lone Star Love Affair." Hopefully Nolea already had some ideas. Serena would definitely have to talk to Uncle Frank. They couldn't ignore the "Lone Star Farce" accusation, but they could put a positive spin on it. After all, what started as a farce had actually turned into a real love affair. Maybe a little dose of the truth was in order.

The conversation with Macy whirled through her thoughts. Serena struggled with the knowledge that she had been wrong about Arlene all these years. The cross she'd clung to as a symbol of her mother's abandonment had, in truth, been the most precious object Arlene possessed. The only thing left of the love she'd shared with Serena's father. No matter what differences the two women had, the cross bound them together in their love for him and the deep loss they had endured in different but equally devastating ways.

Serena thought about her mother, the things she'd said to her in anger, the years they'd missed. Tears sprang to her eyes. In a few weeks when things settled down, she'd set aside some time to talk to Arlene. Maybe come to an understanding if it wasn't too late. She added that to her mental list.

Serena parked in her drive and climbed out, frowning at the sleek Mercedes that sat in front of the house.

"Who's here?" Justin asked.

"I'm not sure." Tyler had said he'd be at the house. Where was the Jeep?

She went in and stopped short at the sight of a man sitting at her table leafing through piles of invoices. "Excuse me? Can I help you with something?"

The man looked up. Serena thought he seemed familiar. "I'm Jeff." He stood and walked to her with an outstretched hand. "Jeff Cooper."

He could be Tyler's reverse twin. Jeff's dark hair and eyes seemed the only difference between the two.

"Thanks for getting here so quickly." She shook his hand, taking note of the expensive watch and high quality shirt. He looked like a guy who drove a Mercedes. "Where's Tyler?"

"He's cleaning up."

She nodded and headed down the hallway, leaving Jeff and Justin to make their own introductions.

Tyler sat on the bed, his hair still wet from the shower. He struggled to bandage his hands.

"Need some help, cowboy?" she asked.

"If you don't mind." He gave her a small smile as she took the roll of tape from him and unwrapped what he'd started.

She knelt in front of him and looked at his hands, still red and raw from the burns. "Are you all right? You look tired." And he did. Both eyes wore smudges of exhaustion underneath.

He nodded. "Nothing that won't heal. How's Justin?"

"He's fine." She noticed he avoided looking at her. Serena sensed his withdrawal. The devastation and loss of his business had to be heartwrenching.

"How did it go with the police?" she asked as she rewrapped.

"Interesting. Thanks for calling Jeff."

Serena could tell from his tone that he didn't want to talk about the fire, and she knew this wasn't the time to push for information. She wanted to say something reassuring, make Tyler feel more than utter hopelessness, but she couldn't think of one positive thing.

"Why is Jeff going through your old records?" she asked.

"He's looking for an insurance invoice or payment. I told him it was a long shot. I don't remember one."

Serena frowned. "Me neither, I wish we'd had time to get all that organized."

"Me, too." He yawned.

"Why don't you lay down for a while, and I'll help Jeff?"

"Thanks."

She could hear the exhaustion creep into his voice; he seemed beyond thinking or worrying. She finished wrapping and laid the bandages aside. Tyler took her hand and cupped it inside both of his bandaged ones. He looked into her eyes. "You know I love you, right?"

"I love you, too," she whispered. His expression conveyed a sadness that pierced her heart. "Tyler, what's wrong?"

A knock sounded at the door.

"Come in," he said, once again avoiding her gaze, shutting her out.

Justin pushed through the door, frowning at the bandages on Tyler's palms. "You okay?"

"Your mom fixed me up." Tyler raised both hands. "Look, ready-made catcher's mitts."

Justin and Tyler both laughed. The boy stared at the floor, his face coloring a bit. "I just wanted to say . . . you know," he glanced at Tyler, "thanks."

"No problem. Glad you're okay."

"Me, too." Justin waved a goodbye, pulling the door closed.

Serena gave Tyler a soft kiss. "Get some sleep."

He murmured an agreement and scooted back on the bed. She left the room quietly and stood outside the door for a minute. Taking a deep breath, she tried to calm her panic. She'd wanted him to say he loved her, but something wasn't right. She believed he meant it and knew their relationship had developed into a deep, almost palpable bond. So much so, that she sensed his emotional distance no matter how small it may be. Why would he choose now to confirm his love for her, yet pull away at the same time?

Maybe he was afraid she'd leave him now that everything he owned lay in a heap of ashes. Serena hoped that was not the case. Surely he knew she'd never walk away just because of this. She loved him, not what he had or didn't have.

Tyler had been through hell in the last 24 hours; they all had. He needed time to adjust and absorb all that had happened, and so did she. Maybe that was it.

Hopefully he'd be ready to talk once he'd slept. If the fire had taught her anything, it was to hold on tight. She wasn't about to let him go.

Jeff gave a frustrated sigh as Serena entered the kitchen. "I can't make heads or tails of this. Where's a good accountant when you need one?"

Serena glanced at the piles. "I haven't made much progress either." They needed help. "But I think I know someone who might be able to get it in order pretty quickly."

"Would you mind asking them?" Jeff turned a hopeful expression to her. "Chelsie called a minute ago. She heard about the fire this morning."

"Is she okay?"

"She's pretty upset. I told her I'd stop by her house for a few minutes this morning, but I didn't tell her anything else." He stood to leave.

"What else is there?"

Jeff lowered his voice. "They suspect arson, but they don't know for sure yet. Tyler's their prime suspect."

"How could they think that?" Her voice inched up a notch. "He wasn't even there."

"Business partner blackmailing him, finances in ruin, his only alibi is a pretend girlfriend." Jeff arched a brow at her in the exact same way that Tyler always did. "I need to get the story on that when I get back."

"You will," she promised.

A minute later, Jeff's Mercedes pulled away, and she stood staring at the piles. Only one person could do this. Serena glanced at her phone. She'd planned to think things through, come up with what she really wanted to say, and gradually work up her nerve. But this was for Tyler, and time was running out. She picked up her phone and dialed.

"Hello?" Arlene's voice paused. "Hello?"

Serena hesitated a moment, the emotion and guilt of the past threatening to overwhelm her. She cleared her throat, "Mom. I need your help."

Chapter 32

As promised, Arlene arrived at Serena's within 10 minutes. Serena held open the door for her and allowed the woman to catch her breath.

How do I start this? Serena wondered. Arlene had been the enemy in her mind for almost 20 years, and now Serena wasn't sure exactly how to climb the walls she'd erected in her heart. Arlene looked around the room and gave Serena a small smile. Was she just as nervous?

"Thanks for coming." Serena led the way to the kitchen giving herself time to think.

She watched Arlene, who clutched her purse to her side as if expecting to be asked to leave at any moment. The last time they'd spoken wasn't a pleasant memory. Serena feared the damage she'd inflicted might be insurmountable. Her mother might reject any attempt to reconcile, and Serena couldn't blame her. She had literally kicked Arlene to the curb the other night.

Maybe she should open with the problem at hand instead of the past. "Tyler's financial information for the restaurant has to be put in some kind of order, by today if possible. The police think the fire is suspicious, and they have questioned him."

Arlene set her purse on the table. "Today? Oh my."

"I'm sorry for the short notice, but Tyler really needs the help." Serena knew Arlene had a soft spot for him. "I'd hoped that maybe we could set aside our own issues for today and work on it together."

"Do you think that's possible?"

Was she asking or telling? Did Arlene want to come to an understanding or was she setting boundaries? Serena's stomach churned. What if she'd really pushed Arlene too far? What if she'd lost the chance to try again? "I'd thought about calling you next week to invite you to lunch or something."

Arlene stared at her.

Serena stammered. "If you're interested. But if not, that's okay, too." And no less than she deserved.

Arlene beamed. "I'd love to do lunch."

Relief escaped Serena in a rush of air. "Good. I know Tyler really appreciates you helping me get this done today too."

"I'm not doing this for Tyler; I'm doing it for you."

Serena's emotions whirled again. At this rate, she'd be a blubbering fool in no time.

"We can do it." Arlene touched Serena's arm. "Together."

The gesture sent a warm charge through Serena. She had gotten used to taking on the world. Doing things herself or doing without. But for once, it felt good to have an ally.

"We also need to try and find some kind of reference to insurance or a premium payment or something." She flipped through one of the piles.

"Of course." Arlene took her reading glasses out of her purse and slid them on, a determined gleam in her eyes. "Now, first things first. I'll gather the invoices up in order, and you can start entering them into the computer."

Serena got her laptop and then followed Arlene's instructions as they went along. The women worked in tandem for more than two hours, putting a large dent in the stacks.

Arlene paused a moment, rubbing her eyes underneath the glasses.

"Would you like a break?" Serena offered. "A cup of coffee or tea maybe?"

"Only if you're having one."

Serena closed the laptop and stretched. "Definitely." Within a few minutes, the coffee pot dripped into the waiting carafe. Strong hazelnut aroma wafted through the kitchen. An awkward silence nestled itself between them once again. *Had it always been this bad?* She had chosen to ignore it before, but now she was very aware of the fact they had nothing to talk about, nothing to share. Serena gathered two cups from the shelf as she searched for something to say, a question to ask, anything to break the quiet. "So, what are your plans once Macy's radiation is finished?"

"I don't know. It's not like she needs me around now, except to hear someone tell her how fabulous she looks every day."

Serena smiled. "She came by the hospital to see Justin."

"So did I."

Serena stopped in mid-pour. "You did? When?"

"You were sleeping."

"Why didn't you wake me?" She set a steaming cup in front of her mother. "I'm sure Justin would have been glad to see you."

"I didn't want to intrude. I've never wanted to intrude."

Guilt twinged Serena's conscience. How many other visits had Justin missed? Serena chose not to have a relationship with her mother, but Justin hadn't been given the option of choosing not to have a grandmother.

"I'm sorry about what I said the other night." Serena expelled a breath full of years of pentup emotion. "And that I let things go on like this for so long. I'm sure you would have liked to see Justin grow up."

"Oh, but I did. I watched from a distance." She cast a knowing glance at Serena's confusion. "I went to his little league games and school plays. Do you remember the year he played a leaf? Must have been first or second grade."

"Second, he twirled until he fell off the stage." Serena laughed. "I had no idea you were there."

"I know. Macy kept me up to date. As long as I stayed in the shadows, you didn't get upset."

Serena stirred her coffee, guilt pressing in on her shoulders.

"I hope you're not upset at me now?" Arlene peered at her.

"No." She blinked at her mother, trying but failing to hold back her tears. "I just feel horrible that I forced you to sneak around like a criminal to see your grandson."

"Don't fret over it, honey." Arlene's eyes glistened as she rubbed Serena's arm. "It's done and in the past. And I consider myself very lucky. I watched you grow too. Into a beautiful, smart, talented woman. You have done for yourself what I couldn't seem to do while you were at home, no matter how hard I tried. You've become everything I ever hoped you'd be. I'm so proud of you."

Emotions tumbled inside Serena. The words seemed so easy for Arlene to say; why were they so hard for her to hear? She had wanted to be angry when Arlene sent her away. She needed to have a reason to fight the world and prove herself to everyone. But some small part of her heart knew the truth. She'd let her mother down. Pride demanded she turn her back on Arlene and everything she represented. It had taken almost 20 years for Serena to prove to herself that she could be the person her mother had always wanted her to be.

"I used to be afraid you would show up one day and be totally disgusted with what I'd become," she said, her voice choked with emotion.

Arlene shook her head. "Even when you were a teenage nightmare, I was still proud of you. That you had an opinion and stood up for yourself no matter what."

Serena laughed through her tears. "I was a nightmare wasn't I?"

"There were times I didn't know if you needed an intervention or an exorcism."

"Both probably." Serena let go of her mother's hand and stood. "Wait here." She got her purse from the living room and took out the cross. The small piece of silver was a precious memento that she no longer felt right keeping. It belonged to her mother.

Serena's heart tugged as she handed the heirloom to Arlene. Though it had been a symbol of past hurt to her for so long, she'd come to cherish it deeply in the past two days.

Arlene graced the cross with a loving gaze. "I knew you'd keep it safe."

"Macy told me what the inscription means."

"My heart lies within you," Arlene whispered.

"Yes." Hearing her mother utter the words made Serena believe. The cross was like a lifeline that tethered their hearts together, no matter what emotions swirled around them in this crisis or any other. The bond refused to be broken. "I feel terrible that I've had it all these years and had no idea how much you treasured it. I want you to have it back."

Arlene glanced up. "No, this is yours." She pushed it across the table to her.

"But..."

"Serena," Arlene gave her a piercing gaze. "When you give your heart away, it never comes back. I loved you before you took your first breath and will continue until I take my last. Someday you'll understand and want to pass this on to someone you love."

Serena reached out and touched the object, allowing the truth of Arlene's words to sink in. This small piece of silver tied her to all she had ever loved and all she would love in the future. Serena took the long chain and slipped it over her head. The cross lay on her chest above her heart.

Arlene smiled. "It looks perfect."

Serena accepted the compliment and the forgiveness. They were very much alike. Arlene had patiently waited all these years, stood in the wings observing Serena and her son. Like watching a movie, she could see and hear but never participate. How had she done it all this time? Arlene said she had admired Serena's strength once; now Serena admired hers. She couldn't comprehend having the grace to stand back and watch someone she loved live her life, make her mistakes, grow away from her. She peered at her mother as Arlene focused on the paperwork once again.

Picking up the stack of bank statements, Serena noticed small detailed notes that had been made on several of them. She held one up. "Is this your handwriting?"

Arlene tilted her head back to see the writing through her glasses. "Yes. I told Tyler he should get copies of all the checks. It was hard to tell what had been paid, or if some had been double paid. The checks are out of sequence. Do you know if he ordered them?"

"Yes, he did." Tyler's sleepy voice drifted down the hall. He appeared a moment later, hair sticking up and sheet wrinkles still pressed into the side of his face. "Hey, Arlene." He smiled at her. She gave him a wink that seemed to convey a kind of secret communication. Serena liked the fact that Arlene had warmed to Tyler, even approved of him in a way.

"I thought you were sleeping," Serena said.

"I was, but my stomach wasn't." He grabbed a box of Justin's cereal and filled a bowl, topping it off with milk before joining them at the table. "The checks are over there," he said, pointing to the living room.

Sitting atop the rolltop desk were two stacks of fat envelopes. Serena hadn't even noticed them in all the excitement. Arlene retrieved them and opened the envelopes, one by one.

Tyler struggled to grip his spoon in his bandaged hand, dripping milk and cereal as he took several sloppy bites.

"Do you need some help?" Serena asked.

"I got it." The distance in his voice was still there. Wincing as he took the next bite, Tyler laid the spoon on the table and tipped the bowl to his mouth.

"It will take a little time to get through all the checks," Arlene said. "But it can be done."

"Why don't you start marking off the checks and I'll start posting the daily deposits into the profit and loss?" Serena suggested.

"Have you seen any insurance yet?" Tyler asked.

Silence descended. Serena hated to tell him no and add more stress to what he already carried.

"Not yet, but we're still looking." Arlene obviously tried to give her statement a positive tone.

The doorbell rang, and work temporarily halted as Serena let Jeff in.

"Good, you're up." He frowned at Tyler's disheveled appearance. "Sort of."

Tyler shrugged off the comment.

"How was Chelsie?" Serena asked.

"Emotional, but I think she's all right. Jim stayed home today." His gaze focused on Arlene. "I don't believe we've met."

"Jeff, this is my mother, Arlene. She's a bookkeeping wizard."

Arlene basked in the compliment. "I don't know about wizard, but I do my best."

"Jeff is Tyler's brother from Dallas," Serena continued. "And his attorney."

Jeff glanced at the stacks of papers still on the table. "Find anything yet?"

"No, we're going over the bank statements now."

Arlene brought one check closer to her glasses. "Tyler, who is Cynthia Gervasi?"

He thought a minute. "I don't know, never heard of her."

"Hmmm." Arlene set it aside and continued sorting through the checks.

"I thought we might go down to the restaurant and talk to the fire marshal." Jeff directed his comments to Tyler. "Maybe they know more by now."

Tyler pushed back and stood. "Yeah, maybe." He shuffled down the hall to get dressed.

He didn't seem any better at all. In fact Serena thought he'd slipped even further into depression. She glanced at Jeff, whose expression mirrored her worry. "Do you think I should go?"

"If you want, but I'm keeping him busy until we get some answers."

Chapter 33

Jeff parked his Mercedes across the street from the blackened shell that only yesterday had been JT's. The three walked across and stood on the sidewalk in silence staring at the devastation. Tyler leaned back and gazed at the sky that stretched unobstructed between the neighboring buildings.

The stores to the left and right still sported their historic charm and genteel grace, unlike JT's, which perched like a rotten cavity amid perfection. Yellow caution tape encircled the burned area, and police guards stood by as several men sifted through the rubble.

Detective Rossnagle observed the activity inside the building and now moved over to their small group. "Mr. Cooper." He acknowledged Tyler and held out a hand to Jeff. Tyler made quick introductions.

Rossnagle showed immediate interest at Serena's name. "I'd planned to contact you this morning, Miss Finley. I have a few questions for you." The man produced a small notebook and pen from his pocket.

Serena turned an annoyed glare on the detective. "Like?"

"Where were you when the fire started?"

"At home."

Tyler detected a slight timbre in her voice. He knew it like a snake's rattle, a warning. He watched Rossnagle closely. The man didn't even seem to notice. Some detective.

"By yourself?"

"With Tyler."

Rossnagle jotted something down and then looked at her. "And what were you doing?"

Serena gave the detective a saccharin sweet smile. "Enjoying each other's company."

Warning number two. Tyler glanced at Jeff, who sensed the impending storm too and struggled to keep from smiling.

"Which involved what?"

Serena narrowed her eyes and the small man, "Hot sweaty sex."

The detective made notes calmly though small beads of perspiration appeared across his bald scalp. "So you were together the entire evening."

The saccharin smile was back. "Yes, detective, Mr. Cooper has fabulous stamina." Serena produced a business card from her purse. "If you have any other questions, you may contact my office and set up an appointment." Her brushoff was smooth but no nonsense.

Detective Rossnagle looked relieved to have an escape from this particular line of questioning. "I'll be in touch."

Serena turned her back on him and focused once again on the men combing through the ashes.

Tyler grinned at Jeff. "I'm beginning to think a female pit bull beats a lawyer any day."

"I'm beginning to think you're right."

Serena gave them both the same smile she'd given the detective. "Problem, gentlemen?"

"No problem here," Tyler chuckled.

"I'm going to take a little walk, see if I can find out anything." Jeff strolled down the sidewalk. Serena and Tyler followed slowly, giving themselves some privacy.

Tyler scanned the rubble, recognizing small bits and pieces. A partially scorched chair covered with melted red vinyl. The old ice machine, its stainless steel covered in black soot, and the jukebox, its window clouded with brown smoke residue. The place seemed as familiar as an old friend, yet as alien as a lunar landscape.

Tyler bent down and picked up one of the horseshoes that had once been tacked to the wall. Most were shoes his and Matt's horses had worn during their rodeo days. It was the only physical connection he had left of his friend. Now that, too, had been irrevocable altered. He tossed the metal into the rubble producing a small plume of ash. This time he had no trinkets, no souvenirs, no reminders. The past was completely and totally gone. In the space of a few hours, all traces of what once was had been wiped from the earth, but not from his memory. He rubbed the soot on his jeans and turned away.

Serena's worried expression greeted him. Looping an arm around her shoulder, he gave a squeeze.

"What are you going to do if we don't find any insurance?" she whispered.

"Start over I guess."

"With what?"

Good question, and one he'd thought about a lot because right now he didn't have a pot to piss in. "Hope."

She smiled and swung her arm around his waist as they walked. Jeff met them at the end of the sidewalk.

"They couldn't say much, but they're still looking awfully hard. I have to think they haven't found anything out of the ordinary, yet."

A white rental car pulled to a stop in front of them. A man in a suit stepped out, looking completely out of place in what was quickly ascending to 100 degree heat. He walked toward Detective Rossnagle. Tyler saw the detective point in their direction. The man approached with the cop tagging along like an eager puppy.

"Are you the owner?" The man looked at Serena.

She shook her head.

"I am. Tyler Cooper."

"James Teague." He shook Tyler's bandaged hand carefully. "I'm investigating an insurance claim on JT's restaurant."

Serena gave an excited squeal. "Oh, Tyler, there's insurance."

Jeff frowned. "You've already received a claim?"

Teague hesitated. "Yes, but maybe my information was incorrect." He pulled a paper from his pocket. "I have the owner as one Krista Langford, and her attorney called in the claim late last night."

"That's some quick service." Tyler stood stunned at the possibility that this might be his salvation.

"It's a big claim," Teague said.

"How big?" Rossnagle pulled out his note pad.

"Two million dollars."

Three people stared at the man in silence, while Rossnagle scribbled.

Chapter 34

Jeff drove back to Serena's. Tyler was completely dumbfounded at the possibility that Krista could have taken out an insurance policy and then burned JT's to the ground. He'd assigned her all kinds of evil attributes in his mind during the past year, but most of her faults were miniscule compared to this.

"Teague said the policy was taken out six months ago, so it would have been after the first of the year." Jeff tried to piece the puzzle together. "When did she show back up?"

"Late April." Krista never had the ability to pick what shoes to wear let alone plan something six months in advance. Maybe she hadn't planned it at all. Maybe someone else had. "Her lawyer probably had something to do with it."

"And that's another thing," Jeff said. "I called a colleague in San Antonio to check out Mark Ricca. He had never even heard of him, so he must not have a practice there. Ricca has to be from somewhere else. And I know a two million dollar policy isn't cheap. I wonder where Krista would ever get that kind of money?"

Tyler searched his memory. "Her Granny is pretty well off, but she never gave Krista a dime that I know of." The old woman had called Krista an irresponsible airhead the last time Tyler saw her. She was right, too. At least about the irresponsible part. But if it was true that Krista planned or even helped plan a con involving two million dollars, the airhead part might not be accurate.

Tyler glanced at Serena. It felt awkward talking about Krista in front of Serena, but she didn't seem bothered by it at all. She gave him a smile.

"Maybe the old lady gave some money to someone else." Jeff stared at the road.

"Like?"

"Didn't you say Ricca had Krista's power of attorney?"

"Yeah."

"Why would she hand over her power of attorney like that unless there was a good reason?"

Serena finally spoke. "Maybe he convinced her grandmother that he was managing Krista's money for her."

Tyler nodded. It made perfect sense. Granny Langford was always after Krista to find a good man. One that could take care of her. And to her, that meant money. Tyler hadn't impressed the old woman much, but Mark Ricca would have fit Granny's idea of perfection to a tee.

Jeff dropped Tyler and Serena off at her house and left to stay the night at Chelsie's. Darkness had fallen, and they made their way up the sidewalk to the porch where June bugs danced and swerved in the light. Peering through the front window, Tyler could see Arlene at the table where she and Serena had spent the better part of the day. "She's still at it."

Serena smiled. "Isn't she great?"

Tyler agreed. One of the few good things that had happened today was the reconciliation between Serena and her mother. He was glad for both of them.

As they walked through the front door, Arlene looked up. "How was the fact-finding mission?"

"Slim." Tyler said.

Printouts lay in neat piles on the table. Serena picked one up and frowned.

Tyler glanced over her shoulder. "Did you finish?"

"Yes, but it's very odd." Arlene said. "Are you sure you don't know this Cynthia Gervasi?"

"No. Why?"

Serena turned the laptop around where they could both see the screen. She pointed. "Look at all these checks to her."

"With increasing amounts each month," Arlene added. "And the profit and loss shows that the restaurant has been making money hand over fist."

Tyler stared at the numbers. His intuition had been right. The volume had been up substantially the last few months. He had been so busy he hadn't had a chance to look at the numbers, but his gut told him he'd been making a bundle. "So where's the money?"

"With this person." Arlene handed him a fat stack of checks. "Someone's been robbing you blind."

Tyler flipped through them, one by one. Different dates, different amounts, all made out to Cynthia Gervasi.

"As near I can tell, someone had a duplicate set of checks to this account."

Tyler's blood boiled, "Krista."

Serena scanned the dates that Arlene had posted for the checks. "Not unless she's been doing it for almost a year."

Tyler stared at the dates.

"Who else would have been able to write checks for you?"

He thought a minute. "Well, no one. Lydia used to write some of them out when we really needed to pay something, but I always signed them."

Arlene and Serena shared a knowing glance. "Tyler, do you think Lydia could have done this?" Serena asked.

Tyler's stomach felt like a sledge hammer had landed on it. How could he have missed something this big? He'd paid attention when the bills were made out and had never seen this person's name. Not once. "Why would she? They aren't made out to her." Lydia had always been honest and upfront about everything. She wasn't great in the people skills department, but that didn't make her a thief.

"It may be a friend or relative of hers," Arlene suggested. "Did anyone other than you two pay bills out of this account?"

"No."

"But it could have been anyone that got hold of a second checkbook, right?" Serena asked.

"I already thought about that." Arlene came around the table and motioned to the screen. "You see how they're made out in different amounts?"

Tyler had noticed. Odd.

"It looks like someone made out checks for you to sign to the vendors, then replaced those checks with ones of a similar amount made out to this Gervasi woman." Arlene handed him a bank statement. "See how the checks you wrote are out of sequence?"

He nodded.

"I would guess they destroyed yours and ran through those instead. So while the restaurant kept gaining more customers and selling more, you got further and further behind with your vendors. It had to be someone who knew those amounts to begin with. And if she was the one getting the mail and answering the phone, she could have kept you in the dark for quite a while."

Tyler couldn't believe it. He thought Lydia treated that restaurant like it was her own, working late covering shifts, doing what had to be done. But she'd just been stringing him along, keeping him in the dark, covering her tracks. Tyler tossed the checks on the table, his temper flaring. "How could someone steal right from under my nose and me not know it?" He felt like the biggest horse's ass on the planet.

"Happens every day." Arlene stuffed the checks back into an envelope. "You got busy, worked hard, and trusted the wrong person without even realizing it."

The phone rang, but neither woman moved. "You want me to get it?" Tyler asked.

"They've been calling all day for a statement on "Lone Star Love Affair." Serena shook her head. "Let the machine get it."

After a few rings, a familiar voice boomed from the answering machine. "Serena, this is Deborah Blackwell from *American Woman*. Congratulations! You're our newest assistant editor! You said you could be ready any time, and I'd like to hold you to that. We need you here in two weeks, if possible. Give me a call, and we'll go over all the details."

Chapter 35

The tension in the room closed in on Serena. How could she be so thrilled and excited, yet devastated at the same time? She'd dreamed of getting this call. How she'd celebrate for days and how she'd be out of Texas so fast it would take weeks for the dust to settle. She hadn't imagined being torn by her emotions. Desperately wanting a future that was rightfully hers, but clinging to the love she'd missed out on her whole life.

Searching Tyler's face she tried to get some idea what he thought. Was he hurt because she'd kept this from him, or angry that she'd consider leaving? Especially now, with the restaurant gone.

His face gave no emotions away. Except that he didn't seem surprised by the call. What did that mean?

Arlene folded her glasses and placed them in her purse. "I think I'll call it a night."

Serena followed her mother out to her car, aware of Tyler's relentless gaze. Once out of earshot, Arlene gave her a big hug. "Congratulations, honey."

"Thanks, but I'm not sure . . ."

"Have a little faith," Arlene glanced back at the house. "Things will work out fine."

Serena nodded her agreement, but the lump in her throat refused to budge. Looking into her mother's eyes, she found they matched hers in teary emotion. "I don't know what to say. Thank you doesn't quite cover it." Words hung in her chest. She admired Arlene, respected her, and yes, even loved her.

"I know." Arlene squeezed Serena's hand. "I love you, too." Watching her drive away, Serena dreaded what awaited her inside. How would she feel if Tyler had kept something like this from her? She'd be angry, very angry. And hurt.

Serena braced herself for some heavy duty apologizing and rejoined Tyler in the kitchen. He'd pulled out a bottle of wine and now searched the cabinets for glasses.

"What's this for?" Not that she couldn't use a drink right now, but this wine was for special occasions.

"I thought we'd celebrate."

"What?"

"Your new job."

Guilt weighed on her. How would she explain this and have it not sound horrible? "Tyler, I didn't think it would really happen. It was like a long shot of a long shot, so I didn't see any reason to . . ."

"It's okay, Nolea told me about it a long time ago."

"Nolea told you? Why?"

"Trying to scare me off, I suppose."

"And you didn't say anything?"

"I figured you'd tell me if you wanted me to know." He popped the cork and poured two glasses. Passing one to Serena he raised his. "Here's to you. Congratulations."

He drank a sip, but Serena set her glass down. "So what now?"

"You go to New York and wow 'em." He tried to joke, but failed to lighten the mood.

"And you?"

He set his glass beside hers. "I don't know."

"You could come with me."

"There's nothing for me there."

"They have restaurants in New York."

"Not my kind. Besides, I don't want to weigh you down."

"You wouldn't." Serena's heart sank a fraction. Tyler gave up so easily. Couldn't he see she'd try anything? Any kind of compromise? He wasn't even considering one.

"I'd be working long hours that are the opposite of the typical eight to five. We'd never see each other. How long do you think you would put up with that?'

"As long as it took."

He shook his head. "You wouldn't, and I'd never ask you to."

"So the answer is no? Just like that?" Her face flamed. How could he throw in the towel like this? How could the last few weeks mean so little to him? And so much to her? "You told me you loved me this morning; now it's hard, so that's it?"

"No, that's not it. I have to get back on my feet. I have my pride too. I don't want to tag along like a lap dog and not ever have anything to offer. You'd end up hating me, and I'd hate myself."

Serena couldn't believe what she heard. She'd have given up anything for this man, and he wouldn't even travel to another state for her. Tyler Cooper didn't posses an ounce of faith in anything including this relationship. Her pride goaded her to leave him in his misery. She'd worked hard for this opportunity, damn it. How dare he rip her heart out by making her choose. Her feet were lead weights anchoring her to the floor. She couldn't leave. She needed him. His strength, his comfort, his love. Tears rolled down her cheeks. "How can I go and leave the best part of me here?"

Tyler circled her stiff arms with his own, holding her until her anger eased. "You've earned this. I won't let you pass it up if I have to hog tie you with duct tape and take you to Grand Central Station myself."

Serena laughed in spite of herself.

"I won't love you any less if you're a thousand miles away." Tyler squeezed her close. "In fact, I'll probably love you more."

"Why?"

"Because you followed your dream, made yourself that person you always wanted to be."

Serena clung to him as his lips brushed the top of her head. Part of her knew he was right. He couldn't come with her, and she'd never forgive herself if she didn't go. But her heart refused to understand why. Why couldn't he go on faith? Trust they could work things out no matter what? Why was the solution never simple for her? Each answer only offered more problems.

"Let's agree to enjoy the next two weeks, and then take it one day at a time," he whispered against her ear. Tyler kissed her tenderly. The emotion between them humming with unspoken fear for the future. Serena slipped her hand into his and tugged him down the hall. She needed to be with him. Feel his heart against her chest, his hands on her body. Take comfort in the only man she'd ever had this kind of bond with, no matter what tomorrow may hold.

Closing the bedroom door behind them, Serena quickly undressed. She came to him, her need to be loved by him pulsing through her body. Tyler shed his clothes and trailed kisses down her throat to her nipples. Serena arched her back as she stood and Tyler dropped to his knees, burying his head in her stomach. He kissed and tasted each part of her, as if committing every nuance of her to memory.

Lifting her up, he laid her back against the pillows and covered her body with his. Serena gasped as he slid inside her, the warmth filling her completely. They both lay still, enjoying the feel of their bodies intimately joined in the love they shared. Gradually they moved together as if they were one being. Slowly at first, then faster as their need grew. Serena moved her hands over Tyler's back, the muscles jerking and straining underneath her hands as he loved her body. For tonight, for this moment, they were closer than any two people on earth. Serena's climax burst from deep in her soul and mingled with Tyler's. They clung together, still joined as their breathing slowed.

Tyler rolled over and pulled Serena close to his side. She slid a hand through the slick matt of curls on his chest. She loved this man. Too much to wound him with demands that forced his pride to surrender. Serena had been allowed to go her own way years ago by her mother and had come back to love Arlene deeply. Would she be able to offer Tyler the same thing?

She wasn't sure she possessed the strength, but she would find it. Serena's heart burned with her decision, begging for consideration, but it was not to be heard. She would love Tyler with all that was in her for the next two weeks, then she would go.

And hope.

Chapter 36

The strategy session for "Lone Star Love Affair" shifted into full swing as the clock struck 10 on Monday morning. Will and Nolea sat across from Serena, and Frank once again occupied the head of the table as editor-in-chief. They were the only four people at the paper who knew the whole truth, and they had to come up with something before the next edition went out.

"Are you insane?" Nolea stared at Serena across the conference table.

"I think it's a fabulous idea." Frank hopped up and paced behind his chair. "Blatant honesty! Who would have dreamed that could be the answer?"

Will gave Serena a wink and a grin. She'd had the idea last night lying in Tyler's arms. Why not tell people what really happened? Lay it all out, detail by detail. She and Tyler no longer had anything to hide.

"What about the backlash from people that feel we lied to them?" Nolea glared at each person at the table in turn as if the entire world had skidded off its track and gone mad.

"Lied, schmied," Frank waved her off. "They'll forget about that part and be swept away in the romance of it all. Besides, we didn't really lie; we ran this as a special advertising series. Once people find out it's real, they'll go nuts." Frank expanded on his idea with his usual flourish, planning photos and additional advertising opportunities to squeeze every drop of revenue from the last "Lone Star Love Affair."

The meeting broke up a few minutes later, and Nolea followed her down the hall, closing Serena's office door behind them. "So, you're going? Right?"

"Of course I'm going. I gave Uncle Frank my notice this morning."

"How'd he take it?"

"He pretended to be hurt, rattled on about how much I'd be missed and how proud he was, but Macy told me that he's been itching to get back to work for weeks now. He was thrilled I'd been offered another job."

"How's Justin doing?"

"Great. He's getting information on cooking schools in the New York area."

"New York is definitely the place for a budding chef. Or so I hear." Nolea beamed. "Do you need me to do something with your house?"

"My mom is going to stay in the house for the rest of the summer until I get settled and Justin can join me. Then she'll sell it." Serena picked up a newswire photo from her desk. "What's this?"

"I did a little research on the guy I saw at the fire. I knew he looked familiar."

"Who is he?"

"You remember that story on a man in San Antonio who was conning women out of their money?"

"And?"

"So this is the same guy. Seems he's been hiding out here with a chick named Krista Langford. Sound familiar?"

"This is Krista's lawyer? The guy who took out a two million dollar insurance policy on Tyler's business? We have to call the police."

"Already did." He may have disappeared by now, but they're looking for him. You can bet she'll never see a dime of that insurance money."

She smiled at Nolea. "Thanks. I know you and Tyler didn't really hit it off."

"You're welcome. And no matter what I think about Tyler, no woman should get two million for destroying someone's business." Nolea propped her feet up on Serena's desk. "So is he going with you?"

Serena shrugged. "I don't know."

Nolea leaned forward. "You really love him, don't you?"

She nodded, her emotions threatening to tumble overboard like they did every time she thought about saying goodbye.

"What's this?" Nolea squinted. "You never cry. Especially over a man."

"I know." Serena swiped a finger under one eye, hoping the mascara stayed in place the entire day instead of streaking down her cheek before noon as it had lately. "I think I've cried more in the last month than I have my whole life. It's a wonder I'm not dehydrated."

Nolea laughed with her. "You know I didn't mean to make things hard."

Serena grinned. "Yes, you did."

"Well, maybe a little hard, but I had your best interest at heart. You can't help who you love, I guess."

Nolea's sincerity touched her heart. They'd been friends so long. Serena found it hard to imagine going to work every day and not having Nolea there to support and encourage her. She was a huge part of the reason Serena was getting this opportunity. It hurt to leave her friend behind. "You can come visit me in New York once I'm settled."

"Bet on it." Nolea stood. "You better get to work on that last article. I have a feeling it will be a barn burner."

Will passed Nolea on the way out, and Serena thought she saw Nolea's fingertips graze his behind. Her eyes widened at Will's grin.

He leaned into the office and whispered, "I owe you one, Red. You were right about playing hard to get. Works every time."

He disappeared as Serena dissolved into a fit of giggles. She couldn't even picture Nolea and Will as lovers. They were the ultimate odd couple. But somehow, they seemed made for one another. Opposite sides of the same coin. She was thrilled for them and hopeful that they could find what she and Tyler had. No matter how short their time might be.

Chapter 37

The last edition of "Lone Star Love Affair" was read by almost everyone in the state and many across the country, having been picked up by news wires from coast to coast. Serena's honest and heartfelt description of how they really met, came to an agreement, and "faked" their love affair was a hit. She ended the article with the fact that the restaurant had burned, and though there was no insurance, they planned to carry on and rebuild. That last part wasn't exactly true, but here again, she hoped it would be.

One unexpected outcome was that it had created an outpouring of good wishes from readers across the city and around the country. People stopped Tyler and Serena on the street asking for autographs and offering advice to make their love last. Donations also poured in to help Tyler rebuild, and while it wasn't a huge amount of money, at least it gave him a start. Still, difficult decisions and choices loomed ahead of them both.

Two weeks came and went so quickly, Serena's heart barely kept up. It was like an Indy car driver racing toward impact, the thrill of the speed with the knowledge of disaster ahead.

Each day she fell deeper in love with Tyler as they talked, laughed, and held one another into the wee hours of the morning. But they couldn't put off the inevitable.

The investigation so far had turned up a big fat goose egg. The fire marshal ruled the blaze an accidental electrical fire with no evidence of arson, which cleared Tyler. Jeff turned over all the financial records of the business, and the police were still looking for Lydia but said it could take months to track her down.

This is it. Serena took a deep breath and scanned the bedroom hoping she'd packed everything. Today it was time. *The last time.* Serena had been up at dawn, to have a last breakfast with both Arlene and Justin. It had been a joyous occasion; she'd see them soon in New York. But it was different with Tyler.

Her bags sat next to the door, ready to be loaded as the clocked ticked. Each second a blow to her heart. She rubbed a finger over the cross that hung at her neck. Did she really have the strength to do this?

"Is this everything?" Tyler scooped up the bags, invading her dread.

She followed him out and climbed into the Jeep. The thick Texas air weighed heavy on her chest, muggy and humid; she would definitely not miss Texas in July. Glancing back, she took in what had been her home, her life, one last time. She was ready to go, but her heart begged to stay.

They drove to the airport neither one saying much. It had all been said anyway. Several times. The reasons why, the arguments, the acceptance. It had to be this way. She knew it, so did he.

Tyler parked, unloaded, and followed her to security, holding her hand until the last second. Serena turned and looked at him. Her heart pounded as she gazed into his stormy blue eyes. "It's time."

He tried to smile. "Those magazine people don't have any idea how lucky they are." Gathering her into his arms, he held her close.

She inhaled his scent, burning his memory into her heart. She wanted to say she'd be back, but she knew it wasn't true. It was his turn, his choice to make the leap of faith or not, and she had to be strong enough to survive if he didn't.

Serena leaned back and pulled the silver chain over her head. It was her most precious possession, but not near as precious as the love they shared. Pressing the cross into Tyler's palm, she said, "If you're ever in New York . . ."

Tyler nodded, moisture glistening in his eyes. "I love you." He grasped the necklace in his fist.

"I love you, too." She kissed him one last time, turned, and walked away.

Chapter 38

Tyler sat on Chelsie's porch listening to his sister's excited chatter inside the house. He couldn't make out the words but expected they were similar to what he'd heard an hour or so ago. James Lohan Jr. had made it through his first month of life. So, of course, Chelsie threw a barbecue to celebrate.

Jeff strolled out on the porch and sat down next to Tyler. "Poor kid's gonna be deaf at this rate. Chelsie hasn't shut up for five minutes since I got here."

"You staying long?"

Jeff shook his head. "Just wanted to be sure everything was wrapped up with the restaurant."

It was wrapped up all right. The police still hadn't found Lydia or any trace of the money she'd stolen. "It's about par for the course. I am the proud owner of a pile of ashes."

"Glad to see you're not bitter about it." Jeff glanced sideways at Tyler and grinned. "You have a little from the donations, and at least Krista didn't get anything. That's one bright spot. Apparently Mark Ricca left her high and dry."

"Couldn't happen to a nicer girl." Tyler shrugged. "We all gotta move on, I guess." Not that the fire left him any other choice at this point.

"You hear from Serena?"

They talked at least once a day, which wasn't near enough to suit him. "Yeah, she's using that Texas charm on those New Yorkers." Serena talked for hours on end about her new job and the life she was making for herself. She'd done it. Decided what she wanted, reached out, and grabbed it. He was proud of her and afraid at the same time. Tyler felt the distance in her voice each night growing further and further away. There was less to talk about, longer lapses in conversation. She was slipping away from him.

"So what are you still doing here?"

Tyler didn't have a good answer. Oh, he had good excuses, but none of them were the real reason. He felt worthless next to Serena. Like a pretender conning her into loving him, when he knew she deserved better.

He knew he had flaws, as a business person, as a partner, pretty much in every area there was a lot of room for improvement.

"You know I haven't seen Mikayla since the day she left me standing at the altar," Jeff said.

Tyler remembered but was shocked Jeff brought it up. It didn't seem like eight years had passed since that awful day, and Jeff had always refused to talk about it until now. "Coopers sure do throw interesting weddings."

"That we do." Jeff laughed. "It's the Cooper curse."

"I always wondered what happened with you two."

"Ahh, it was stupid. I had just opened my own practice, and we agreed that once we got married, we'd wait five years to start a family. But that morning she said she'd changed her mind, she wanted kids right off." Jeff's voice trailed off, lost in the memory. "We argued, and I refused to budge. Next thing I knew she was doing a sprint back up the aisle of that church and out the door."

"You would have never gotten where you are today if you'd had a family that soon."

"Don't kid yourself, little brother. I'd trade that Mercedes for a mini-van in a heartbeat."

"What happened to her?"

"Don't know. She's probably a soccer mom out in the suburbs somewhere."

"I'm not letting Serena go, just waiting until things get better for me."

Jeff got up to go inside. "And when will that be?"

Tyler didn't answer.

"Me and Mikayla could have had half a little league team by now."

Tyler sat alone on the porch. Shadow brushed against his leg and lay down in front of him. He glanced at the dog's pitiful expression. She had moped around since the day Serena left and so had he. "Don't look at me that way." He reached down and scratched Shadow's ears. "I miss her too."

All the reasons he'd had for staying failed to convince him he'd made the right choice. He had to decide. Either go after what he wanted, or sit here and let it slip away. How had Serena put it? Imagine yourself in the life you want and work to get there. Baby steps, she'd said. It sounded easy but felt like leaping off a cliff.

Tyler closed his eyes and imagined him and Serena together, side by side, running a new and improved version of JT's. The image quickly faded as doubts crowded in. It had taken years to start JT's, and look how that had turned out. Serena was all wrapped up in her new job now, her new life. There might not be any room for him anymore. One thing was for sure. Daydreaming on his sister's porch wasn't getting him anywhere.

Tyler shook hands with Jeff and gave Chelsie a quick hug. Climbing into his Jeep, he whistled for Shadow. He steered the vehicle onto the highway. A large green sign read Highway 287 North. That's where he wanted to be: North, with Serena. Tyler missed his exit to Serena's old house and kept driving. The hardest thing about faith was taking that first step.

Chapter 39

Serena gazed out her office window on the 10th floor. A slight haze surrounded Central Park several blocks away, its lush green an oasis in the late summer heat of the city. Even after six weeks, the view seemed surreal, as if someone had taken the imaginary picture that she'd had in her mind all these years and glued it to the window.

"You ready for this meeting?" Deborah stuck her head into the office. Ten years older than Serena, she exuded New York fashion from her black leather designer jacket to her tall spiked heels. Nolea would love her. Deborah joined her by the window.

"I don't think I'll ever get tired of looking at this." Serena smiled.

"Miss Finley?" The receptionist carried a small wrinkled paper bag at arm's length. "This was just delivered for you."

"Is it ticking?" Deb gave the bag a suspicious glance.

The girl set it down, leaving them alone with the offending object. Serena peered at it. There were staples along the top. Picking it up, she jiggled it gently.

It had something in it. Something heavy. She tugged on the paper, popped open the staples and dumped the contents onto her desk.

The cross tumbled out, its bright stones reflecting the light.

"Wow." Deb said. "That's beautiful."

Serena's breath caught in her throat. *Tyler's here.* She grabbed the necklace and ran down the hall to the reception desk. "Who delivered that bag?"

"A guy in a cowboy hat. I told him you had a meeting."

Serena ran toward the door.

"Where are you going?" Deborah yelled after her.

"Sorry, there's something I have to do." Serena clutched the cross in her hand as she waited on the elevator and pushing the down button repeatedly. "Come on, come on." She couldn't believe he was here. He'd done it, finally taken the leap. She had almost convinced herself he'd never come for her. She rode down and burst through the front entrance into a sea of people. Where was he? She scanned the sidewalk to the left and to the right. A cowboy hat should be pretty easy to spot on a street in Manhattan.

A dog barked, drawing her attention. Shadow. She peered through the throng of people toward the park. A beat up cowboy hat floated through the crowd toward Central Park. Serena bobbed and weaved her way through the people hurrying to catch him. She'd waited weeks for him and wasn't waiting one more second.

Arriving at the park a few minutes later, she saw him in the distance on the lush grass. "Tyler!" She yelled.

He turned around and grinned at her.

Serena kicked off her heels and sprinted across the grass. She leaped into his arms and he caught her, laughing as he kissed her.

"I can't believe you're really here." She gazed into deep blue eyes that had haunted her dreams for the past six weeks.

"I couldn't stay away. You have to understand I'm still trying to get things together. But I love you, and I'm willing to do anything to make this work."

"I love you, too," she whispered. They kissed, sealing the promise between them. She'd somehow found the strength to let go, and he'd found the faith to believe.

Chapter 40

Four Years Later

Tyler threw more wood into the fire pit. The ribs would be smoked to perfection in another 30 minutes, just in time to feed a restaurant full of people.

Serena weaved her way through the kitchen, talking and laughing with the staff. Tyler smiled. They all loved her, and so did he.

She'd been right about almost everything. Tyler had attended culinary school in New York right alongside Justin with the money he'd received from the donations, and now not only could he cook better, he knew every nuance of running a successful restaurant including how to pay the bills!

Though Serena had been a big hit at *American Woman* magazine, it hadn't taken her long to realize the city really didn't suit her—or Shadow. As soon as culinary school was complete, they had all come right back to Cranfield.

Serena grabbed Tyler's arm. "Come on, you're the man of the hour. They can handle this."

He followed her out to the front of the restaurant where all of their friends and family had gathered. Justin and several servers passed champagne to all the guests. Thank God they'd volunteered to help; the crowd had already grown larger than expected.

Jeff raised his glass for a toast. "Here's to my little brother," he nodded toward Serena, "and my new sister-in-law. May their venture, Cooper and Company, be a huge success." Shouts of agreement filled the room. Serena grinned at Tyler, love radiating from her face. She wore the silver cross around her neck as she had since the day he arrived in New York. The dream of the restaurant had happened much faster than he'd imagined. It was hard to believe that just a few years ago he'd stood in the rubble of what was JT's thinking his life was over, but this was more than he'd ever hoped for.

No one could have made him believe that this was even possible. No one except Serena. He'd never be able to thank her enough, love her enough. Putting his arm around her, he pulled her close. "Are you ready for this Mrs. Cooper?"

She grinned. "Absolutely."